KIRIATH'S QUEST

Also by Rick Barry
Gunner's Run

KIRIATH'S QUEST

RICK BARRY

JOURNEYFORTH

Greenville, South Carolina

Library of Congress Cataloging-in-Publication Data

Barry, Rick (Richard C.), 1959–
  [Into the Grishnazi's lair]
  Kiriath's quest / Rick Barry.
       p. cm.
  First published under the title: Into the Grishnazi's lair.
  Summary: When the evil Grishnaki ambush Prince Kiriath and his
  father the king, Kiriath sets out on a quest to bring his father home, no
  matter the cost.
  ISBN 978-1-59166-905-0 (perfect bound pbk. : alk. paper)
  [1. Fathers and sons—Fiction. 2. Kings, queens, rulers, etc.—Fiction.
  3. Voyages and travels—Fiction.]   I. Title.
  PZ7.B28038Ki 2008
  [Fic]—dc22

                                                              2008020566

Cover photos: Craig Oesterling; DigitalVision/Getty Images/(mountain);
PhotoDisc/Getty Images/(mountain); www.iStockphoto.com/ranplett/
(old paper); www.defcon-x.de/(wood grain)

Design by Craig Oesterling
Page layout by Kelley Moore

© 2008 by BJU Press
Greenville, SC 29614
JourneyForth Books is a division of BJU Press

Printed in the United States of America

ISBN 978-1-59166-905-0

15   14   13   12   11   10   9   8   7   6   5   4   3   2   1

For Pam, Jessica, and Josh

PUBLISHER'S NOTE

Kiriath's Quest is a fantasy, the kind of novel whose job it is to remove life's problems from their normal setting and put them into relief, making the lessons easier to see and to remember.

As a fantasy, it contains some fanciful elements, including objects and events that contradict the laws of the natural world. Such events and objects are part of the background that put the truly important themes into that relief. The reader must decide how he will respond to those elements.

If he can accept the fantasy as emblematic of life and as a useful vehicle of truth, he can judge it on those bases. He can enter into the story ready to weigh what he reads there against what he believes is good and right.

The issue, then, becomes not what kind of book *Kiriath's Quest* is, but rather what it teaches about moral growth. Does the book have snakes that fly? Then the reader asks himself how those snakes serve the book in providing a journey to truth.

Thus jewels that can capture sounds and orbs that explode are simply parts of the story metaphor. Though such things would seem strange indeed in the world as we know it, they are not so in their own world, the world of the book.

When the reader leaves that world and returns to his own, if he is better equipped to live there, then the fantasy has served him well.

CONTENTS

CHAPTER 1

AMBUSH

Lifting his eyes from the cobblestone roadway, Prince Kiriath admired the glinting walls and spires of Shiralla, situated on a broad shoulder of the mountain high above.

He called to Jekoniah, who rode the steed beside him. "Father, look. See how the morning sunshine—"

A loud *chink,* as of something beating metal, split the morning air. In that same instant, the prince felt something strike beneath his cloak.

King Jekoniah immediately looked at his son with alert, questioning eyes. "What was that sound?"

"Something struck my breastplate, here under my cloak!" Kiriath circled his horse to scan the ground, then pointed to the roadside. There lay a slender shaft with a crudely chipped arrowhead bound to its tip. "A black arrow."

"Grishnaki!" Jekoniah muttered in disbelief, his eyes straining to pierce the underbrush.

Another arrow split the air between them.

"To Shiralla, Kiriath. Quickly!"

As one, the two men spurred their steeds toward the city, their horses' hooves clattering wildly against the cobblestones. Kiriath glimpsed several large, hulking silhouettes under the trees to their right, but there was no need to speak of them. They had to be

1

Grishnaki, for only Grishnaki chipped heads for their arrows and spears from stone. But how many of them were there? How had they penetrated so near Shiralla?

Unexpectedly, about a score of Grishnaki scrambled onto the road ahead, bows raised, faces leering.

"Ambush!" Kiriath cried.

Father and son reined in their horses. From the direction they had come another mob of Grishnaki were quickly loping up the road, some with bows, others wielding stone maces, bludgeons, spears, or roughly fashioned swords of wood.

Not one of them less than seven feet tall, Kiriath noted to himself.

An arrow whistled past his ear.

"To the ravine," Jekoniah called. "The swinging bridge is our last chance."

"I'm with you."

Leaping a ditch, horses and riders flew between the roadside birch trees and down a narrow footpath. From behind a boulder, one massive Grishnak leaped out, a stone mace in his upraised hand.

The prince snatched his sword from its sheath, and struck the descending arm just below the wrist. The blow struck home. Although the prince didn't turn to see what damage he had done, the howl of pain in his wake told him it had been enough.

"This is not a mere raiding party," Jekoniah shouted. "They strike only at you and never at me."

Kiriath understood his father's meaning. "They won't take you. Not while I'm alive!"

Jekoniah's only reply was to point to the path ahead.

Ahead of them the last trees ended, and the ground fell away sharply. The path descended toward a deep ravine, spanned by a solitary bridge of rope and planking. Oblivious to the danger, a field laborer was just stepping off the near end of the bridge, an empty sack slung over his shoulder.

"Back!" Jekoniah boomed. "Go back! The Grishnaki are upon us!"

The field hand froze in place as if transfixed by sorcery. The only sign of life was in his wide, dumbfounded eyes. However, as Grishnaki came spilling out of the woods, the man flung down his sack and sent the bridge dancing to and fro as he scrambled across it.

"You cross first, Father," Kiriath said as they reached the chasm. "I'll follow."

"Do not wait long," the king called. He swung out of his saddle and started toward the bridge.

From the fast-approaching horde, a spear came streaking toward Kiriath's head. Involuntarily shutting his eyes, the prince arched backward in the saddle to dodge the weapon.

After the missile had sailed past, Kiriath defied the enemy horde with a grim smile. Within moments, he thought, he would be on the far side of the ravine, where he could slash the rope supports to the bridge. He and his father would be safe. Then, turning to see his father's progress, he stifled a cry.

King Jekoniah lay on the threshold of the bridge face down, unmoving, one arm dangling over the edge. For a long, frozen moment the spear that had narrowly missed Kiriath teetered on the bridge, then slid off and disappeared.

"Father!"

The king moved slowly, struggling to rise.

"Father!" Kiriath shouted again.

As the prince began dismounting, the fleetest of the attackers dashed past and planted himself between the prince and the king. Clutching a heavy wooden bludgeon with both hands, the creature squinted at the prince and twisted his cracked lips into an ugly grin.

As Kiriath's horror gave way to anger, he felt a great strength surge within him. Throwing himself back into the saddle, he shouted, "Back to your hole, black-heart!" He spurred his steed forward and, grasping the hilt of his sword with two hands, as did the Grishnak his bludgeon, he slammed it down with all his might.

Steel thudded into wood as the Grishnak intercepted the blow with his weapon. Instinctively the creature stepped backward. The smile was gone, and his bloodshot eyes flashed with hatred. Hefting the bludgeon again, he croaked a single word between clenched, crooked teeth.

"Die!"

Kiriath heard more enemies pounding down the slope from behind, but he had no time to look. A putrid stench from the Grishnak assailed his nostrils even as he met the foe's lunge. His steel arced downward to meet the attack. This time the handle of the wooden bludgeon clove in half under the prince's blade.

The creature dropped to one knee for but a moment. With little more than a pointed chunk of wood left in his claws, the Grishnak leapt up to drive it in as a dagger. Too late—for Kiriath was already stabbing downward. The Grishnak screamed as he thrust himself onto Kiriath's blade, then fell limply to the ground.

The prince felt strong hands grappling at his legs and waist. He slashed wildly, blindly hewing at the giants that sought to wrench him from his saddle.

Neighing loudly, Kiriath's mount joined in the fray. She reared up on her hind legs and came crashing down on one of the enemy. But as she reared up again, Kiriath glimpsed another Grishnak swinging a massive club at him. Striking the prince on his breastplate, the powerful blow tumbled him from his saddle. But instead of hitting the stony ground squarely, Kiriath felt his chest smash into rock, while his legs fell into—nothingness.

The ravine!

Even as his hands grappled for a solid hold, the sparse grass between his fingers wrenched loose, and the prince felt himself plummeting downward. Gray rock streaked past his eyes.

Another second, and Kiriath slammed into a rocky crag. He shot out his hands, desperate to grasp a crack, a knob, anything to halt his descent. But his efforts were vain: the angle of the rock was too steep, and he fell plunging through air once more. Sickeningly fast, the ground rushed up toward him.

Convinced that he was about to die, Kiriath thrust out his arms and legs, catlike, waiting for the end.

CHAPTER 2

NIGHT COUNCIL

As consciousness gradually seeped back into the prince's mind, his first sensation was of pain. His body ached, and dried blood coated the palms of his scuffed hands. He could feel a light tickling, as if ants crawled over his arms and neck, and he heard flies buzzing about his ears.

As the mist in his thoughts slowly lifted, he realized that he wasn't on his bed in the Citadel but sprawled on the ground under a hot sun. He opened his eyes to find himself peering between blades of deep grass. Kiriath tried to swallow but couldn't. His parched throat didn't have enough moisture for the effort.

Aching, the prince rolled over and looked up. Seeing the rock wall of the ravine towering above him brought his last waking memories flooding back to him. Not until then did he marvel that he was still alive.

The Grishnaki, he recalled, scanning the empty heights above. *And Father! They must have him. I have to get out of here . . . help him.*

With an effort, Kiriath pulled himself first to his knees and finally to his feet. He paused long enough to run his fingers over his body to search for broken bones. There were none, but he found bruises in abundance. He winced when he touched his forehead. One spot there was particularly tender.

Must have struck my head on the way down, he thought. *At least nothing is broken.*

The delicate trickling of water caught his attention, reminding Kiriath of his thirst and of the brook running through the ravine. Wading through briars toward the brook, he had gone only a few paces when he spotted something glinting to his left: the sword he had been holding as he toppled from his horse.

A faithful piece of steel, you are. He retrieved the weapon. *Come with me. There may be work for you yet.*

With that he sheathed the blade and continued on to the brook. Within moments Kiriath's thirst was quenched, and he was able to think more clearly. He surveyed the heights around him.

I must have lain here all day, he mused. *It's well past noon. Yet it was barely first light when the Grishnaki attacked us. I must find a way out of here if I'm going to help Father.*

But search as he might, Kiriath could find no spot where he could hope to scale the rocky face. Even if the fall had not weakened him, the sides were almost vertical. And even though the supports on the bridge had indeed been slashed, leaving it dangling down one wall, the closest end was still well above his reach.

Perhaps Father managed to escape after all. But then he reconsidered. *No, the bridge was cut from the side where we fought. The Grishnaki must have done it to keep anyone from following them.*

Finding no other recourse, Kiriath started trudging up the ravine. At its upper end, he knew, the ravine became much more shallow and narrow. One portion of Shiralla had actually been built over it, with the mountain brook running under the walls as a constant source of cool water for the city. Wary of the Grishnaki, the builders had constructed a heavy iron grating that allowed water to flow through but barred any intruders from entering. It was toward this point that Kiriath now made his course. The ravine would lead him directly to the city, and from there he would be able to hail one of the sentinels on the wall.

What was left of the afternoon sun slid steadily across the sky and disappeared from sight while Kiriath felt that he was traveling at scarcely better than a crawl. Trudging along the floor of the ravine was more difficult than he had expected. He hadn't been on its bottom since he was a boy, and the paths he remembered had long since overgrown. Also, fallen boulders littered the ground. Near the brook, the boulders were fewer, but there his boots oozed deep into the black mire, slowing him even more.

Here and there he sometimes glimpsed a lizard darting into its hole. Everywhere chest-high thickets of briars and matted vines resisted his efforts to push through. Gaunt poplars also barred his way. But still he pressed on, the uncertain fate of his father burning in his mind. Once he thought that he heard the noise of hoofs pounding in the distance above. He shouted for help, but mocking caws from the crows that inhabited the ravine gave the only reply.

The fading light was deepening into dusk when Kiriath slashed his way through some bushes and encountered an obstacle he didn't remember at all. At a point where the ravine narrowed, a section of the rock wall had broken loose and tumbled to the bottom. A heap of shattered rock stood as a barrier twice the height of the prince. At this barrier's midpoint the brook poured down in a miniature waterfall, ending in a foamy pool.

Kiriath leaned on this new hindrance for a moment to catch his breath. "Happy are the birds who can fly," he said to himself. "But, if climb I must, then climb I will."

With that, he started scrambling up the crumbly stone in front of him. Many of the jutting handholds that he reached for broke loose as he grasped them. Within moments, however, Kiriath was heaving himself over the crest. Just in front of him was another, larger pool of water where the fallen stone had formed a natural dam. But his heart leaped within him when he raised his eyes. Just a few hundred yards ahead stood Shiralla, the capital of the kingdom and a fortress of silent strength, with lamplight twinkling from hundreds of windows. Shadowy figures moved back and forth atop the ramparts.

Kiriath felt renewed strength at the sight of his home. Edging along the pool of water, he found that the final barrier had been overcome, and he rapidly strode toward the city.

As Kiriath approached the grating where the brook issued from under Shiralla's wall, a voice rang out from above. "Halt! You, near the brook. Who are you, and what's your business outside the king's wall by night?"

Three other sentinels joined their comrade, who already had an arrow fitted to his longbow.

"Your eyesight is worthy of praise, Rylon," Kiriath called upward, "but don't loose your arrow too quickly. I'm Kiriath, son of Jekoniah. I was attacked by Grishnaki this morning, and it has taken me this long to return on foot."

"Prince Kiriath! This is good news. We thought you had been captured! Is the king with you? Is he all right?"

"He is not with me. I wish he were. But this is not the place for discussions. Can you send someone with a rope? I've already wasted too much of the day in this miserable ditch."

"At once, my prince," Rylon replied.

"While we're waiting, send word for Urijah to meet me in the council chamber," Kiriath went on. "The queen and my sister too. And Commander Carpathan, Bered, and Captain Brand, if they're in the city. Even bid old Nethanel to come. It's past his time to serve as Counselor, but strange things are afoot, and I'd like him to attend this discussion as well."

Rylon spoke a word to another sentinel, who hurried off. "All will be done. But Captain Brand has not yet returned. He and most of the others have been out searching for you and King Jekoniah since we received the report that you were under attack. Carpathan has only just returned."

Before long Kiriath saw three men with a torch appear on the cliff above. One of them carried a coil of rope over one shoulder.

"Shall we pull you up, Prince Kiriath, or will you climb the rope?"

"Hold the rope fast, and I should be able to climb out quickly enough."

The men did as they were bid, and soon the prince was scaling the wall. He walked up the side with his feet while his hands gripped the rope. The ravine walls were scarcely fifteen feet high at this point and not so steep as farther down the mountain, so he gained the brink fairly quickly. As strong arms stretched out to help him up, one of the men gasped.

"My prince, you look as if you've done battle with all of Darkon's legions at once."

"Not all of them, just more than I could handle. But give the rocks and thorns of the ravine the credit for shredding my clothing."

"Shall we send for the healers?" another asked, still eyeing him doubtfully.

"No, thank you. I'm tired and bruised, but not much worse."

As the group passed under the arch of the city gate, Kiriath saw that tidings of his return were already spreading. Many off-duty defenders of the city were turning out to welcome him back and to rejoice in his escape. A few merchants, tradesmen, and their families also lined the street to greet him as he strode up to the Citadel.

Kiriath tried to walk nobly, as was expected of the prince of Xandria. Still, the friendly smiles of the onlookers gave way to wide-eyed amazement when they saw his battered condition.

When the prince reached the entry to the Citadel, he released his escort to return to the wall. Stepping under the crossed spears of the King's Guardians, he felt oddly out of place walking across the sky blue tiles and up the marble steps in his stained and ragged clothing. When he shoved open the heavy door to the council chamber, Queen Vandrielle and his sister Ariana were already there.

"Kiriath!" they exclaimed in unison as each rushed up and took a hand. They looked him over in wonder.

"What happened to you?" his mother asked. "And tell us what's happened to your father."

"If he's alive, the Grishnaki have him. But let's wait for the others to arrive before I recount the full story."

Kiriath saw the tears well up in his mother's and sister's eyes. They had clearly been afraid of that possibility, and now he had confirmed their fears.

"You must be hungry," Ariana said, changing the subject. "Let us send for some supper."

"I'm hungry, but that can wait. I've called for the counselors, and Carpathan, Bered, and Brand. Things are happening that I can't explain. We need to talk and to lay our plans."

Just then the door swung open, and two men stepped inside. They were both clad in dusty military garb: gleaming steel breast-plates and red cloaks, with swords hanging at their sides.

"Kiriath!" said the foremost and huskier of the soldiers. He clapped the prince on the shoulder. "I've spent most of the day chasing through woods and vales searching for you and Jekoniah. I couldn't believe it when they told me you were back. But I'm glad to see that you are."

"I, too, am glad, Lord Kiriath," replied the grim-faced Bered, who followed Carpathan. "But where is the king?"

"Yes, what of the king?" repeated a voice from the doorway. Somberly, an ancient man with a short staff stepped over the threshold. His snow-white hair settled about the shoulders of his linen robe. Around his neck hung the silver medallion of a counselor.

"Nethanel," Kiriath said in greeting, "thank you for coming. I realize, of course, that your term as Counselor to the King is ended and that you are in your resting years. But I summoned you because your advice was always sound in the days when my grandfather was king, and in this hour, Xandria needs all the wisdom she can muster. As soon as Urijah arrives, I'll answer all of your questions about what happened to us this morning."

"Here I am," called a man bustling into the chamber. He, too, wore a silver counselor's medallion, but unlike the older Nethanel, this man wore a tunic and breeches rather than a robe. Also, his short black hair showed only a few flecks of gray. "Pardon my lateness. I only just received the summons to come."

"You're not late, Urijah," Kiriath replied. "We've just arrived ourselves. Now, what happened to Father and me is something I can't explain in one or two words. Truthfully, I don't even know the end of the story. Come, everyone take a seat. After we've told each other all we know about the day's events, we'll discuss what must be done."

Kiriath took the chair at the head of the table, where Jekoniah would normally sit. To his right were Queen Vandrielle; his sister, Ariana; and Counselor Urijah. To Kiriath's left sat Commander Carpathan; Bered, the chamberlain of Shiralla; and, lastly, the aged Nethanel. A single lamp on the table cast the shadows of the little group onto the richly carved paneling of the room.

"I know you all have as many questions as I do, so I'll begin by explaining what happened to Father and me."

Before the prince could continue, the sound of running feet and clinking metal echoed from the hallway outside. The door re-opened quickly, and a young man clad in a chain mail shirt slipped into the chamber. Glancing around, he shot the prince a quick grin of relief.

"Sorry for interrupting. Just arrived back for a fresh horse when I heard that you were here." He slipped into an empty chair at the far end of the table.

Despite the gravity of the moment, Kiriath inwardly smiled at his friend's disheveled appearance. It was obvious that he had been riding long and hard.

"Glad you could join us, Brand. We were just about to begin. I'll make my tale short, for there isn't much to it," Kiriath continued. "As I think some of you know, my father had lately become somewhat . . . restless. He felt almost as a prisoner in his own home, as he put it. He was feeling inactive and craved a change in his routine. I thought this time of depression would pass, but it grew as the weeks went by."

The queen nodded her head.

"So when Father approached me some days ago about our taking a morning ride without any Guardians, I didn't wholly reject the idea. I hoped that the fresh air would improve his spirits, as indeed it did. But without any warning, a band of Grishnaki attacked from the trees at the foot of the mountain. We sped up the road but found ourselves cut off by another band. Having no other escape, we made for the rope bridge. Father tried to cross first, but a spear meant for me struck him from behind."

The queen's eyes locked on Kiriath, and Ariana caught her breath. Giving the prince their full attention, the men remained motionless as they awaited the rest of the story.

"Although I can't be sure, I don't believe he was seriously hurt," the prince went on. "I have thought about it all afternoon as I struggled to hurry back here. Father was wearing his helmet and a mail shirt, so he was well protected. But the spear was extremely long and heavy, even for one of the Grishnaki's. I believe the sheer weight and speed of the thing caught him from behind, perhaps stunning him with its force. Also, I'm sure the spear didn't pierce him, for I saw no blood. It would have lodged where it struck instead of falling away as I saw it do."

"But you did not leave him." Lady Vandrielle spoke with the confidence that came from knowing her son.

"No, I didn't. The Grishnaki surrounded me before I could get to where Father lay. During the fight, one of them knocked me from my saddle, and I fell off the cliff into the ravine. That's all I remember until I awoke at the bottom of the cliff this afternoon."

"You lay at the foot of that cliff all morning, Kiriath?" Carpathan asked.

"Yes. The Grishnaki must have assumed I was dead."

"Then I beg your forgiveness. I stood on the very spot where your battle took place and even looked into the ravine. Please forgive me for whatever carelessness kept me from seeing you." Carpathan bowed his head in shame and self-rebuke.

"There's no need to forgive when there's no fault," Kiriath replied. "I doubt if you could have seen me even had you known I was there. A ledge of rock that I struck as I fell would have shielded me from your eyes. Besides, my cloak is green, and the grass where I fell was tall. You would have needed the eyes of an eagle—or a sorcerer—to spot me there. Anyway, I spent the rest of the day hacking underbrush and plodding up the ravine."

The elderly Nethanel spoke next. "Carpathan, I suggest you tell your part of the tale, so the prince and the rest of us will know what has been happening since you left this morning."

Carpathan nodded, and all eyes shifted to him.

"I was in the dining hall with fifty or sixty of my men when the door warden from the west gate rushed in, all out of breath. He declared that a worker on his way to the orchards had been to the swinging bridge, where he saw King Jekoniah and the prince fleeing from Grishnaki."

"Yes," Kiriath agreed. "We did see a man. I had forgotten about him."

"Well," Carpathan continued, "I scarcely believed the report at first, but a quick check showed that neither you nor King Jekoniah were in the Citadel. Lady Vandrielle affirmed that you had left Shiralla before first light."

"Folly it was, though it didn't seem so at the time," the prince muttered.

"Bered," Carpathan said, motioning to the silent man to his left, "ordered the trumpeters to blow the call to arms. Within minutes of hearing the report, I had talked to the man that brought in the news and was riding with a troop of men down the south road to find your attackers. Bered gathered enough men to take down the west road and around to the other side of the ravine. We knew that in the time a man on foot could reach Shiralla from the swinging bridge, the Grishnaki could cover a lot of territory.

"As we approached the ravine, it was obvious there had indeed been a fight along the path in the woods. We found the severed hand of one Grishnak. Three dead ones lay in the clearing near the bridge. We also found your dead horses, both shot through with many arrows."

"Only the most wicked of hearts vents hatred on his foe's animals." Anger mingled with disgust in Ariana's voice.

"True," Carpathan agreed. "But for myself, I'm glad that the enemy continues to fear and hate our horses rather than try to master them. A Grishnak on horseback would make a formidable foe. Then too," he added, looking at the prince, "judging by the hoof prints on one Grishnak body near the cliff, they had good reason to fear yours today."

"Is that the end of your account, Carpathan?" Vandrielle questioned.

"Most of it. I would add that the rope bridge had been cut by the time we arrived. When we started tracking the trails to and from the clearing, we found that there must have been more of the enemy than we had guessed, probably several hundred in all."

"Several hundred?" Kiriath repeated in astonishment.

"Surely hundreds of Grishnaki could not penetrate so far into Xandria without being seen," old Nethanel objected. "Not even by night. At least one of the patrols ought to have seen them. How is this possible?"

The expressions on Ariana's and Vandrielle's faces showed that they shared the elder counselor's surprise. The younger counselor, Urijah, sat motionless, save for a slight knitting together of his eyebrows as he fastened his eyes on Carpathan.

"How it's possible, I cannot tell," Carpathan answered, "but I've spent most of my life resisting Grishnaki. I've learned how to track them and to recognize the signs of their passing. Now I would stake my position as Chief Defender on the fact that there were at least two hundred of them at the foot of Mount Shiralla this morning. Maybe more. They did not come all together, though; that much was clear. For myself, I believe that five bands came separately by slightly different routes. All of them eventually reached various parts of the forest on the south road."

"But came from where?" the queen asked. "The Valley of the Grishnaki is so far to the northwest. They did not simply fly here. How could they travel this far in a single night without being seen from one of the garrisons, towns, or by one of your patrols?"

Carpathan shook his head gloomily. "I don't know. It's a mystery to me."

"I believe I can help shine some light on the mystery," Brand said. "But let's see first whether Bered has anything to say of what he found on the westward road."

For the first time, Bered broke his silence. "There was nothing at all to be found on the west road, nor in the orchards near the ravine. I thought this strange, for if Grishnaki had indeed traveled so far, I would have expected them to come by that way. As Vandrielle said, Dar-kon's lair is to the northwest. When we reached the ravine, the rope bridge had been cut from the far side, where Carpathan's men were already searching. I expanded our search westward, but there was no trace of their having come or gone that way."

"Then that confirms something," Brand said. "Following the Grishnaki trail out of the forest was difficult because, as Carpathan has said, there were many bands of them. Each group entered the forest from a different route; and when they left, each group struck out on an entirely new trail instead of backtracking the way they had come. So the woods were full of the signs of their passing.

"Then a scout found a place where two trails joined south of the forest. We followed their footprints all the way to the Gray Bogs. I couldn't believe that they had walked straight into the swamps. I thought it a trick to hide their trail. So I sent half my men one way along the edge of the Bogs while I took the other half along the other way. We found places where three other trails entered the Bogs. The men of the Highmount garrison told us that they had not seen so much as a single Grishnak in weeks. In my opinion, they must have waded through the Gray Bogs and then circled around to the northwest on the wild side of the Ironridges."

"Yes," Kiriath said, "I recall now that the Grishnaki who attacked me had a foul stench about them. Not that any of them ever wash, but it was like the putrid odor of the Bogs."

"Aye, and all the bodies we found stank worse than usual," Carpathan added.

"I had no time to think about it then," Kiriath went on, "but their crossing the Bogs might explain that. Urijah, Father has sent you to accompany border patrols in that district. What do you make of this news?"

Counselor Urijah cleared his throat. "No one could have expected it, my prince. For three hundred years, indeed, since the founding of Xandria, the Gray Bogs have been a natural defense, since Grishnaki bodies simply can't swim. Of course, we have known for a long while that the Bogs have been slowly drying up. Still, no man has ever crossed them without a boat. Who would have thought that the Grishnaki could do it?"

"Brand," Ariana began, "did you try to follow any of the trails into the Bogs? There has been less rain this year. Perhaps—"

Brand shook his head. "The Bogs are much lower; that's true. But they're still too deep for a man on foot, and I wouldn't dare take a horse into that slime. Even the Grishnaki must have been up to their chins in scum unless they've learned new tricks."

"But the Ironridge Hills are tall and wide," Queen Vandrielle remarked. "They're almost small mountains. If the Grishnaki took that route, surely they could not have circled all the way back to Vol-Rathdeen even by this hour."

Carpathan looked toward the ceiling, silently calculating. "No. Even with their loping run that gobbles up the miles, they could not travel that far so swiftly. It must have taken them a good part of the day just to reach the Bogs. They may still be near the Ironridges, or perhaps in the wilderness just beyond." He paused for a moment. "But that knowledge does not help us. They will be safely inside their valley before we could send a troop to intercept them. Besides, Dar-kon will have his warriors protecting their retreat. To send any men over the border tonight would be sending them into a trap."

Kiriath rubbed his chin. "Xandria is not safe if the Grishnaki can cross the Bogs. We'll need new fortresses near there and will have to expand the patrollers' routes. But what of the present?

The Grishnaki have our king—and my father. What will we do about it?"

Heavy silence descended upon the room. Clearing his throat, Bered said at length, "Perhaps, before we ask what we will do about it, we should ask what *can* we do about it? We don't even know the Grishnaki's purpose in all this."

"They may not have a purpose," Urijah pointed out. "Or perhaps not a clear one. It may be that this was simply a raiding party sent by Dar-kon to torment us or to strike fear into our people. Suddenly finding our king unprotected would be reason enough to capture him alive without any thought of what they would do with their prize."

"Judging by their arrows and spears, they certainly had no thoughts about capturing me," Kiriath noted. "Not until they surrounded me did they try to pull me down alive."

"Who can say?" Ariana asked. "They may even have come to capture you, Brother. Everyone in Shiralla knows that you often ride at dawn. If the Grishnaki tortured this knowledge out of someone—say, a captured hunter—they might have come hoping to seize a prince and then passed you by when they saw their chance to snatch the king instead. But the thoughts of Grishnaki are black. Who can know them?"

"Aye, they're black," Carpathan agreed. "And I'm always finding new and darker corners in them."

"Regardless of why they came in the first place," Queen Vandrielle said, "they have Jekoniah now. We have to do something. What will they do to him, and how can Xandria respond? I want to hear definite answers."

The elderly counselor Nethanel shook his head. "No one can be sure of what they will do. But I believe there are only two likely possibilities. On the one hand, they may torture and kill King Jekoniah for their own evil pleasure and for our distress."

Vandrielle raised one eyebrow.

Noticing her reaction, Nethanel added, "I do not predict this. I present it only as one possibility. It would be in keeping with their barbaric nature. On the other hand, they may try to barter with us. That is, hold the king captive until we pay some ransom to get him back."

"But what would they want of us?" Brand asked. "The Grishnaki seem more bent on destroying than anything else. Even gold and silver hold little attraction for them, except maybe as metal tips for their arrows and spears."

"I was not speaking of money. Dar-kon may try to get something else from us. Food, for example. You know that Grishnaki do not grow any food of their own; they hunt for it. So they could demand that we supply them with cattle, venison, or other meats. Or they could demand that we pull back our borders and never patrol outside the realm again. But these are all just guesses. No one can be sure. When I was young, I used to think Dar-kon was stupid. But as I grew older, I began to realize that he has a certain shrewdness, even cunning, in a malevolent sort of way."

"So either they kill Father," Ariana concluded in frustration, "or they hold him hostage for barter. My blood boils to attack and teach Dar-kon a lesson."

"Vengeance?" Urijah asked. "Xandria has never made war for vengeance, nor to improve the Grishnaki's education. King Jekoniah himself supports that principle."

"Urijah is right," Nethanel agreed. "Vigilant strength for defense has always been our principle. Besides, attacking now would only ensure the king's death. Even if they do not intend to kill him immediately, we could not hope to win him back through arms. They would chop off his head before our men could reach him."

"Nor could we hope to take an army into the Valley of Grishnaki," Carpathan added. "The entrance to the valley is wide but very defensible. Knowing the territory, they would have all the advantage. Even if we did force our way into the valley, how could we hope to do battle underground, in Vol-Rathdeen itself? Horses cannot be used for fighting in caverns, and on foot the enemy would have the advantage in size and strength."

"So we still have the question," the queen persisted. "What can we do?"

"All that we can do," said Bered. "Remain alert and strong—and wait."

Kiriath nodded and stood up. "I don't like it, but I see no other choice. The Grishnaki have seized control in this game. The next move seems up to them."

Queen Vandrielle stood too. "It's a filthy game that reduces Jekoniah to a mere token, ready to be cast away. But let us wait then and remain ready for anything. If Dar-kon is going to make a move, he will not waste time doing it.

"Now, my son," she added, "you have fulfilled your duty to your father and king. I will have a meal prepared while you wash and refresh yourself."

With that, the queen and Ariana slipped out.

Nethanel and Urijah made for the door as well. "Thank you for coming," said Kiriath, clasping a hand on each one's shoulder. "No advice would be worth listening to without the wisdom of the king's counselors."

"We have but done our duty," Urijah stated.

"Doubtless, the days that come shall see need of further counsel, Prince Kiriath," Nethanel added. "I realize I am aged and have not served in the office of Counselor for a long while. But like Urijah, I am still yours to command if I may be of service. Call for me day or night."

The two departed, and grim Bered approached the door. Kiriath raised his hand, signaling for him to wait. Then going to the door, the prince silently closed it and turned to the remaining three.

"Stay a minute and remain seated, if you will," he said.

Bered, Carpathan, and Brand exchanged glances, then obeyed the prince's request.

"Every step of the way back to Shiralla, the possibility of Father's being a prisoner of the Grishnaki burned within me. It occurred to me that, if they decided to kill him outright, there would be nothing we could do to stop them. But if they keep him captive, there might still be a course of action open to us. It would be dangerous, though, for the person involved, so I wanted to discuss the idea with you three first."

"All right," said Carpathan, "but shouldn't we call back Urijah and Nethanel? Giving advice is why they are here."

"No, let's not involve them for the moment. Yes, yes, I know it's true that especially Nethanel knows the Grishnaki's history, and Urijah is the official Counselor. But you, Carpathan, as Chief Defender have had much experience with Dar-kon's legions through strength of arms. The same can be said of you, Bered, since you grew up and fought in the Western provinces. I include you, Brand, not only because you're like a brother to me, but also because you have spent as much time leading border patrols as I have. Probably more. It's your joint military experience with the foe that I want to draw upon now."

Brand reached a hand to the lamp on the table and turned up the wick, brightening the light in the chamber. "All right, Kiriath, you have us all curious now," he said with a hint of a grin. "I can tell when you're scheming. Let's hear your plan."

CHAPTER 3

KROLL

The next day, Kiriath was in his chamber pulling on his boots when a knock sounded on the oaken door. "Come in."

A man wearing the red and black garb of the Citadel Guardians stepped in. "A message from Westrock, Prince Kiriath. They have received an ambassador from Dar-kon."

Kiriath stood up at once. "An ambassador, did you say?"

"Yes, although I have never heard of Dar-kon's using any ambassador other than the spear and the arrow, that is what this Grishnak calls himself. He says that he comes to parley arrangements for the release of King Jekoniah."

"What kind of arrangements? Where is this ambassador now?"

"As for the arrangements, my prince, we do not know. The Grishnak refuses to discuss Dar-kon's terms with any but Lady Vandrielle. A score of riders from the garrison are escorting him here now. The creature refused to ride on horseback but consented to be carried in a field wagon. They should arrive within three hours."

"In three hours by field wagon?" Kiriath asked in disbelief. "From the frontier?"

"The news is not fresh. The messenger arrived in Shiralla almost two hours ago, and it is already approaching the seventh hour of the day."

"The seventh hour!" Kiriath exclaimed. "How could I be such a sluggard? Why was this news not brought to me at once?"

"The queen forbade it. She thought rest a better medicine for your recent ordeal than news. Not until a few minutes ago did she bid me to rouse you and give you the message. She also said to tell you that she would have a morning meal prepared for you in the dining hall, where she awaits you."

"Thank you, Naimer. You may go."

The Guardian bowed and left. Kiriath snatched his sword belt from the bedside table and hurried out, buckling it about his waist as he strode toward the end of the tiled hallway. He then descended a winding staircase to the ground floor. Striding down another corridor, he soon came to the dining hall.

Long rows of tables filled the hall, all empty, save one at which Queen Vandrielle sat in silent contemplation. Hesitating at the sober-minded look on her face, Kiriath opened his mouth to speak but then closed it again. Presently she sensed his presence and beckoned him closer.

"Come, Son, your food is growing cold. You must regain your strength. We can talk while you eat." She motioned to a platter beside her.

Kiriath sat down and sliced into a thick slab of ham. Noting her drawn face and the circles under her eyes, he said, "You look weighed down with your thoughts. I'm sure you couldn't have slept much. Is there more news about this emissary from Dar-kon than I've been told?"

"No. You know as much as I do. I'm simply afraid of what may be inevitable. According to the message from Westrock, the Grishnak courier says he comes to parley terms for Jekoniah's release. Still, in my heart I know that Dar-kon would not go to such efforts for any prize that Xandria can easily afford to lose."

Here Vandrielle rose and stepped to the stained-glass window, as if able to peer through its opaque thickness. "But if the price is too high to accept? What then? It would be a grievous blow for Xandria to lose one whose leadership has prospered and strengthened the kingdom so much. Of course, being his wife, I would suffer an even greater blow. Yet . . ."

She paused, her tension showing in the white knuckles of her clasped hands. Then, lowering her voice, Vandrielle continued, almost as if speaking to herself. "Yet as queen of the realm, I may have to reject Dar-kon's terms and let your father suffer whatever hideous death the Grishnaki can devise."

Kiriath pushed back his platter, stepped over to his mother, and placed an arm around her shoulders. "Let's wait awhile before we cast aside all hope. We haven't even heard the terms yet. 'A people who feel defeated . . .'"

"'. . . will be defeated,'" Vandrielle finished. "I know. So has your father often quoted. Do not worry about me, though. I share my thoughts with you only because you are my son. The queen is expected to show no weakness to anyone outside her own family. Neither Dar-kon nor the people shall see the battle in my heart. I think I should tell you, though, that if your father does not return, I have decided not to rule Xandria."

"But why not?"

"Oh, I know the people would follow me, and in this present distress I will do all that a queen must do. But if Jekoniah does not return, there would be no heart left within me. I would step down and pass all authority to your hands."

His mother's words suddenly reminded Kiriath of what his father had said on their last ride together: that the prince would know what it was like to be king before many more years. His father had spoken in good humor, but now Kiriath could almost feel the invisible responsibilities of the kingship descending on him with their full weight.

"We talk of such things too soon," he said at last. "Let's wait for Dar-kon's mouthpiece. When you receive him, I think I will listen to his message from out of sight. If the Grishnaki don't realize that I'm still alive, let's keep that bit of news a secret. We may find some advantage if Dar-kon believes he is dealing with a distraught woman who is deprived of both husband and son."

Vandrielle gave her son a wan smile. "I thought you might wish that," she said. "As soon as I received news of the Grishnak's coming, I sent back a rider to acknowledge the message and to charge the captain of the escort not to let your name be mentioned in the creature's presence. Indeed, traveling all the way from the frontier, the captain himself could not know that you returned last night."

Kiriath forced a chuckle. "Ever since I was a boy, you have been able to read my thoughts. What's your secret?"

"No secret. All mothers can predict their children's thoughts at times. Besides—your father would have done the same."

A little over three hours later, tidings arrived that the field wagon carrying the Grishnak emissary was winding up the west road to Mount Shiralla. By Bered's orders, all available men-at-arms in the city were on duty along the walls and towers or in the streets. No hint of military weakness was to be visible.

Commander Carpathan led a troop out to meet the wagon outside the city. This news amused Kiriath, for he realized that Carpathan did so neither because he feared the Grishnak nor to honor him, but because all Grishnaki retained a primitive fear of horses. Making this representative of the enemy as uncomfortable as possible was as much sport as Carpathan could derive to vent his frustration.

The procession entered the gates of the city, proceeding directly to the Citadel, as Queen Vandrielle had bidden. Many of those that had stood in the streets to welcome Kiriath now watched from behind windows. Here and there, a courageous lad ventured outside to get his first glimpse of a genuine Grishnak, only to be pulled back inside by a scolding mother.

Inside the Citadel, Vandrielle and Kiriath waited in the Praetorium. The prince couldn't help thinking how odd it seemed to see his mother sitting alone, in silent expectation, on the oaken judgment bench atop the dais where he had never seen anyone but his grandfather and father sit. Nethanel and Urijah sat on smaller chairs to the left and right of her. Standing to one side, Brand and Ariana also waited in strained silence.

At last, one of Carpathan's men entered. "Lady Vandrielle," he called. "Dar-kon's ambassador has come."

"Let the creature enter," Vandrielle said.

"By your leave, Mother, I'll examine Dar-kon's minion unseen," Kiriath reminded.

Vandrielle gave her son a half nod, and the prince slipped behind a tapestry that hung in front of a small alcove. He pulled the tapestry close to the wall and left just a slit through which to watch.

Soon two of the king's guards entered, followed by the Grishnak, then Carpathan and Bered, and two score soldiers. One of the men carried a primitive wooden sword, which the prince knew belonged in the Grishnak's belt.

Kiriath saw nothing unusual about this particular Grishnak, unless perhaps he sensed a slightly greater intelligence than he normally did in these creatures. Never before had the prince experienced the leisure of examining one of the foes so closely. Normally he glimpsed them from afar, perhaps across a river. Up close he had seen them but rarely, and then only in the heat of combat.

The young prince could see that the creature was tall, though not exceptionally so for one of his race. The Grishnak's head was crowned with scraggly hair that resembled matted twigs more than anything else. The ambassador held his eyelids half-closed, as if feigning boredom or indifference, while those partially concealed eyes slyly flitted right and left as he clumped across the Praetorium. His raiment was of crudely fashioned deerskin, with a matching belt girt around his waist. His feet were likewise shod with deerskin, bound in place by strips of leather.

As it always had in the past, the thickness of these creatures' limbs caught Kiriath's attention. Observing again how Grishnak skin resembled flexible bark more than flesh, he thought this creature's arms and legs bore more similarity to a cedar tree's branches than to the limbs of a living being. The mouth, though, reminded Kiriath of a dog's as canine-like fangs protruded from leathery lips.

When the procession reached the foot of the dais, the two lead guards divided and stood with their spears butted on the floor, one at each side of the dais.

Bered took one additional step forward. "Lady Vandrielle, I present the ambassador of Dar-kon, chief of the Grishnaki."

The queen fixed her gaze on the Grishnak without speaking. The Grishnak did not bow or offer any word of greeting. However, after a long moment Kiriath sensed with satisfaction that the creature was becoming uncomfortable under her stare and at last dropped his eyes to the floor.

Finally Vandrielle released a single word: "Welcome."

The Grishnak raised his eyes again. "I am Kroll-Tahn-Su, from the tribe of Gahb, of Vol-Rathdeen—the Fortress of Night! I will permit you to call me Kroll."

To the prince, the rumbling grating of the Grishnak's voice sounded as if each syllable were gurgling up through a throat full of gravel. Hearing it, Kiriath swallowed unconsciously.

What would it feel like to speak with such a voice? he wondered.

Vandrielle gazed at Kroll for another prolonged moment and gave no indication of what she was thinking. At length she said, "It has never been the custom of our people to receive armed ambassadors, Kroll. Please surrender your weapon for now. It will be returned when you leave Xandria."

For a moment the thick lids of Kroll's eyes slid down even farther, his eyes becoming little more than slits before he reopened them to their normal half-lidded position. "If you are not blind," he replied, motioning to the man to his rear, "you can see that this horse-boy already has my sword."

"I weary easily of games," Vandrielle answered. "That bulge inside the bindings of your left boot—do not tell me that your leg is shaped so."

As before, Kroll's eyes narrowed, but they remained locked on Vandrielle's. Then, wordlessly, he stooped and pulled a small wooden dagger from the location the queen had mentioned.

Murmurs of surprise came from many that stood by, and the soldier bearing Kroll's sword hastened forward to accept the smaller weapon as well.

Within his hiding place, Kiriath grinned broadly and nodded with approval at his mother's discernment. If he had harbored any doubts of her strength as a leader, she had completely dispelled them.

"Now we may speak," the queen said. "What message does the ruler of Vol-Rathdeen bid you to deliver today?"

"You have a choice, O woman," he replied in his gravelly voice. "You can get your man-kon back, or you can let us keep him. But choosing the latter means you will never see his flesh again—at least not in one hunk." Here Kroll opened his eyes wide for the first time, as if to add venom to his words.

"Say on," Vandrielle answered, unflinching.

Kroll appeared disappointed by her attitude. He seemed unsure how to react to this uncommon woman.

She may be the first woman he has ever seen, Kiriath thought. *Only men man the border garrisons.*

"Dar-kon will trade your leader-man back to you," Kroll continued. "And the price is small. Yes, quite small."

"You use many words to say little, Kroll. We assumed you would say this much long before you arrived here."

Behind the tapestry Kiriath felt proud of his mother. He wasn't sure that he himself could have handled the matter better. Directly across the room, he could see Ariana, also with a twinge of a grim smile on her lips. It occurred to Kiriath then how much like their mother Ariana had grown. He looked more closely at her. Certainly she had always resembled the queen, with wheat-colored hair curling about her shoulders and a silver circlet above her brow. The way she stood and walked were also reminiscent of Lady Vandrielle. But there was a certain other indefinable quality he had not fully remarked before. An inner strength of will or character it was. Kiriath shifted his gaze to Brand at her side. Perhaps it was her love for his friend that had hastened the change in her? But now words began rumbling from Kroll's mouth, drawing back Kiriath's full attention.

"All we want is . . ." Kroll stopped, as if groping in his mind for the proper word. "Only . . . knowledge. Nothing else. The Grishnaki are growing, learning. We have new needs. We have outgrown wood and stone for our tools. We want your people to teach us the secret of steel crafting."

Outraged mutterings filled the hall. Defenders looked at each other with disbelief and anger. Aged Nethanel nodded to himself, as if he had expected something of this sort, though his younger counterpart, Urijah, intently followed the exchange without moving. On the judgment bench, Vandrielle raised a single eyebrow in her typical way.

"I do not know how much history the Grishnaki share with their young, Kroll," the queen began. "Years ago, our ancestors came to this shore and found your fathers wandering the hills in quarreling tribes, half-starved and naked as they hunted and fished with their bare hands.

"Our people had never seen a Grishnak before, but they soon perceived that your hearts were darkened. In their innocence, they thought to enlighten your nature by dwelling with your kind as friends, by giving them knowledge and teaching them new skills. So it was that our people taught your kind how to fashion tools and better ways to hunt and to fish. In addition, they had intended to teach your Grishnaki fathers how to create iron, steel, and many other useful things. But they learned their error too late. Teaching the mind cannot shine light into the heart of a being given over to darkness: it merely provides new avenues for him to channel his evil.

"Using what we had given them, the Grishnaki united under Dar-kon's grandfather and attacked us, recklessly killing and pillaging. If your fathers had waited until our people had shared all our knowledge instead of just a little of it, our race would no longer exist. Our knights of old resisted your warriors—barely—and not without much loss of life on both sides. Since that time, sharing any knowledge with Grishnaki has been outlawed in our realm.

"Personally, I could not begin to explain anything about steel making, nor could King Jekoniah whom you hold captive. That is the work of our steelsmiths. But even if we could, we would not share that knowledge with your kind. It is forbidden. You Grishnaki jealously guard your elixir of long life. Steel making is something that we, in turn, must hold as a secret."

Kroll crossed his thick arms in front of him. "Now who uses much speaking to say little, O woman?" he rumbled. "I do not speak of what was. Only of what is and what will be. I said you have a choice: you have your precious little secrets, but we have your man-kon."

Kroll paused, as if to see what impact his words were having, then continued. "What is knowledge? Nothing! You cannot eat it. You cannot drink it. We could ask for more. Much land, much meat. Or we could even demand golden-haired mates for our warriors." Even as these last words tumbled from his mouth, the Grishnak swung his leering face toward Ariana and ran his slimy tongue over his lips.

Behind the tapestry Kiriath clenched his teeth.

"Impudent—" Brand began.

"But we do not!" Kroll bellowed before Brand could finish. "A little more learning is our only price. After we receive this skill, the man-kon will be yours—alive. Dar-kon has promised. Dar-kon has spoken."

"How do we know the king is even still alive?" Counselor Urijah called from where he was sitting. "You could be bartering with an empty sack."

Kroll gave the counselor a sidelong glance. "I speak the words of Dar-kon, and today Dar-kon speaks only to the woman-chief."

"It is my counselor's duty to raise questions as well as to give advice," Vandrielle said. "Although spoken by him, the question is also mine. Please answer."

"I cannot prove his life," Kroll responded. "But his heart still beats. In Vol-Rathdeen. To make your choice easier, before your smiths teach us to make steel, Dar-kon may suffer one or two of your kind to see him from afar—but not to speak to him. When our Grishnaki return to us from their learning, then your chief one will come home to you."

"That means our king would be your prisoner for many days, possibly weeks or months. Are you certain that a guest of Vol-Rathdeen can remain alive for so long?"

More than a hint of sarcasm gilt the queen's tone. However, the question seemed to please Kroll. As if remembering something, he raised his twiggy eyebrows and curled his mouth up at the corners, revealing crooked teeth that matched his yellow fangs. "It has happened before—at times," he said smugly. "Oh, yes, it has happened."

Kroll showed no intention of elaborating, and Vandrielle did not care to learn the meaning behind his humor.

"Dar-kon sets a large price for the return of one man," she stated.

"A large price indeed," came a voice. Breaking his silence, Nethanel leaned forward in his seat. "One man alone—even a king—is hardly worth the secret of Xandrian steel. Why does Dar-kon not offer more than one man's return for such valuable knowledge?"

Odd question, the prince thought from his alcove. *But he's a counselor. He must have his reasons.*

Kroll hesitated, as if pondering how to reply. His half-closed eyes slid from Vandrielle to Nethanel, then to Urijah, and finally back to the queen. At last he said, "Because these two speak for the woman, I will answer. If such a question came, Dar-kon bade me to add one last word. Besides returning the man-kon, the Grishnaki will share a secret too. Many generations of men-kind have been born and buried since your people sailed here across the great water. But my father's father was there to see that day. Woman, you spoke of the Grishnaki's elixir of long life. Your dead fathers wanted it. Teach us to make steel, and we will even give you the elixir. We will teach you to number your years as the Grishnaki."

When Kroll finished, the hall was silent. Men turned their eyes to the queen to await her response.

"For myself, I care only for the life of our king and not at all for secret elixirs," she said. "I suppose Dar-kon expects a speedy reply to these terms?"

Kroll held up one hand, spreading wide his seven thick fingers. "Seven days," came the gravelly reply. "You have seven days to weigh these matters. When the sun rises on the seventh day, Kroll will come to the fortress where he met these." He gestured toward the men from the border garrison.

"Westrock," Carpathan said.

"Yes. That is your word for it. Westrock. The seventh day after today. When the sun rises. Choose well."

"So far, Kroll," Vandrielle said, "you have spoken only of King Jekoniah. Yet we know that Prince Kiriath was with our king when your Grishnaki brothers captured him. Why do you say nothing of returning the prince?"

Now Kiriath watched Kroll's visage even more closely. Once more he saw the ambassador's eyes become hooded as his eyelids descended, almost as if Kroll feared the queen might see into his thoughts if he fully opened those eyes. After scrutinizing her face, he slowly moved his head to the right then left, the upper part of his body turning with it, and the smudge of a smirk appearing.

"Why would Grishnaki need the son when we have the father? We do not have the young one. But I was not there when your chief-man was invited to Vol-Rathdeen. Perhaps the son had an accident. Search for him. I hope he is not hurt—or dead."

Kroll practically spat out this last word. He seemed disappointed when his words failed to disturb the tranquility of Vandrielle's face.

"My duty is done," he concluded. "Seven days. No more. Darkon has spoken." He took one step backward and fixed his gaze on the wall, waiting.

"Carpathan," the queen called. "Arrange for a new escort to return Kroll to the border. Have the Westrock men remain and rest in Shiralla for now. They can ride back tomorrow. Also, if Kroll requests food or drink or anything to refresh himself, give it to him. Let it not be said that we ever mistreated one who comes in truce."

"All will be done as you say," Carpathan replied. He bowed and turned about, the other defenders following his lead. Kroll loped out among them, seemingly trying to ignore his escort.

As soon as the Grishnak was out of earshot, Kiriath thrust back the tapestry and strode to his mother's side. Brand, Ariana, Nethanel, and Urijah likewise gathered around the queen, who sat staring at the doors through which Kroll had disappeared.

"That Kroll is loathsome," Ariana declared with a shudder. "And why does he call Father *kon* and *man-kon*?"

"I thought you knew," Kiriath replied. "To them *kon* means *king*."

"That is how the Grishnaki first pronounced the word when the colonists began teaching them our tongue," ancient Nethanel elaborated. "Even when they gained a better grasp of our pronunciation, the corrupted version remained. So *Dar-kon* is not one name; it means *King Dar*."

"The only Grishnaki words I know are the curses they hurl across Border River," Brand remarked. "But you were right about their intentions, Nethanel. It's a ransom they want. A hefty price too."

"What shall we do, Mother?" Ariana asked.

Vandrielle glanced at her daughter but did not respond. Instead, Nethanel quietly spoke for her.

"Xandria cannot afford to give the knowledge of steel making to the Grishnaki, not even in exchange for ten kings. That law must not be broken. Your mother realizes this. So, too, does your father in Vol-Rathdeen. To give them steel would give them a terrible advantage in battle. We would be handing them the weapons with which to slaughter us."

"Would we indeed, Nethanel?" Urijah questioned. "Consider. Eventually, the Grishnaki would become stronger for war, but they could not become masters of metal crafting overnight. It would take them quite a while, perhaps years, to perfect their skills and create enough weapons and armor to become a worse threat. But in those same years Xandria could also grow stronger for war. What I mean is, with their secret elixir of long life, one Grishnak lives for many of our generations, but their females bear offspring much less frequently than among us. If we knew how to create that elixir, the total number of men to defend the kingdom would increase because our men-at-arms would live three, maybe four, times as long as they do now. It could be argued that such knowledge itself may be worth more than steel and the ten kings you mentioned. And do not forget that it is Jekoniah's neck that is on the chopping block."

"You surprise me, Urijah," Nethanel returned. "Do not forget yourself that the Grishnaki are unworthy of our trust. Over the years our ancestors have tried to negotiate with them many times. Ten separate treaties have been made. Each time the Grishnaki broke those agreements. The lesson of history is that the Grishnaki cannot be trusted to fulfill any promise. I do not believe we would receive either the king or the elixir. Besides, how many years would it take to know if the elixir they give us is genuine? Only time would reveal that."

"But there is a chance," Urijah persisted to the queen. "In my opinion, they would not dare to cheat on this bargain since they obviously want steel."

"Dar-kon might dare anything," Nethanel declared wearily.

Kiriath studied his mother's face and felt pain for the struggle he knew was raging in her heart. As much as she wanted to accept Urijah's counsel, the prince could see that she had already abandoned all hope of seeing her husband again. Dar-kon's price had been too high.

"We cannot negotiate with the Grishnaki on their terms," the prince stated. "However, we may yet save Father and restore the king to Shiralla."

"But how?" Ariana asked for all of them.

"I will go to Vol-Rathdeen and bring him back."

Urijah dismissed the idea with a flip of his hand: "Impossible." He suddenly seemed to realize how impatient his response must have sounded and lightened his tone. "Prince Kiriath, let no one doubt either your valor or your faithfulness to your father. But, as has already been stated, any armed assault against Dar-kon would be fruitless. His position is too strong. The very entrance to the valley is walled up. The valley walls are honeycombed with defended caves. Even the most stalwart defenders could not hope to battle their way into the main caverns of Vol-Rathdeen quickly enough to locate Jekoniah and then escape with him."

"He's right, Kiriath," Vandrielle agreed.

"Yes, he is," the prince said. "Any armed assault would be a foolish effort. That's why I intend to sneak in—on foot."

Comprehension dawned in his sister's eyes. "You're not thinking of walking into Vol-Rathdeen alone?"

"Not exactly alone," Brand put in. "I'm going with him."

Nethanel remained silent, his eyes closed in contemplation as he stroked his white beard. But Urijah spoke up quickly. "What new folly is this?" he asked. "The king has been taken; our prince proposes to make himself vulnerable in the enemy camp, and one of our finest captains says he is going along? Kiriath, please reconsider. This is not wisdom."

"But wisdom dictates that we examine every option—no matter how daring—before we timidly yield to our foes or let them slaughter our king. The Grishnaki were able to capture Father because they did the unexpected—they penetrated our border in a place and in a way we never imagined they could. Brand and I will do the same to them. My idea is to head north. When we are far past our northernmost garrisons, we'll circle around to the far side of Vol-Rathdeen, approaching the enemy from a direction no Xandrian has ever used."

Nethanel, his eyes still closed, continued leaning on his staff and listening to the prince's bold proposal. A stranger might have thought him tired, but Kiriath knew from experience that the aged counselor was seriously weighing this strategy.

"That road holds its own perils," the queen observed. "The Deserted Kingdom lies to the north, and it is said that mysterious things happen in those Lowlands. In addition, the wilderness to the north is not wholly empty. Dar-kon's folk often roam north of Xandria. Farther yet, loose tribes of wild Grishnaki still wander the land."

"It's not safe to approach the Valley of the Grishnaki from any direction," Brand agreed. "But the difficulties of this path would be to our advantage. The harder the road, the less thought the Grishnaki will give to finding us on it."

"In addition, the Grishnaki see strength only in large numbers," Kiriath went on. "They hunt in packs, and they watch for large movements of our men. By stealth, two men without horses just might be able to slip into their valley by night."

Urijah shook his head. "Suppose you do get as far as the valley. You cannot see in the dark. How will you find King Jekoniah inside their caves?"

Kiriath glanced again at Nethanel. As yet, the elderly advisor made no sign of his thoughts. "No, we can't see in the dark. But neither can the Grishnaki. They use torches to walk by night and light their camps with fires. My guess is that torches light their caves as well. Brand and I are both tall enough that, in Grishnak clothing, we might be able to pass through torchlight unchallenged."

Urijah remained unconvinced. "What about freeing the king? Even if you overcome all other obstacles, you cannot hope to walk up to the Grishnaki's prize prisoner and simply stroll out unnoticed."

"Unforeseen problems lie around every corner," Brand said, directing his words to the queen. "But so do unforeseen opportunities. We do hope to disguise Jekoniah Grishnak-fashion as ourselves, but past that it is difficult to lay plans. Certainly all of Dar-kon's legions would be alerted before we could escape very far. But by using caution and hiding in the daytime, we might reach Border River safely."

Throughout this debate Queen Vandrielle listened without comment. She studied the faces of her son and Brand. "This is not a mission I could send any man on," she said. "Least of all my own son."

"Nor could I," the prince agreed. "That is why I decided to go alone. I dared not ask even Brand to come along, although I'm glad he volunteered to join me. Carpathan and Bered have also heard the plan. They have some misgivings, but both confess a sliver of possibility in it."

Kiriath saw hope intertwining with fear within his mother. "If you forbid me, Mother, I will obey. But how many years would it take me to forget that I let the Grishnaki murder my father while I had a chance to save him?"

"Nethanel," the queen asked, "have you nothing to share?"

As if summoned back to life, Nethanel opened his eyes, straightened himself to full height, and drew in a deep breath. "There is a chance. How much of one I cannot judge. Perhaps only the glimmer of a chance, but a chance nonetheless. The prince rightly discerns the ways of the Grishnaki. He knows, too, the risks."

"If this were my decision to make, it would be an agonizing one," the queen said. "I could not send either of you into Darkon's caves without fear. *Vol-Rathdeen* means *Fortress of Night*. Even the name reeks of evil. Kiriath, you are old enough to rule Xandria, so you are old enough to make this choice. I will say neither stay nor go. The decision is yours. Just remember—if you should attempt this, and the Grishnaki discover you, your death will be as hideous and painful as the enemy can contrive to make it.

"And Brand," she said, turning to her son's companion, "No friend could be called unfaithful for not going on this errand. A friend such as you have proved yourself to be is worth more than much gold. My heart is heavy, but I am glad Kiriath has such a friend. If you still determine to attempt this, may the light that shines in you both sustain you in the darkness ahead."

Brand seemed uncertain how to respond. Without a word he simply bowed to the queen.

At Brand's side, Ariana wiped her eyes and then hastened out of the hall.

CHAPTER 4

UNDERCOVER

Kiriath stepped from his room and silently swung the door shut behind him. Night still reigned over the Citadel, dispelled only here and there in niches along the walls, where lanterns glowed. The prince shifted the pack he carried over his shoulder and set off down the corridor.

Arriving at the circular stairway, he descended, step after step, with scarcely a sound. With the assurance that comes from years of usage, Kiriath descended through alternating lantern light and darkness, running a hand along the cool stone wall as he did so.

Reaching the ground floor, he drifted past the darkened entrances to several adjoining halls. At last he arrived at his goal. From beneath the door at which the prince now stopped shone a soft orange glow. He lightly tapped a knuckle on the door.

A second later the slit of light at his feet winked out, and the latch clicked. As the door opened, he could just dimly make out Brand's silhouette.

"Ready?" Kiriath breathed.

"Yes," came the answering whisper. "Let's be off."

As phantoms, the two companions floated down the corridor. Only the slightest rustle of clothing and an occasional scuff of leather soles on the floor tiles betrayed their passing.

"This way," Kiriath whispered when they arrived at the dining hall. He led the way through the arched entrance.

Although a popular place for meeting and eating during the day, the hall was void of life at this early hour. It awaited the return of day in an almost eerie silence. Blue-tinged moonlight oozed through the stained-glass windows.

"Over here," signaled the prince, approaching the empty fireplace at the head of the hall. "Now I'll show you something that no one outside my family has seen since the builders of Shiralla died."

As Brand looked on, Kiriath stretched both arms up to the ancient shield of Kanadon, first ruler of Xandria, that hung above the hearth. Almost reverently, he removed it from its pegs and set the shield on the nearest table.

Stepping back to the fireplace, the prince ran both hands along the spot that the shield had covered. His fingers stopped; then he pushed. The stone beneath his touch yielded and sank into the wall. At the same time a muffled click sounded from somewhere nearby.

Kiriath saw Brand jump, startled, and he chuckled lightly. "Just the lock," Kiriath explained.

He replaced the shield and turned his attention to a portion of the wall just left of the hearth. He pushed here also, and a four-foot-high section of stone swung open, revealing a low doorway. Brand stared wide-eyed.

"Kanadon's best-kept secret," Kiriath said. "He believed a monarch should always have the means to leave his home unnoticed. He also thought a ruler should have a safe way to lead soldiers into the Citadel should it ever be captured by an enemy."

Brand nodded. "I have been wondering how King Jekoniah slipped out of the Citadel without the door wardens' knowing of it. Now I see."

"Yes, Father and I passed through here just two days ago. It seems like much longer though."

Kiriath put his hand into the deeper gloom of the secret doorway and pulled out a lantern. Next he located a flint and sparked the lantern to life. "Follow me."

"It's your passage. Lead on."

One after the other, the two companions stooped and stepped through the opening. The air inside was damp and musty. Kiriath's lamp revealed a small landing from which rough steps descended sharply. On a stone shelf sat another lantern.

"There are lanterns at the other end too," Kiriath explained, "so one may both come and go and still have light. Now push the door shut behind you until the clasp catches."

Brand grasped the rusty bar protruding from the door's backside and heaved. With a slight creak, the wall swung back into place. Once again they heard the metallic click of the lock, louder this time than it had been from the dining hall.

Side by side, the two men proceeded down the steps. Because of the steepness of the descent, each kept a hand on the wall, for there was no banister. After they had descended some forty steps, the stairs ended, and a tunnel stretched before them. Here and there water dripped from the walls and puddled along the floor.

"We can talk normally now," Kiriath announced. "No one will hear us."

"We're facing east, but where does this passage lead?"

"Two places," came the reply. "About halfway down the tunnel, you'll see steps branching up to the left. They lead to another stone doorway that actually opens on the inside of the city wall near the east gate not far from the stables."

Brand thought for a moment. "Where those old holly bushes line the inner wall?"

"Exactly. That's why Father never allowed the hollies to be cut down. Some people think he's just a sentimentalist like my grandfather, but they both wanted to keep the exit disguised."

"Ah," Brand said, comprehension in his eyes. "I, too, assumed that he must have a fondness for the holly. I never suspected."

"The other exit is about a thousand paces beyond the east gate," Kiriath continued, "in a place where a clump of birches surrounds an outcropping of rock. The doorway there is simpler in design. It's nothing but a boulder that fits snugly into the tunnel's mouth."

Brand stepped over a puddle and laughed. "If that's the rock I'm thinking of, I may have sat on it once, while Ariana and I picnicked under the trees."

"It may be the same one. Ariana knows of the tunnel. It would be like one of her jokes to let you sit there, atop one of the ancient secrets of the city."

"But have you always known about this? When we sported about the mountain as boys, I was certain you knew no secrets that I didn't."

"You're right; I knew nothing that you didn't. Not until I was out of my boyhood years did Father bring me here. Ariana has known of it for even longer than I."

"And with good reason," Brand said with a grin. "After all, the king's son was known as quite a boaster in his younger days. If you had found out about this passage too early, the whole kingdom would have heard of it long ago."

Kiriath grinned back. "That's probably true."

Presently, Kiriath pointed out the steps leading up to the door near the stables. After that point, the passage tilted downward at a steeper angle. At last the glow of the lantern fell upon steps ascending directly in front of them.

"The tunnel ends here," the prince announced.

Mounting the steps, they arrived at a small landing at the top, just as had been inside the Citadel. The far end of the landing ended in a damp rock wall. But four feet above, in the ceiling, the underside of a boulder just wider than a man bulged downward.

Kiriath set his lantern in the niche prepared for it and blew it out. Complete darkness flooded the tunnel. Bracing his shoulder against the stone, the prince heaved, and the stone rolled away, revealing starlight through the gap. A cool breeze swirled down to greet them.

"When Father first showed me the tunnel, there was a larger stone here. It took both of us to move it. Since then, though, we've replaced it with this smaller one so that one of us alone could pass through if need be."

After tossing out his pack, Kiriath grasped the lip of the exit and heaved himself out. Then he turned and took Brand's hand, pulling him up as well. A large hillock of rock jutted up behind them, shielding them from the watchful eyes of Shiralla's sentinels. Around them on the other three sides birch trees gleamed palely in the moonlight.

Brand watched as Kiriath replaced the entry boulder. "The very stone," he said, amused. "And Ariana knew it all along."

The two men picked up their packs and started down the mountain. The birches soon ended, and the friends angled onto the eastern road. At the horizon, the black sky eased into blue, where it signaled the approach of dawn.

"Now that we're away," Brand said, settling his pack onto his back, "how about telling me what you wouldn't discuss last night? Do you really think it necessary to dress as hunters and to sneak out of the city unseen?"

Kiriath glanced at his friend and likewise shifted his own pack onto his back as they trudged along.

"Necessary may not be the word. Let's say prudent. If we are to have any hope of freeing Father, we'll need absolute secrecy. Something . . ." Kiriath's voice trailed off before he resumed. "It's hard to say what it is, but in the back of my mind I hear or feel a warning that all may not be right in Xandria. Almost like a trumpet call heard from so far away that one cannot be sure if it's genuine or just the wind."

"And with good reason," Brand replied. "No one could have foreseen a Grishnaki attack at the foot of Mount Shiralla. It's like a man's suddenly discovering that the lock on his door has been broken for a long while without his knowing it."

"Something like that. But this may be more serious. What I sense is more like a servant inside the home who has unlocked the door and told highwaymen the best room to plunder."

Brand immediately caught his friend's meaning. "You suspect treason? But who? How?"

Kiriath just shook his head. "I have no facts, nor anyone to accuse—just a gnawing uneasiness in my stomach. I'm not convinced that the Grishnaki just happened to capture Father the first time they carried out a raid across the Bogs. Nor can I fully believe that I was the prize they originally wanted. Even though Father loves me, Dar-kon surely realizes that Father would not barter away the knowledge of steel craft for me if it meant endangering the kingdom. Even as I talk now, I feel more strongly about it: Dar-kon wanted our king and expected to wring his will from a grief-stricken queen. Whether I was captured or killed didn't seem to matter as long as I didn't return to Shiralla."

"And you think someone from Xandria may have given or sold Dar-kon information?"

"Perhaps. Someone either from the city or from somewhere else in this district, I fear. My habits for morning rides have become public knowledge. Anyone who cared to take note might know where to find me at sunrise. Why someone would do it, I can only guess—torture, or blackmail, perhaps, or greed. The Grishnaki have gold to offer the witless."

"I'm not so sure," Brand countered. "It's hard to conceive of such a thing—that any man or woman of Xandria would betray us to a black-hearted Grishnak. No one but you knew about King Jekoniah's going riding that morning, did they?"

"I don't think so. Mother did, but, of course, I don't suspect her. I can't help wondering, though, if Father confided it to anyone and was overheard. I like the idea no better than you, but let's not fall into the philosophy of the common people. Men are not totally good and light and Grishnaki totally evil. Grishnaki have a bent toward destruction and a lust for wickedness, but from history we know that some have occasionally shown unexpected mercy. And while we don't like to think about it, all men—from the king to the lowliest beggar—have at least a strand of darkness in their hearts. There's no evil that a man couldn't fall into, given enough temptation and the belief that he could get away with it."

Brand grinned his usual grin. "The brown cloak and pack make you look like an outland huntsman, but the lecture sounds like one of old Nethanel's discourses. Still, with that much I agree. Even in Shiralla, which we call the City of Light, thievery and other mischief sometimes happen, usually under the cloak of darkness. Still, I'm not totally convinced that the enemy has a cohort among our own people."

"Nor am I convinced for that matter. I just fear that it might be true. But, come; let's quicken our pace. Sunrise already approaches. I'd like to be far from Shiralla before full daylight. Mother and Ariana are going to play-act that I'm still in my room and hurt more than was suspected, while Carpathan carries on as if you were away on a border patrol for him. But even so, near Mount Shiralla anyone with sharp eyes and a quick mind might guess who we are, especially with this bandage on my brow."

With that, Kiriath and Brand stopped talking and hastened their pace down the road, which now veered northeast. Thinking both of the city that they left behind and the enormity of the task before them, each one was silent. The sun, indeed, soon rose, but for some time no one passed them along the road. News of the recent Grishnaki raid had apparently discouraged early-morning traveling.

The day wore on, and the two continued their brisk pace. Past scattered farms and over bridged rivers and streams the road led them, until Mount Shiralla was but the nearest of several mountains looming in the distance behind them. The friends hurried through tiny hamlets too, where byways and side roads intersected the main highway.

Toward noon the travelers at last cleared the summit of a grassy knoll and looked down upon the port city of Greensea. Beyond the city, ocean waves danced and glinted under the cloudless sky. White sails of fishing boats dotted the water. A refreshing sea breeze rose and swept through their hair.

Brand turned to his friend. "Time to decide the next road to take. Do we continue on to Greensea for the noon meal, or shall we strike northward from here? Whichever way we go, we'll need to eat soon."

"I've been considering that. While my heart tells me to forget my body and hurry to Father by the swiftest road, my mind knows I must be patient as well as stealthy. We'll need our full strength on the road ahead of us. Let's go straight on to the city. We can buy a hot meal and rest our feet a bit as well. I'm used to riding. This walking stirs up my appetite!"

"Are you sure you won't be recognized? That princely face of yours is well known throughout Xandria."

"I already have a solution for that problem."

The prince put a hand into the pouch slung from his belt. With a deft motion he slipped a band around his head and adjusted a black patch over his left eye. He stepped back for Brand to examine his whole disguise. "So what do you think? Will anyone suspect me as Kiriath, the prince, or will I pass undetected as just another outland hunter?"

Brand shook his head slowly. "As I live and breathe, that completes the disguise. Yes, I would believe that you spend your days skulking on the frontier and tending traps, but only when you're not gambling and jesting somewhere with a pack of rogues." He laughed. "If I weren't in disguise myself, I'd be afraid to keep company with such a dubious-looking character."

"You hardly fit the description of a nobleman's son yourself today. Passing you on the street, I doubt that I would glance at you twice if you were to pull the hood of your cloak up. Off to Greensea now. We'll be eating cold food out of our packs by tomorrow; let's hurry to an inn while we may."

Kiriath took a step forward, but Brand shot a hand to his friend's shoulder.

"Wait," Brand whispered. "One moment." He narrowed his eyes, staring past Kiriath, back down the road they had just traveled.

Kiriath looked too but saw nothing, save for the bushes, maple trees, and meadows that lined either side of the road. He looked again at Brand, who still stared into the undergrowth at the foot of the knoll.

"What is it?" Kiriath asked, his mind flashing back to the ambush he had escaped two days earlier. "Not Grishnaki?"

"I'm not sure what it was," Brand answered. "I thought I glimpsed something brown slipping off the road into those maples down there. Probably just a deer, if it was anything at all. Certainly not a Grishnak though. Even if one ever mastered the art of walking quietly, I'd recognize one of those hulking brutes."

At last, smiling, Brand relaxed his gaze and turned away. "Your talk of traitors has me jumping at shadows. Come, every minute we stand here is another minute Jekoniah spends as a prisoner. As you say, let's take a quick lunch at an inn, then be on with the journey."

Within the hour two brown-cloaked strangers were strolling through the bustling marketplace of Greensea. Now and again a vendor in a stall called out to them, promising an especially low price on fresh fish, vegetables, or handcrafts. Each time, the strangers merely smiled, shook their heads and melted back into the throng.

In a side street they eventually found a quiet-looking inn with a weathered sign reading "The Blue Whale." Going inside, the friends found an old but clean establishment with a gray-headed innkeeper who seemed to rival his inn for age.

The innkeeper regarded them with curiosity, then ushered them to a table in the deserted dining room.

"Either hunters or gold searchers, I'd say, from the looks of ye," the man said as Kiriath and Brand sat down. "Come from the outlands at any rate, I'd warrant."

"Hunters," Kiriath replied. He didn't mention that his father was the only prize for which they would hunt. From behind his eye patch he hoped his disguise looked more natural than it felt. "Right now, though, all we're needing is a quiet place to rest our feet and a meal of fresh Greensea perch."

"Then that's just what you'll get," the man said, with an enthusiastic clap of his hands. "No one in the city offers better'n you'll get in the Blue Whale. Now, how about some ale to whet your appetites?"

"No, thank you," Brand replied. "It clouds the mind and loosens the tongue. I always like to keep a firm hold on both. A hot cup of sandalroot tea would be more to my liking."

"And mine," Kiriath put in.

"Hot tea it is then," the man said, looking at them a trifle more closely, "though I can't remember the day I ever saw a hunter turn down ale for tea. But I'm forgetting my manners. My name is Gaius. Gaius Pitalus. And your names are . . . ?"

The two friends hadn't expected the question. Brand stirred uneasily.

"Call me Jathan," the prince answered, using the old-language word for *hunter*. And this is . . ." He hesitated just a moment before his mind seized upon a name for Brand. "Killdeer," he finished.

The corners of Brand's mouth curled up slightly at the long-forgotten nickname from his youth.

"Jathan and Killdeer," Gaius said, repeating the names. "Good, solid hunter names. Ah, well, I'll be seeing to your meal. My daughter Beuthinda—a fine gal if'n ever there was one—she'll bring your tea as soon as the kettle's hot."

Gaius bustled out to the kitchen, leaving the two men alone. Immediately the friends heard the sound of excited voices talking quietly on the other side of the kitchen door. More than once Kiriath noticed the door crack slightly, then quickly close again.

Each incident was followed by a high-pitched giggle and more of the same excited whispers.

Before long, Beuthinda appeared with platters. Although she was well past the flower of youth, Kiriath, judging by the ample supply of rouge coating her cheeks, thought that the woman must be clinging to her younger years. The prince couldn't guess which scent Beuthinda wore (he suspected that it was a mingling of several) as she leaned over to set his saucer before him, but it was so overpowering that he found himself holding his breath.

Chattering excitedly about the weather, her father's cooking, the recent good fishing, and assorted pointless subjects, Beuthinda fluttered in and out as she fetched silverware, napkins, and a honey jar and generously interspersed her nonstop talk with more giggling.

Each time she disappeared into the kitchen, the same excited whispers Kiriath had heard at the first immediately ensued. Had they been recognized so quickly? Cocking his head toward the kitchen door, Kiriath threw a questioning look at Brand, who raised both eyebrows and shrugged with complete bewilderment.

Finally, Beuthinda scurried in with the teakettle. But as she stepped forward to set Brand's brimming cup before him, she tripped on a warped floorboard, spilling the scalding drink into his lap and causing him to leap up in astonishment. Embarrassed and more crimson-faced than ever, she helped him to dry off as well as she could, then rushed from the room.

Shortly afterwards Gaius returned with the perch. As it turned out, however, the innkeeper fulfilled only half of his bargain. True, the perch was tasty to the tongue and well prepared, but the two friends were not to have a quiet place to rest their feet. Gaius pulled a stool up to the table and plopped himself on it, repeatedly asking if the food was to their liking, bewailing the slowness of business, and hinting that he wouldn't mind hearing some firsthand accounts of their experiences outside the border. When no tales were forthcoming, however, he turned his comments to the recent events of King Jekoniah's capture and the rumors of a Grishnak ambassador up at the capital.

"What do you two make of all these events?" he asked.

The unanticipated conversation had at first annoyed the friends, but this latest twist alarmed them. Kiriath acted disinterested and hoped the man wouldn't penetrate his disguise.

Brand attempted to end the subject. "Who can know what it all means? Men that are not royalty have other matters to think about."

"Ah, you're right there, Master Killdeer," Gaius agreed, a gleam in his eye. "And what could an unwed man like yourself consider that's more important'n his choice of a good woman? Nothing. That's what I say."

From that point on old Gaius began to heap Brand with praise for every virtue—both real and imagined—that his daughter Beuthinda possessed. The only concession he made was that she was perhaps a tad on the clumsy side. "But her other fine points more than make up for that," he declared.

Finally seeing the true purpose for the innkeeper's keen interest in two strange men, Kiriath smiled openly. While Brand did his best to keep his mouth full of food, Kiriath joined Gaius in bemoaning the plight of the unwed man. He also pretended to recall fictitious moments when Brand himself had sighed for want of a wife. This comment spurred Gaius to redoubled efforts in persuasion. At last, however, Brand was compelled to explain that, while he was not yet betrothed, he had already taken a fondness for a certain maiden and hoped to win her hand in marriage some day.

"Hmm, 'tis a pity," Gaius said. "Such a fine, strong man you look—and fair spoken for a hunter at that. I wouldn't 'ave minded a bit if you'd taken a mind to come courtin' my Beuthinda. Ah, well. If you'll excuse me, gentlemen, I've enjoyed our little chat, but I'd better see to cleaning up the kitchen. Enjoy the rest of your meal."

When Gaius was out of the room, Brand frowned at Kiriath. "Now I know how a hunted animal feels. I think you were actually enjoying that."

"I was. Besides, I didn't want him going back to the subject of the king and the Grishnaki. The best way to keep his mind away from it was to let him have his say. Maybe if you had worn your own bandage and eye patch, you would look too unwholesome for a father to approach. I notice he showed little enough interest in me."

"I would have, if I'd known the ordeal that was in store for me. Though I daresay we would make a curious-looking pair of one-eyed wanderers. At least now I understand the riddle of an inn that serves fine food, yet remains empty of men!"

After the meal, Kiriath and Brand stepped back into the street and made their way to the north quarter of Greensea. They blended into a crowd of people leaving the city, and Kiriath noted with satisfaction that the gate wardens gave them but a cursory glance.

Outside the gates, the two men slackened their pace, which allowed them to fall behind the main throng.

"Let's try to avoid any conversations along the way," Kiriath said when they were well behind the group. "Even though I doubt that anyone would connect us to our real identities, Gaius isn't the only one talking about Kroll and Father's capture."

"Yes," Brand agreed. "I've caught mention of the names King Jekoniah and Dar-kon many times in the city as well as from that group ahead of us. But travelers make friends quickly. The only sure way to avoid everyone is to leave the road. We could make our way north along the seashore almost as quickly as we could by road. That would save us from having to climb hills for a while too."

"Let's do it," Kiriath decided.

The two friends continued walking for about another mile, until they had passed all the houses and shops that overflowed Greensea's crowded walls. Then veering off the road to their right, they strode across several hundred yards of low, rolling dunes that were sparsely covered with grass. On the far side, the mounds leveled out into a wide strip of beach, becoming at last a hard, smooth floor of damp sand slanting into the waves of the sea.

"I'm always amazed at how even the wind near Greensea carries a salty taste. It's invigorating!" Brand said.

"Good. Perhaps that will help us keep up a good pace while we march alongside it."

At that, the companions picked up the pace northward along the ocean. They made no efforts to conceal their tracks here. Indeed, it would have been difficult to do unless they were to walk within reach of the waves' restless groping. But the wind blew steadily now; no tracks could remain in that fine sand for long before being erased forever.

A multitude of pink and white shells littered the shoreline. Some were cracked and ugly, while others lay whole and glistening in the sunlight. Broken chunks of bleaching driftwood, twisted into bizarre shapes and washed smooth by their journeys from unguessed shores, littered the shore in abundance.

"The sea must not care for mankind," Brand remarked. "It removes all signs of men's having been here before. I feel as if I were walking along a shore no other man has ever set foot on."

"Perhaps it doesn't like us," Kiriath returned. "Enough fishermen have lost their lives on it over the years. And then there was Old Illandria across the waves. I've often wondered what it must have been like."

"What? To live in the Old Kingdom?"

"That, too, but I mean that last day there. I can't fathom what it must have been like to feel the ground pitch and sink and to see a gigantic wall of ocean water hurtling toward me."

"Nor can I," Brand agreed. "Such events would make the most stalwart man lose his heart—or his mind. If I remember the chronicles rightly, fewer than a couple hundred survivors from the Old Kingdom were plucked from the ocean when ships from the colony arrived, looking for Illandria's coast. And of those few who had been in high places and managed to cling to drifting logs or wreckage, many could not speak for a long while. Others babbled nonsense, while others yet who had not been greatly injured died from the shock of witnessing such a cataclysm."

"And all that remains of a once vast and prosperous kingdom is this remnant in Xandria, its former colony. Now, after so many years, we still cling to the shore of a continent we barely know and ever expect more harassment from the Grishnaki."

"Ah, the Grishnaki," Brand said. "Illandria may not have been paradise, but at least they knew peace. Tell me, did Urijah or Nethanel give you any information that might help our quest?"

"Not much. I talked to both of them last night. They agreed that many men have seen the entrance to the Valley of Grishnaki, especially before their tribes united under Dar-kon's grandfather. But none that have actually ventured into it have returned to describe what they saw. The rest you already know; the main entrance to Vol-Rathdeen itself is supposedly a yawning cave in the rock wall in the center of their valley. Up and down the valley on both sides it is said that there are smaller caves where Grishnaki warriors live and keep watch. But how much of that is fact and how much is myth, we don't know."

Brand picked up a shell and hurled it at a circling seagull in frustration. "I'd hoped that all their learning would yield some hidden knowledge that could help us."

"Urijah still seems to think our whole scheme impossible," Kiriath said. "Nethanel was a little more optimistic. He did have one thought that might prove helpful. According to his guesses, several thousand Grishnaki must inhabit the central cavern, even after subtracting those that supposedly dwell in the valley's secondary caves."

"Hardly encouraging, since the main cavern is our destination," Brand pointed out.

"But listen to this," the prince went on. "Grishnaki breathe fresh air like us. Probably more than we do, since their bodies are so large. But according to Nethanel, one entrance for such a cave would be too small for sufficient air to circulate. The large number of Grishnaki breathing in there would soon render the air foul and unusable. Any torches or fires inside would make the situation even worse."

"Then there's at least one other entrance?"

"That's Nethanel's guess. He thinks that either some of the peripheral caves must adjoin Vol-Rathdeen or that there are some smaller openings or vents in the mountain above the valley."

"So we may not have to pass their main defenses after all? That's encouraging news. Now if only we can find one of these other openings."

"That, and we'll have to hope that they are big enough for us to pass through," Kiriath added. "Nethanel cautioned that the air may simply flow through cracks in the rock that are too small to be of help. At any rate, the Grishnaki have dwelt in the region for years; if there is a back door into their realm, Dar-kon will have concealed it or stationed warriors to watch it."

"If Nethanel's theory turns out to be true, let's hope they have only tried to hide it. Grishnaki wits have never been much to brag about. I'd rather match minds against several of them at once than to do battle with any one of them. What do you make of Urijah, though? It's not in keeping with his nature just to shrug his shoulders and say that a task can't be done. Did he have no suggestions or thoughts to offer whatsoever?"

"He did have one suggestion in the form of a gift—albeit a grim gift. I wasn't going to mention it right away."

The prince opened the pouch on his belt and took out two small, square bottles of thick yellow glass. A cork securely stopped the mouth of each one. He handed one of the bottles to Brand. "One for you, and one for me."

Brand took the bottle Kiriath offered and held it up to examine its contents. Inside was a dark brown liquid. "I don't understand," he said at last. "What is this?"

"Dorminia juice," came the reply. "It's squeezed from the Dorminia Lotus and boiled down until potent."

Brand knit his eyebrows together and looked at his bottle again. Puzzlement was still in his eyes. "Sleep water? I know the healers sometimes use it on their charges to deepen their sleep, but how can it benefit us? Does Urijah expect us to put the Grishnaki guards to sleep so we can stroll into their home?"

Kiriath shook his head and returned his bottle to his pouch. "Urijah explained that Dorminia juice causes sleep only in its fresh and diluted form. Undiluted and aged, it brings swift unconsciousness followed by a painless death. His opinion was that, should our mission fail and the Grishnaki discover us, a sudden death at our own hand would be more desirable than the torturous end that the enemy would invent for us."

With a grunt, Brand took a final look at the glass object in his hand, then likewise slipped it into the bag on his own belt. Together the friends continued along the beach in silence.

CHAPTER 5

UNEXPECTED ENCOUNTERS

After hours of fast striding, the two men noted that the beach began to narrow. The sandy dunes on the left gave way to stone-strewn hills that marched down close to the sea. In the distance ahead they could see where the ocean dashed and broke against rugged cliffs.

"Time to leave this path," Brand said. "The cliffs ahead block the way."

"Right," Kiriath agreed. "Besides, the sun is sinking. We'll be warmer camping in the hills than here by the sea."

Turning their backs to the ocean, the companions pushed inland, angling north and west. The sun settled into a bank of clouds, igniting them into an orange brilliance. For a while the friends could hear the incessant surging of the ocean waves behind them. As the hills surrounding them became taller, however, the sound gradually diminished until it was replaced by the whisper of the wind in the treetops.

"There's the first star," Kiriath announced, pointing to a steady gleam above where the sun had set. "May fortune also shine upon our errand."

"What is it the children say?" Brand asked as he searched his memory. "Upon whom first star shines its light, to him will be his heart's delight."

"You have a good memory. I'd forgotten that one. Right now my heart's main delight would be to have Father free and safely away from the Grishnaki's clutches." He paused. "Unless I'm mistaken, though, Ariana holds more than a small place of delight in your mind."

Brand grinned. "I won't deny that. Your sister is quite a woman."

"So how long are you going to draw out the courtship? I've been expecting an announcement of betrothal for weeks now. Certainly, as your friend and the brother of the damsel in question, you can tell me? Or are you reconsidering our good innkeeper's offer of Beuthinda?"

"Hardly that. Even if I were as old as Beuthinda, my nose isn't durable enough to survive her perfumes." Brand's tone became graver. "The truth is that Ariana and I were betrothed three nights ago. Jekoniah was to make the announcement the very next day. But the Grishnaki came, and by then it wouldn't have been appropriate to say anything. Lady Vandrielle knows, too, of course. But for now thoughts of wedding ceremonies must wait. King Jekoniah raised me as a father ever since the Grishnaki murdered my parents long ago. Even if he were not king, my duty would be to go to him. For Ariana, though, who must stay behind and await the outcome of our trip, that decision is harder to accept."

"I saw anguish in her eyes when we announced our plans yesterday. No wonder she was so hurt. Have you spoken to her since then?" The prince paused. "Or maybe I shouldn't ask. It's really none of my affair."

Brand waved his hand, as if to brush away the thought. "That's all right. She wouldn't mind. Besides, talking it out might help me to settle the matter in my own mind. Yes, I spoke to her, but only briefly. Surely others could have—and would have—come with you had they known your plan. But my conscience wouldn't let me stay home. She said she understands even though the idea rips her heart asunder."

"Who could blame her?" Kiriath asked. "The first man she ever loved has been seized and is in danger of death. Now the second one could remain safe, but only as long as he doesn't attempt to rescue the first one. No woman should be so torn."

"Yes, exactly," Brand agreed. "She desperately wants our mission to succeed, but dreads that it won't. More than my own death, I'm afraid of what may happen to her if we don't come back. But enough morbid talk. It's growing too dark to continue much farther tonight. We'll be tripping over roots and stumbling into tree trunks if we don't halt soon."

"You're right. My impatience keeps pressing me. I'd hoped to be nearer the frontier before we halted." Prince Kiriath pointed forward to a slope on their left. "That looks like a stand of pines up ahead. Let's see if we can make a soft cushion of pine needles to sleep on."

When the friends arrived at the spot, there was indeed a thick mantel of dry needles covering the ground under the pines. Only an occasional weed or small bush pushed up through that natural mattress.

By this time the daylight was gone, but a full moon was rising, which flooded the area with light to see. Both men tossed down their packs, and Brand spread his cloak on the ground for a sheet. Straightening it, he sat down and pulled off his boots while Kiriath removed the water flask from his belt.

"I'm going to freshen my water at that stream down below," the prince announced. "Want me to take yours too?"

"Yes, if you're going," Brand replied. He tossed his own flask to Kiriath. "As for me, I've found out that I was born to travel on horseback. I'm going to lie here and rest my feet while I have a bite of dried beef."

"And think of Ariana," Kiriath added. The prince felt a handful of pine needles pelting his back as he set off for the stream.

Even as the prince made his way down the hillside, the first beams of light from the rising moon helped him to pick his route. Walking leisurely now, he gazed up at the disk of the moon and marveled at how large it appeared as it loomed just above the treetops. Next he paused to ponder the stars studding their black dome. Stars had intrigued Kiriath ever since he had been a boy. He studied again the first star they had observed earlier and wondered why it shone with a steady beam rather than flickering like most of its fellows. Sighing, he shrugged his shoulders and pushed on to where the ribbon of a stream glinted at the hill's base.

Near the water's edge the chorus of crickets around Kiriath lapsed into silence as he approached. The nocturnal song gradually resumed, however, as he knelt on a mossy bank and dipped Brand's water flask into the water. Replacing the cork, he next filled his own flask and tipped it to his lips. As he swallowed, the prince gazed skyward again as a cloud crossed in front of the moon and deepened the darkness. Once again he pushed his flask beneath the water before capping it shut.

Refreshed, the prince stretched himself on the bank with his face just inches above the glimmering surface. Lifting handfuls of the wetness to his brow, Kiriath tenderly removed the bandage that was there and daubed his forehead where it had been injured in his fall into the ravine. The wound was healing as cleanly as might be hoped, but it had begun to throb during the afternoon's march. Kiriath resolved to say nothing about it to Brand.

After all, he reasoned to himself, *someone going into the Grishnaki's lair has more to worry about than a little headache.*

Plucking a broad plantain leaf, he dunked it into the stream, put it to his forehead, and rolled over onto his back, content to let the cool moisture soothe his pain. At first Kiriath was aware only of the rising and falling notes of the crickets. Gradually, however, he noticed another sound. Slowly he discerned the noise of something—or someone—moving nearby. Cautious steps were advancing through the thick grass, punctuated with the snapping of a twig. The crickets quieted again. After several paces, the footsteps would pause for a moment, then resume, growing closer.

Kiriath's first thought was that Brand had changed his mind and decided to join him, possibly to give his feet a soaking in the stream. But uncertainty checked the prince's impulse to call out. Dropping his leaf bandage, he sat up and scanned the underbrush. Ears straining, he breathed as shallowly as possible through teeth that were ever so slightly apart.

Hurry up, Kiriath willed the slow-moving cloud that was still obscuring the moonlight.

The footsteps continued advancing, pausing every few moments, then drawing closer again. Kiriath ruled out the likelihood of its being Brand, for his friend would have no need of such stealth. Next the young prince's mind considered the possibility that it might be a mere animal—a fox, perhaps, or a badger?

But it also occurred to him that a few wild jackals still roved in sparsely populated corners of Xandria. When they were hungry, these creatures could be vicious.

Noiselessly, the prince pulled himself into a crouch and drew his sword, making a faint ringing sound as he eased it from its sheath. The footsteps abruptly halted.

For what seemed a long while Kiriath waited, motionless as his eyes strove to penetrate the shadowy thickets.

Another twig snapped off to Kiriath's left. He sprang to his full height and took two quick steps in that direction, his sword raised and ready. What sounded like a choked cry of surprise was followed by a thrashing of underbrush. He took one more step in time to glimpse a dark shape scurrying across a patch of moonlit grass.

For a fleeting moment, Kiriath considered pursuing the figure but quickly decided against it. He didn't know the terrain. More importantly, he wasn't sure who or what the mysterious visitor was, nor how many more might lie in the shadows downstream. Finally, with a last glance around him, he started climbing the hill again at a fast pace, ever looking around and behind him as he went.

When he arrived back at the pines, Brand was lying down and resting.

"I was considering coming to search for you," Brand called. "The stream wasn't all that far. Lose your way in the dark?"

The prince sat down and recounted his experience at the stream. In the heavier gloom under the pines, he couldn't discern the reaction on his friend's face, but Brand let out a low whistle when he had heard the whole account.

"And you never caught more than a glimpse of him?" Brand questioned. "Are you sure that it was a man and not a Grishnak?"

"No. I'm not sure of anything except that it ran upright on two legs and wasn't an animal. I wouldn't have thought a Grishnak could skulk so quietly, but then again they've already fooled me once this week."

"Whoever it was knows that at least one person is camping here. I don't like it."

"Nor I," Kiriath agreed.

"Let's move to some other spot while the night offers some protection. I'd hate to wake up and find that some skulking robber had killed me while I slept."

Kiriath cocked his head. "Was that supposed to make sense?"

"It was supposed to, even though it didn't. My mind is too tired to work right. You get the idea. Let's move."

Without another word, the prince and his companion reslung their packs onto their backs. They also tried to smooth out the covering of pine needles, but in the darkness they couldn't be sure that they were not increasing the signs of their having been there, so they soon gave up the effort.

Leading the way, Kiriath took them deeper into the pines. Traveling under the trees at night was slow going. From left and right dead limbs often grappled at them. Rotting stumps and logs lay in their path, ready to trip a careless foot. Occasionally, however, a dagger of moonlight stabbed down through the boughs, which helped them to navigate. For lack of a cane, Kiriath pulled out his sword and began circling it before him as they edged along.

About an hour later—they couldn't be sure how long—the pines thinned out until the companions finally stepped into a moon-swept meadow.

Kiriath returned his sword to its sheath. "We've not traveled nearly as far as we could have in daylight. Still, anyone but a hound would have a hard time tracking us before sunrise. I think we should be safe enough if we find a concealed place to spend the rest of the night."

Brand stifled a yawn. "I'm ready for that. Let's see what sort of bed we can find to replace the one we gave up."

The two friends trudged along the meadow's edge. Finding no better hiding place, they eventually wormed their way into a gigantic old clump of lilac.

Kiriath broke off a branch that stuck in his face. "Not as comfortable as our last stop, but at least we're hidden here. We shouldn't have to take turns keeping watch."

"Yes, we're certainly hidden," Brand agreed, twisting another branch out of his back. "We're crazy to stay in here, but only another crazy man would think to find us encamped in a bush. Whether or not we can actually sleep, though, remains to be proved." He paused, as if reflecting. "I shouldn't complain. This must be luxury compared to whatever sleeping arrangements your father has."

The remainder of that night passed uneventfully. As Brand had predicted, the two friends did not sleep comfortably, and they often woke to bend back offending lilac branches or to reposition themselves. They were, however, able to rest well enough to prepare themselves for another long march.

When daybreak arrived, Kiriath and Brand decided not to make a fire to heat a meal. Instead they breakfasted on their provisions of dried meat and dark bread.

Heading cross-country, they resumed their course northwestward. At first the terrain was much the same as it had been the previous evening—rolling sylvan hills and an occasional meadow. As the sun approached its zenith, the woodland gradually gave way to a plain covered with knee-deep grass. Little clumps of cattle or sheep leisurely grazed here and there, but there was no competition among them, for the grasslands looked almost endless. The hills they had left paralleled their course on the right and grew ever larger as they went northward. In the distance ahead of them, the line of hills cut across their path and merged into a range of low mountains. Twice the friends passed within view of small, walled farms, but each time they gave them a wide berth. They had no time for either idle gossip or friendly hospitality.

As they made their way across the grassland, Brand turned to survey the countryside they had just traversed. "No one following us," he commented, "but a person could. Every step we take across this land leaves a trail. See there? We are like two ships in a green ocean, leaving wakes that anyone could trace."

Kiriath threw a backward glance over his shoulder. "Yes, but it can't be helped. Not unless we veer miles out of the way, and we can't afford the time. Kroll gave us just seven days. Today is already the second, and we're not even out of Xandria yet."

"I know. I just have a funny feeling about that stranger you saw by the stream last night. It's bad enough knowing that we're walking toward the Grishnaki's hole. It's worse thinking that some mystery man might be stalking us from behind."

"But, as we approach the frontier, the terrain will leave fewer signs of our passing. Besides, it may be that no one was following us at all. Whoever I saw last night might not have been a threat. He could have been a lost traveler or even a real hunter on his way to the border. Or, at the worst, a wayfaring thief, in which case he wouldn't be willing to track us over so many miles."

"Perhaps. But the farther and faster we travel, the more at peace my mind will be."

Kiriath and Brand didn't run, but the fast pace they struck now fell just short of a trot. Mile after mile they strode, taking advantage of the level terrain. Around the eighth hour of the day they halted for a brief lunch. They spared only a few minutes to munch on some dark bread, dried meat, and a fistful of raisins, followed by a cool swallow from their water flasks.

Barring the way ahead, the purple mountains loomed larger but were still at least a full day's march away.

Brand pointed a finger toward the mountains when they resumed their march. "After we cross the border, how far north do you think we should go before we head west?"

"That's a good question. I've been thinking about it for a while." Kiriath paused, as if reflecting. "Dar-kon's valley is almost due west of those peaks. To approach from an unexpected direction, I think we had best push past the mountains for a full day. That way we could be sure to approach Vol-Rathdeen from a northerly route."

"Like Lady Vandrielle said, such a course means passing through the Deserted Kingdom." Brand spoke evenly, making his observation into a statement rather than an objection.

"I'm afraid so," Kiriath agreed. "But if we cut straight west anywhere near the border, there will be too much risk of running into Grishnaki out patrolling or hunting. But I wouldn't advise that we go any farther north than a day's march, because we would be more likely to encounter one of the still-wandering Grishnaki tribes. They may quarrel with Dar-kon's folk, but they certainly wouldn't love us either. As things stand, the way I propose barely leaves us any room for delay."

"So be it then. I can't think of any better routes."

The friends pressed on. Even though they traveled with the hoods of their cloaks up to protect them from the burning rays of the sun, the wind caressing the plain kept them cool. From time to time they exchanged a few words, but for the most part they saved their wind for walking. The mountains didn't seem to draw any nearer, yet the plains gradually slanted upward. Whenever Kiriath glanced backward, he could see that they were markedly higher than where they had walked hours before. The sore spot on Kiriath's forehead still ached a little; however, the pain was not so intense now. The wound seemed to be healing.

Late in the afternoon they came upon a dirt road stretching toward the peaks before them. Both of them realized that this was the way to the northern border fortresses.

"Hoof prints," Brand noted as they followed this course, "fairly fresh ones too."

More hours on this road showed no other sign of traffic until near dusk, when the friends became aware of movement in the distance behind them. In the waning light they could make out riders on horseback and several field wagons coming up the road. Kiriath threw back his hood long enough to replace his eye-patch disguise. Brand merely rubbed a little dirt from the road onto his face and pulled his hood a shade lower. He had never served in the northerly districts himself, but among Xandria's border guards there was always the risk of running into an acquaintance.

When the company drew within forty feet of them, the man on the lead horse raised his hand high, with fingers spread wide. As one, the company halted while the leader prodded his mount forward to Kiriath and Brand.

"I am Elead," the man said, "assistant commander for the Watercliffe garrison and surrounding outposts. Who are you that travel toward the border at nightfall?" He leaned forward in his saddle, trying to get a closer look in the fading daylight.

"Hunters," Kiriath called, lowering his voice slightly. "We come from the South and go to see how the game is in the North. This is Killdeer, and I am Jathan."

Elead nodded. "Not long ago I would have said that hunters were safer in the southern lands. But since the Grishnaki now grow bold on all of Xandria's borders, I suppose there is no more risk here than there. You are the second and third hunters we have met on the road today. We picked up a young one named Jaykin, who rides in the last wagon. Would you care to join a comrade of your trade and ride awhile? We would be happy to carry you as far as Watercliffe."

Kiriath and Brand looked at each other, hesitating. Accepting Elead's offer would greatly speed up their journey, but they didn't want to risk exposing their identities to anyone lest rumor spread.

Elead chuckled. "You hunters—stubbornly proud and independent to the end, you are. Come, there's no lack of honor in riding a supply wagon, especially when the only other choice means growing shorter by walking your feet off."

Kiriath nodded and reached up to clasp Elead's hand. He was used to soldiers who offered him favors because he was the prince, but this man's friendliness to a stranger struck an agreeable chord in him. "Thank you, Elead. We will accept your hospitality. To tell the truth, we're too foot weary to be proud right now. If your wagons have room for two sojourners, we'd be grateful for some sleep and the protection of your men."

"Fine, then. If you wish hunter conversation, as I say, the one called Jaykin sits on the back of the last wagon. But if you wish to sleep, climb in the first. It is less full, and there are sacks of flour you can lie on."

While the two friends clambered up the back of the first wagon, Elead gave the order to light the lamps. The wagon drivers opened boxes under their seats and distributed lamps to the soldiers riding escort. These were then lit and mounted on the fronts and backs of the wagons. In this way, most of the group was able to ride in flickering circles of light that dispelled the night.

Elead stopped by the first wagon and gave Kiriath and Brand each a peach. "In the North we use lights as long as we are inside the kingdom's borders," he explained. "But if you pass Watercliffe, I advise that you not strike fire at night. In the Lowlands trouble comes unrequested. No need to give it a special invitation."

"Yes," Brand answered. "We, too, have spent time in the king's service. It's the same on the southern frontier."

"Excellent. Then I won't worry about you. Now Jaykin, back there, is different—unusually soft and quiet for a hunter, I think. Young too. Ah, well. I counsel travelers, but I can't make their decisions for them. Rest well for now. I'll see you at Watercliffe."

Elead trotted his mount to the front of the column and whistled two quick notes. Just as the company had stopped instantaneously, they now started forward again as one body.

From where he lay in their wagon, Kiriath looked at Brand. "I like this Elead," he said. "He leads his men well and cares about people who aren't his obligation."

"Two good traits for a leader," Brand replied. "Xandria needs more like him." Then, calling to the driver, Brand asked, "How long 'til we reach Watercliffe?"

"Not for hours," came the reply. "Should be past midnight before we arrive."

With that, the wagon fell silent. The only sounds were the rhythmic thudding of the horses' hooves in the dirt and the steady creaking of wagon wheels. For a while Kiriath watched the stars overhead or the lamps swinging from their hooks as the wagon rolled along. His thoughts continually returned to Vol-Rathdeen, wondering exactly what the place was like and how his father was faring with his captors. Ere long, though, he felt his eyelids growing heavy. So, settling back with a sack of grain for a pillow, Kiriath, the prince of Xandria, drifted to sleep in a field wagon of supplies.

CHAPTER 6

WATERCLIFFE

Kiriath snapped awake as the wagon ground to a halt. It took him but a moment to collect his thoughts. He quickly remembered Elead's hospitality and knew where they were.

"Must be Watercliffe," Brand said, rousing himself.

Kiriath nodded. Their wagon had halted outside a long, low building from which wafted the scent of fresh hay. Two lamps hung on either side of the wide double doors. The prince started to mention that he hadn't been to Watercliffe for several years but caught himself. In disguise, it was best not to mention that he had ever been there at all.

Their driver jumped down from the wagon, and Kiriath and Brand followed his example. "This is our stabling area," the driver explained. "Watercliffe itself is up higher." He pointed above to the night-filled pass between two much higher mountain peaks that blotted out the starry sky behind them. "Because the way up is so steep, we keep our horses here and climb the rest of the way on foot. Elead should be along shortly to lead you up."

As if on cue, Elead strode out of the stable. "Lael," he said to the driver, "fetch that other hunter. Jaykin is his name. I'll take all our guests up myself."

"Right away, sir," Lael answered, and disappeared into the night.

"Watercliffe is the last hospitable place you'll find in the North," Elead informed his guests. "Past this point are the wild Lowlands. The hunting is good out there, and there is gold to be found. However, life in the Outlands is rugged—and dangerous. I first came here three years ago, and of the three or four dozen men who have crossed into the wilds here, I can remember at least ten who have never returned."

"Any idea what happened to the ones who didn't come back?" Brand wanted to know.

Elead shrugged. "Eaten by animals maybe, or killed by Grishnaki. No one knows. No clothing or bones have ever been found. One thing I can tell you, though: strange happenings occur in the Lowlands. Some of those who did come back vowed never to step over the northern border again."

"Most people in Xandria have heard unusual tales from the North," Kiriath said. "But most of them believe that the border defenders weave many of the stories themselves to impress the maidens or to frighten listeners."

"They're wrong!" Elead exclaimed. He realized that his response had been overly energetic and laughed at himself. "I apologize. I don't normally contradict our guests. But those that sit in the comfort of home and hearth and laugh at the accounts of the Northern Guard should try coming on a patrol or two with us. Not that odd happenings always take place, but they are frequent enough."

He peered through the night to where his men had begun unloading the wagons. "Lael should have been back with that other hunter by now. I wonder what's keeping them?"

"You mention odd happenings," Brand continued. "Have you yourself ever witnessed anything unusual? Other than hunters' vanishing, I mean."

Kiriath watched Elead stare at Brand for a long moment before answering. "Aye," the assistant commander answered finally. "I've seen many strange things—and peculiar animals too. I don't mention all of them to my family at home in Quintepolis. But if you doubt my word, I'll tell you about one incident that froze the marrow in my bones."

"All right," Brand agreed, "let's hear it."

"A little less than two years ago," Elead continued, "Commander Heth was leading a patrol in the Outlands. We do that every few weeks to make sure there's no Grishnaki build-up. I was on his patrol. Because we had pushed farther north than usual, Heth decided that we would encamp for the night and return here the next day. We posted sentinels and, since we were a large patrol, we went ahead and lit watch fires around the perimeter. No one could have approached unseen. But at dawn, we found one of our men dead at the base of a tree right in the center of the camp."

"Dead?" Kiriath and Brand repeated together.

"Aye," Elead confirmed, lowering his voice. "But not just dead: his body was withered and shriveled up like an old prune, with little holes here and there in his skin. Eerie, it was. If I hadn't known that this man was well liked and respected by everyone in the garrison, I might have suspected some sort of poison, but as it was . . ."

"None of the sentinels heard anything?" Kiriath asked. He could tell by Elead's tone of voice that the man wasn't simply trying to frighten two naïve travelers.

"Not a sound. We never did solve the riddle. The men don't like to talk about such things either. Living on the border makes many of them more superstitious than they'll admit. Almost as if talking about unusual happenings will bring more down on us."

"A strange tale," Brand commented. "Perhaps we'd better wait until we've been in the wilds ourselves before we make any judgments on it."

"Well said," Elead agreed. "Here comes Lael at last, but without Jaykin, I see."

The wagon driver joined the trio of men in the circle of lantern light. "Sir, I've searched and inquired everywhere. The hunter Jaykin is not to be found."

"Not to be found? What says the man who drove the wagon Jaykin was in?"

"It's a mystery to him too. The hunter never spoke to him along the way, and the driver assumed he slept. But when we stopped here, the hunter was no longer in the wagon."

Turning to Kiriath and Brand, Elead said, "You two. Do you know anything about this Jaykin? Ever heard of him before?"

"Nothing," Kiriath replied. "I've never heard the name before tonight."

"Nor I," Brand put in.

"Odd. Very well, Lael. You're dismissed. But before you turn in, leave word that if anyone sees Jaykin, he is to be brought to me. I should like to ask him a few questions."

"Yes, sir," Lael replied.

"I'll show you the way to Watercliffe now," Elead said. "You can sleep the rest of the night in safety and be off in the morning if you like. Follow me."

Taking a lantern, Elead led the way past the stable to a point where the building abruptly butted against a natural rock wall. Up a cleft in the rock ran steps hewn out of the stone. The passage was barely wide enough for two men to walk abreast, but the three men now climbed single file in the circle of Elead's light.

"Be careful," the second commander said. "The way is steep. Watercliffe was built for defense, not for comfort. Except by air, this is the only approach on this side of the mountains. On the far side of the pass that the garrison straddles is a sheer drop."

"But the mountain peaks tower above your outpost on both sides," Brand called from the rear. "Couldn't the enemy scale one of them from the side and so descend upon you?"

"No," Elead answered, "wherever nature didn't form a natural barrier, our stone-cutters fashioned their own by carving and shaping the mountainside until Watercliffe became impenetrable."

"So how do you get your mounts down to patrol the wilderness beyond?" Brand asked.

"We do it," Elead said cautiously, "but that is all I can say. Because you've been in the king's service, you know that each garrison has secrets that may not be discussed, not even with former defenders of the realm. This is one of ours. Let that be sufficient reply."

"Of course," Brand said, "excuse me for letting my curiosity get ahead of my senses."

"Not at all."

Kiriath said nothing but smiled inwardly. Being the son of the king, he knew the answer to Brand's question and had been through the secret pass before. But as far as he could recall, his companion, having served primarily on the western and southern borders of the realm, had never visited this particular garrison.

"Enough of this snail's crawl. Let's stretch our legs!" Elead struck a fast pace up the stone stairway and led the two higher and higher for what seemed hundreds of steps. Kiriath had always taken pride in his strength and endurance, but he felt even his legs begin to ache. He marveled at Elead's ease in pumping one foot higher than the other at such a quick rate—almost tirelessly, like the gears in a mill. The rough, uneven steps made the climbing yet more difficult. Behind him, Kiriath heard Brand, too, puffing louder than normal. The prince was on the verge of asking their guide to slow down when they suddenly reached a landing that was bathed in light from torches overhead. Here Elead stopped altogether. He turned to face Kiriath and Brand.

"Well done, sirs Jathan and Killdeer." He laughed his now-familiar laugh. "You two are the first to follow me all the way here straight off. And with packs too. Most newcomers beg for a rest less than halfway up."

Still breathing hard, the two friends did not answer. Looking up the remainder of the stairs, Elead turned away again. "Elead, assistant commander, and two visitors," he called upward.

"Pass," came a voice. "Welcome back, Elead."

Again Elead led the friends up the remaining steps, but more slowly now. When they arrived at the top, Kiriath saw a guard-house built beside the cleft. Beneath an awning in front of the building was a wooden bench on which sat several archers with bows in their hands. From their position, they could look or shoot down upon the landing. Nearby a great horn hung from a cord, presumably an alarm to be sounded in case of danger.

"Mostly a formality," Elead explained. "But even though we believe Watercliffe to be impregnable, we take pains to keep it that way."

Elead guided his guests up to the fortress. The well-worn pathway led directly to massive iron-bound doors that formed the entrance, now standing open with two soldiers positioned outside. Even under moonlight, Watercliffe appeared to be solidly built of stone blocks that loomed up three stories high, with a central watchtower rising still higher. An orange glow shone from several narrow windows midway up the wall, but the topmost level was completely darkened. Out of the night came the powerful sound of rushing water.

Brand whistled in awe. "Your fortress is quite a feat of engineering. Doesn't lightning pose a danger to your men so far up?"

"No. The double peaks on either side of us bear the brunt of thunderstorms. We are fairly sheltered here. Still, it's not a good idea to be out on the mountain when lightning bolts are flying. Even though lightning strikes hundreds of rods higher, it can send death racing down the mountainside in rain water. I'm told that the garrison has lost men that way before."

Elead led the men inside. Just beyond the doorway, stairs mounted up to the next level. To the left was a darkened hallway, but through an open door on the right a fire crackled in a hearth.

"Normally Commander Heth likes to meet anyone passing through the region. But it's late, and Heth needs his sleep. He presses himself too hard at times. I'll let you rest for the remainder of tonight, but first let me show you something."

Elead showed the way up the steps to the second floor, then down a dim corridor. Here he pushed open the shutter of a tall window. "This, gentlemen," he announced, "is why we call our outpost *Watercliffe*."

From a cleft in the mountainside above them, a stream of water poured into the air and cascaded down in a rippling rope of white. Moonbeams reflected from each droplet, which gave the whole waterfall the illusion of being millions of miniature, sparkling diamonds. From this window, Kiriath couldn't see Lake Ephron below, but a rising mist showed where the falls tumbled into it. He had admired these falls before in the sunshine, but by moonlight, he concluded, they were even more breathtaking.

"It's beautiful," Brand uttered under his breath.

Still gazing out the window, Kiriath nodded.

"Indeed," Elead said, "we never tire of the sight. It's smaller now than usual, and it dwindles down to nothing in the winter. Through the rest of the year, though, Ephron Falls helps us to remember the beauty of the land that we protect from Dar-kon."

The mention of the Grishnaki ruler broke the spell surrounding the falls. Kiriath was reminded that this would be their last night of security until they either succeeded or failed in their mission.

"It grows late," he said to his host, "and we hope to get an early start tomorrow."

"Yes, of course," Elead answered. "Your beds should be ready by now."

He took his guests down the stairway again and into the darkened hallway they had passed upon first entering the fortress. Elead stopped at a room with three beds and a few sparse pieces of furniture. A lone candle cast a feeble light.

"This is the closest thing to a guest room Watercliffe has," Elead said, setting down his lamp. "Humble accommodations, but better than you'll have when you leave us. If you care to wash and refresh yourselves, there are washbasins in the chamber at the far end of the corridor. If you desire conversation or anything else, the night watch will be at the front door, or there are often three or four men in the meeting hall, where you saw the fireplace. Is there anything else I can do for you?"

"Nothing, thank you," Kiriath answered. "Your hospitality has been more than we could have hoped for. We're grateful."

"It's not often we on the border have an opportunity to show hospitality to our citizens. Rest well. I expect the commander will see you off in the morning if I'm not on hand."

"A good man," Brand said after Elead had closed the door. "I like him more all the time."

"So do I," Kiriath agreed. "If he continues in the king's service, Elead is certain to rise. He has the stuff of a worthy leader in him."

The two friends wasted little time before climbing into bed. They realized that the days ahead would be long and tense. Rest now became vitally important.

Kiriath had slept for he knew not how long when he awoke to the muffled sound of voices and footsteps. Realizing it must the change of the watchmen, he rolled over and closed his eyes again, glad for the feel of the pillow's coolness against his cheek.

This time, however, the prince did not resume his deep slumber. Rather, he drifted into an uncomfortable dreamscape of constantly shifting faces and places. In the end, Kiriath saw himself in a dim cave, standing on a ledge that hung over rippling black water. He knew some kind of danger was rushing toward him, but in his dream he couldn't see who or what it was. Frustrated and anxious, he wanted to look in his pack, for he seemed to know that something there could help him. But there was no time, and he couldn't recall what was supposed to be there anyway.

Suddenly, he felt himself plunging toward the black waters below, though he wasn't sure whether he had fallen, jumped, or been pushed off the precipice. Frigid blackness engulfed him. Despite his efforts to swim, Kiriath's body sank deeper into the wetness. He felt as if he were suffocating in living, liquid silk. When at last he felt that his lungs would burst if he didn't breathe, he opened his mouth and inhaled. But rather than sucking in water, he jerked awake to find himself breathing air. His heart was pounding, and a chill sweat covered his body.

For several moments he lay still, while trying to decide whether the dream held any meaning. Finally he decided that it didn't and rolled out of bed. Light was gleaming under the door now. Brand heard his friend stirring and rose as well.

"It's later than I planned to get up, I'll warrant," Brand said. "But I suppose that means we needed it."

"Yes. Neither one of us is used to continuous marching under the open sky. Still, last night's ride has saved us from walking many furlongs. Come, let's wash and breakfast. After that, it will be time to bid farewell to our host—and to the kingdom."

Within the hour Kiriath and Brand were finishing breakfast in the fellowship hall. They sent word to the garrison commander that they would soon be ready to leave. Shortly Elead appeared. He was accompanied by an older warrior, whom they understood to be the commander of the garrison.

"So here are our two guests," said Commander Heth, clasping each of their hands in turn. "My apologies for not greeting you last night."

"Not at all," Kiriath answered. "Even the best commanders can't stay awake all day and all night both."

"Right you are," Heth replied. "Although if I could manage the trick, I'd have almost enough time to accomplish all that I'd like. As it is, I'm off even now. I need to make rounds of the surrounding outposts. Not that my men are slack, but defenders that don't know when to expect their commander's visits tend to be especially vigilant!"

Brand reached into his belt pouch and pulled out a bronze talent. "Before you go, let us repay the garrison for the meal and its kindness to two travelers."

"No need," Heth replied. "We consider it part of our duty to receive the few wayfarers who wander abroad."

"And we consider it our privilege to repay a good turn," Brand persisted. "Add this to the garrison's strongbox. Having served in the South, we know that no garrison is overflowing with provender."

Elead chuckled. "Which is as polite a way as any to say that defenders of the realm enjoy few dainties."

Heth nodded and took the coin. "I accept your talent. Elead spoke well of you, and now I shall do the same. Watercliffe extends help to all who pass this way, but few stop to consider our welfare or to repay any kindness. Here, Elead, add this to the stores until your next trip to Quintepolis."

He handed the coin to Elead then bowed to his guests. "And now, sirs, I must hasten on my way. I like to know of everything that happens within a league of both sides of the border—a job that keeps me busy. Which reminds me—Elead, has there been any word on that other hunter? Jaykin, you called him?"

"No, sir. No one has caught sight nor sound of him."

"Hmm. Curious." He turned back to his guests. "Anyway, Elead will see you off. Farewell!"

After Commander Heth departed, Kiriath announced that they, too, must be on their way. When they retrieved their packs from their room, however, they found them heavier and more bulging than before. Kiriath opened his and found that at least a dozen golden pears had been added to the top. He raised one eyebrow toward Elead in a silent question.

"A small gift," Elead explained. "Your packs were unusually thin for men going into the frontier. But pears from the five hills of Quintepolis give as much energy as flavor. Besides, your bronze talent more than paid for the breakfast. Keep the gift. All I ask is forgiveness for opening your belongings without your bidding."

"A pardon easily granted," Kiriath answered. "Our thanks, Elead."

As on the previous night, Elead again guided the two friends. This time, however, he led them out of the stronghold and down a moderate slope to where a cliff dropped away sharply. From there they could see both Ephron Falls high above and the lake at the base of the cliff. Mist from the cascading water reflected the morning sunlight and stretched a rainbow over the pass. Smaller mountains loomed nearby, but from here Kiriath could easily see the Lowlands beyond.

"Xandria is something of a plateau compared to the northern lands," Elead explained. "You'll descend farther than the wagon brought you up. From where we stand, there's only one direct route into the Outlands." He picked up a coil of rope that was knotted to a rusty iron post in the ground and flung it over the cliff. "Allow me to lead you one last time." With that, Watercliffe's assistant commander grasped the rope and backed over the cliff, with his feet braced against the rocky face. When he had almost touched the bottom, Kiriath followed him down, and lastly came Brand.

"You now stand outside of Xandria," Elead announced at the bottom. "This is where I must leave you. A stream flows from the far end of Lake Ephron. It's the shortest way to the Lowlands, if that's your goal, but cautious men stay in the mountains. Beyond this point I can give you only four pieces of advice: keep your eyes open, don't veer to the west, don't stray too far north, and never advertise your presence with loud sounds or lights at night. Hunters who do all four may live to prosper."

"Thank you again for everything," Brand said, clasping Elead's hand. "You're an asset to the kingdom."

"Thank you. Certainly, I've met few other huntsmen as courteous as yourselves."

Elead seemed to hesitate before proceeding. Kiriath sensed that something else was on the man's mind.

"Jathan . . . Killdeer," Elead said slowly. "As I was growing up, my father always stressed a particular lesson over and over. 'Walk circumspectly,' he used to say. 'Keep your eyes open, always looking beneath the surface to see what a thing is, and not simply what it appears to be.' These words have helped me through the years. Often I have detected things others do not observe. Some things that seem to be shiny and extravagant on the outside turn out to be quite simple or common beneath the surface. On the other hand, things that look commonplace are sometimes quite special—almost royal, you might say."

The prince observed Brand lift his chin slightly at this last sentence.

"I just want you to know," Elead continued, "that even were the prince of Xandria and a trusted friend to pass this way—peculiar though that would seem to me, especially in days like these—I couldn't wish to aid them more than I want to help you two. Now, is there anything at all that you lack for your . . . hunting?"

Kiriath shook his head. "You've treated us better than two strangers could expect. I can think of nothing more that you can give us now, except hopes of good success."

"That you already have. Farewell then. May we meet again."

"May we meet again," Brand repeated.

With powerful arms, Elead started climbing quickly up the rope.

"Do you think he knows, Kiriath? Or do you suppose he is merely guessing?"

Watching the man climb, Kiriath nodded his head. "He knows, Brand. He knows."

CHAPTER 7

A Living Myth

Kiriath and Brand had no trouble finding the stream trickling from the far end of Lake Ephron. Having refilled their water flasks, they started trudging alongside it. The stream itself had washed all the soil from its rocky bed, but on each side green grass grew. Trees, too, became more abundant as they descended.

As foretold, the stream from Ephron flowed fairly straight to the Lowlands ahead. But what had at first appeared an easy few hours' journey out of the mountains actually took much longer. At times the matted underbrush hemmed in the stream, which almost forced the friends to walk in its waters. In other places the stream unexpectedly raced down steep inclines. In those spots Kiriath and Brand, having no rope, were forced to go out of their way to locate a safe descent to the bottom. Eventually, however, they could see the rolling Lowlands, not in occasional glimpses, but as a steady goal ahead.

Sometime after midday, the companions came to a spot where a lesser rivulet joined their watercourse. Here they sat down to rest and to eat some of the golden pears Elead had given them. Heedful of the advice not to advertise their whereabouts, they conversed quietly as they ate.

"Well, Brother Kiriath, when do you think we'll spy anything *odd* in this northern wilderness?"

"Not soon, I hope. Better yet would be not at all. We have time for only one adventure on this trip, and Vol-Rathdeen still lies far away."

"Yes," Brand agreed, "this is the third day of the seven Kroll gave us. We've made excellent time so far, but if we don't have Jekoniah out of that pit within four more days—"

"I know," the prince cut in.

"Do you still plan to bear north as far as we can travel before sundown? Perhaps we could buy some precious time by angling westward this afternoon."

Taking a last bite from the core of his pear, Kiriath reached into the stream, half lifted a large stone submerged there, and tucked the core under it to hide the signs of their passing. "It's tempting to start west today, but we'd better not. If I wanted to run into a Grishnaki band, that's exactly how I'd do it. But since we need to avoid being seen at all costs, we'd better stick to our original plan."

Finishing their meal and brief rest, the two hoisted their packs onto their backs and resumed the northward trek.

The jagged teeth of the mountains gradually softened into rolling wooded foothills. The stream from Lake Ephron eventually veered off to the east, winding its way into another long, nameless lake.

Neither of the friends spoke much. Whether or not it was his imagination working tricks on him Kiriath could not tell, but as they traveled, an ominous attentiveness seemed to surround them. He almost felt as if their surroundings—the bushes, the trees, the squirrels—were all noting their passing. The prince sensed no particular animosity in the air, simply an inexplicable curiosity and awareness from objects that should have been incapable of such.

"Elead's tales are playing mischief on me," Brand muttered under his breath. "I feel there's something uncanny in this region, growing more eerie the farther we press."

"I know," Kiriath agreed. "I can almost feel eyes looking at me. But each time I turn my head, there's nothing to be seen but woods, sparrows, and a rabbit or two."

"Imagination or not, let's hasten all the more. It's taken longer than I would've expected to get clear of the highlands."

However, Brand's wish to pick up the pace proved nearly impossible. While they had been in the vicinity of the mountains, the two had stumbled across two overgrown trails and an old campsite, all apparently made by patrollers from the Watercliffe garrison but long since abandoned. Those trails, though, snaked east and west among the hills, not northward as the prince and his friend now went. The farther north they progressed, the more difficult it became to march with either stealth or speed. Fallen leaves and twigs so carpeted the floor of the forest that only rarely could they place a boot in a spot that did not crunch or crackle under their weight. Small vines, too, stretched across their path, seemingly trying to trip their feet. Thus passed a frustrating afternoon of much toil with lessening progress.

Toward sunset Kiriath, perspiring, drew his forearm across his brow. "What do you think? Have we gone as far as we had hoped?"

"I doubt it," Brand returned, "although it feels like we've gone twice as far. This wilderness fights against us. But then again, Grishnaki would have just as hard a time roving here. Maybe we don't need to go a normal day's march north before we head toward the west."

"An agreeable thought. I wish these trees would thin out."

A light snapping noise to their rear captured both men's attention. Instinctively, they whirled and crouched, eyes searching the branches and the underbrush behind them. Simultaneously Kiriath's and Brand's right hands flew to their sword hilts. Moments dragged past. A woodpecker began his rhythmical knocking on a dead tree. Two chipmunks raced across the ground, paused to look at the motionless men, then disappeared into a hole under a rock.

At last Kiriath straightened. His eyes met Brand's. "Perhaps nothing," he murmured. "Or perhaps just a dead branch falling to the ground."

"Perhaps," Brand replied, but there was no conviction in his voice. "Let's go a little farther while we may. Evening will be upon us soon enough, and I wouldn't mind getting out of these woods before bedding down."

The prince wondered if Brand was thinking of Grishnaki or if he, too, was recalling the furtive shape from two evenings ago.

With a final glance around, Kiriath touched a hand to Brand's shoulder. "Time flies. So must we."

So on the two plodded. The trees never fully ended before dusk gathered, but they did become less dense. Brand pointed out the dry bed of a brook crossing their path and suggested they encamp just beyond it. Any pursuer, he contended, could not step on the gravel in the dry watercourse's bottom without making a noise.

On the far bank a half dozen ancient willow trees clustered together. The willows were neither particularly broad nor tall, but they formed an ideal hiding place. Each tree's long, slender limbs grew thickly, drooping right to the ground. Indeed, so dense were these living curtains that they could be parted and entered, leaving one inside a green, leafy dome from which he would be invisible on the outside. Best of all, a man keeping watch from inside could lift aside enough fronds to see out without betraying his position.

Brand volunteered to take the first watch. "Maybe my imagination is conjuring phantoms," he declared, "but more than once today I've thought I heard a footfall behind us."

"If there were anything to hear, you would hear it," the prince affirmed. "Your ears are sharper than mine. Though I dare say I can see better than you on a moonless night."

"Go to sleep then. If I need your owl eyes, I'll shake you before my watch is up. But if there's anyone prowling on two legs out there, I'm going to get my hands on him."

"Just warn me before you start wrestling with strangers," Kiriath said. As was his custom, he lay on his back, one hand crossing the other over his stomach.

The wind gently lifted and swayed the branches above, winking out some stars while revealing others. Kiriath noted with satisfaction that Brand had his knife in hand and was soundlessly trimming away part of the inner willow curtain. In this way he would be able to peer out without constantly holding the willow limbs aside.

Alone in his thoughts, the prince struggled with his own doubts. Were they wasting their time? What if there was only one way into Vol-Rathdeen? What then? They would still have to try to sneak in at night disguised as Grishnaki. But what if the passage were too well lighted or too well guarded? And assuming they could sneak in and find Father, what then? Could they seriously hope to free a prisoner of the Grishnaki, escape, and evade the pursuit all the way back to Xandria? Here in the wilderness, his plan seemed more futile than it had in Shiralla. Perhaps Urijah had been right to regard their quest as impossible. Was the prince leading his friend into certain death?

But even in the midst of doubt, Kiriath's resolve grew firmer—either he would rescue his father, or he would fail trying. He could not turn back without at least making the attempt. After all, if he did not try, his father's death was certain. *Who knows?* he thought. *Brand might not even need to go into the Grishnaki's valley. Against a whole legion of Grishnaki, two of us wouldn't survive any longer than one. I could always post him to guard my retreat.*

At this thought Kiriath felt a burden lift from his heart. He decided then that, if at all possible, he would enter the Grishnaki's stronghold alone. Then, if he perished, at least he would not cause the death of his best friend. That matter settled, the prince rolled over and let his mind wander.

Inevitably, however, his mind drifted back to Vol-Rathdeen. He had heard the name all his life, but what exactly was it? Just a valley with caves riddled throughout its rock walls? Or would there be one massive cavern where all or most of the Grishnaki dwelt together? Over and over these and similar questions rolled through his thoughts until he drifted into slumber.

Kiriath could not tell how long he had slept when he felt a firm hand squeeze his shoulder. For half a second he imagined himself underground with a Grishnak bending over him—but no, that had been only a dream.

"Owl eyes," said Brand's voice, barely audible. "Come over to my window. Tell me what you see."

Kiriath knew his companion would not wake him as a jest. On hands and knees, the prince crept to the spot where Brand had kept his watch.

At first Kiriath's eyes remained sleep-blurred. He could discern nothing but thin clouds scurrying across the moon's hazy outline. As he blinked, though, his vision cleared, and he became aware of a movement in the direction from which they had come. Kiriath blinked again and concentrated on the spot. There could be no doubt. The silhouette of a cloaked man stood on the far side of the brook bed, against the deeper blackness of the forest beyond. The figure turned first one way and then the other as if searching for something.

"The same one you saw before?" Brand breathed.

Kiriath could not be certain. He shrugged his shoulders, realizing at the same moment that his friend might not be able to observe the action in their shadowy hiding place.

The mysterious shape stooped and touched a hand to the ground, then looked straight across the channel.

"He's onto our footprints," Kiriath said. "Too small for a Grishnak, I think, but he could spell trouble. We'd better take him."

As the two friends watched, the stranger halted, as if in doubt. Next he stepped into the waterless channel. As Brand had predicted, both men distinctly heard booted feet crunching on gravel despite the intruder's obvious efforts to move stealthily. As the dark figure drew nearer, the moon suddenly broke free of the clouds that had enshrouded it, revealing that the mysterious figure was indeed cloaked and outfitted as a man, and not a Grishnak. He was, in fact, appareled very much like Kiriath and Brand, except that he carried a quiver and longbow on his back rather than a sword on his belt.

When the hooded one gained the near bank, mere feet from the willow, Brand sprang out. "Got you!" he shouted, lunging at the newcomer's waist.

Kiriath was right at Brand's heels, but not close enough. No sooner had Brand flung the newcomer down backwards than the stranger let out an exclamation and shot his feet upward, catching his attacker in the stomach. In the next instant Brand's own momentum helped to send him tumbling head over heels. Scarcely a second later, the stranger was halfway to his feet, ready to flee back the way he had come.

"Stay!" Kiriath commanded. "Or feel steel in your back!"

The stranger froze in place. Slowly he straightened and turned toward the prince. The hood of his cloak hung low, obscuring the eyes, but moonlight illuminated the stranger's face from his cheekbones down to his chin. Kiriath found those features disturbingly familiar.

"I meant you no harm," the newcomer uttered. "Let me go."

To the prince, even the stranger's voice had a familiar timbre to it. Something in it, though, was unnatural. Did he detect a feigned huskiness in the voice? Was this a youth trying to sound older or stronger? But then, what youth could have countered Brand's attack so decisively?

"I meant you no harm," the cloaked one repeated. "Let me go in peace."

"Perhaps no harm was meant," Brand said, brushing himself off, "but both my pride and body have received a bruising." He looked at Kiriath. "This one is skilled in Tara-Ni combat. Only two people have ever succeeded in flipping me through the air so quickly: you and . . ."

Brand did not need to finish his sentence. Kiriath knew that Carpathan, their former Tara-Ni master, was the only other person to better his companion. But this slim figure standing before them was certainly not the broad-shouldered Carpathan.

"Why are you staring? Let me go."

"Answers," Kiriath said. "First give us some answers, and then we'll decide where you go. What's your name?"

After a brief silence the reply came: "Some call me Jaykin."

Brand grew more interested. "Elead's missing hunter."

Kiriath nodded. More interesting to him, however, was the hauntingly familiar quality in the speaker's voice. "Not everyone who wishes may learn the Tara-Ni method of defense. Under whom did you study?"

Again no answer was immediately forthcoming, but Kiriath pressed the point. "Speak. Name your instructor."

The stranger sighed. "Carpathan of Shiralla."

This time the pretended depth of voice disappeared, and Kiriath realized to whom he spoke.

Brand, too, guessed their visitor's identity, for he immediately stepped forward and cast back the hood. "Ariana!" Brand exclaimed. "As I live and . . . Just what are you doing out in this forsaken place?"

"What am I doing? My duty to my father, just as you two are doing."

Kiriath sheathed his weapon. "So you are Jaykin, the mystery hunter who jumped wagon just before Watercliffe? Are you also the one I saw by the stream two nights ago?"

"Yes. I had hoped to wait at least one more full day before revealing myself. But my tracking skill isn't as good as I'd hoped. More than once I lost the trail. Other times you nearly discovered me."

"But what's the purpose?" Brand asked. "Do you know how dangerous—"

"Yes," Ariana interrupted, "I know the danger as well as both of you. And I know my own duty. Kiriath, my veins run with the same blood as yours. I've received learning and training that only the children of kings receive. And Brand, you know how I love you. But I would rather die myself than sit in front of the hearth doing needlework and waiting to hear whether my men folk live or perish. Jekoniah isn't just my monarch; he's my father. Only two people in Xandria may say as much. So who can dictate that a son may attempt a rescue and a daughter may not? I had no choice but to follow and try to help. If you live, I'll live with you. But if you die, we perish together."

"Father would not wish you on this errand," her brother stated flatly.

"Perhaps not," Ariana returned, "but in matters where the king has not decreed otherwise—whether by letter or by principle—a citizen of the realm is at liberty. My destiny is bound to yours and to his and now to Brand's."

Brand stood with arms crossed, shaking his head. Kiriath tried to frown. He couldn't help admiring his sister's daring. She looked as he had once seen his mother during a hunting expedition. But the strength in Ariana's voice now resembled more that of the monarch who was her father.

"Well, Brand, what do you think? Can she join us? After all, you're the one espoused to marry our latecomer."

"I, in turn, should mention that she's of your kin and that the arguing ought to be kept in one family. But if I weren't so angry to see her marching stubbornly into danger, I'd kiss her to show how proud I am of her spirit."

"Being her older brother, I'd feel obligated to tie her onto a horse and send her back to Xandria—if only I had a horse to do it. Back home I could argue that the prince's orders carry the weight of law in the king's absence and order her to the Citadel. But Xandrian law means nothing outside the border, where we now stand."

"Then I can come with you? You won't try to send me back?"

"I doubt that you'd go," Kiriath said. "If you're going to be out here, I want to keep at least one eye on you. Even if you were a man, I wouldn't send you away alone in this uncharted country."

"Nor I," Brand agreed. His eyes met hers and showed fierce emotion. "But even though I love you, you're the last one I would wish along on this quest. I don't know what kind of foolish . . ."

Ariana was the first to break eye contact as she shifted her gaze to the ground.

"But from the other angle, who knows?" Brand continued. "Another pair of hands with a bow might be some help. You ranked seventh in Shiralla's last Festival competition, as I recall. Besides, I was growing weary of having only so-called Jathan's face for company."

Ariana brightened again.

"Careful there, Killdeer," Kiriath warned, "or you may find yourself in another round of Tara-Ni before the night is spent. But seriously, Ariana: you are to stay with us and take no unnecessary gambles. For all your training as King Jekoniah's daughter, you're still short on experience when it comes to Grishnaki."

"I know that," she replied quietly, "but the Grishnaki also lack experience in dealing with kings' daughters."

"Clever," Brand remarked. "But come; the night is wasting. Take a corner of our bungalow, Arie," he said, using her familiar name. "You must be exhausted." As befitted propriety, Brand moved his own belongings away from Ariana's, to the far side of the willow.

Fatigued though she looked, Ariana insisted that she take a turn standing watch. When it came time, however, Kiriath let her sleep. He knew she must have been hard put to follow their trail and catch brief snatches of sleep along the way. Furthermore, the next day would bring few stops for rest.

At dawn's first gray light the prince woke his sister and Brand. A light dew lay round about outside, but their willow roof had kept them dry. After a brief, cold breakfast, the trio set out.

Kiriath was certain they had not traveled as far north the previous day as he had planned. For this reason he chose a course that angled them both west and north. Although he wanted to reach the Valley of Grishnaki as quickly as possible, he still distrusted his own impatience and didn't want to choose an overly direct route. By going at least somewhat northward for one more day, he felt confident of eventually descending upon Vol-Rathdeen from the rear, where no man had ever appeared.

Today the hiking proved less difficult. The rolling countryside had fewer steep hills, and the forest thinned out to scattered patches of poplars, elms, and maples. Occasionally, the little group would even stumble upon wide, open fields teeming with orange and brown wildflowers. They avoided these, however, whenever possible, lest hostile eyes see them from afar.

Near midday Kiriath called a halt on the edge of a large pond in a glade of oaks. Normally he would have pressed on for another hour. Ariana, however, looked weary. Better to eat and make a voluntary rest, he thought, than to march his sister to unnecessary exhaustion. Still, he concluded, she showed endurance and held a good pace. Indeed, some defenders of the realm might have fared worse than his sister. Merely having trailed them alone and almost unseen from home had been no simple feat. Although she spent most of her days in or about Shiralla, Ariana was proving tougher than he would have expected.

"Not a bad spot for a picnic, Kir," Brand said, chewing a strip of dried beef. "A still pond almost large enough to be a lake, just enough trees for a bit of shade, and scenic peaks welling up to the south. A shame this place isn't in Xandria."

"It is nice," Ariana agreed.

"Too bad we can't stay to enjoy it," Kiriath replied. "We need to press on as soon as we've had a bite and a sip of water. Since this region is uncharted, I'm not sure how to gauge whether our speed has been good or poor."

"And even half a day late . . ." Brand let his words trail off. There was no need to finish, and he didn't want to be a dismal reminder of the king's possible doom. A minute later, though, he spoke up with a new topic.

"Kir, I'm no expert in the history of early explorations, but shouldn't we have come across the Deserted Kingdom by now? I mean, I always had the impression that ruins stretched all through the territory we've been in today."

The prince shrugged. "I'm not positive. I knew we wouldn't reach it until we were well clear of the northern mountains. Still, I expected to see some crumbling walls or other traces of it before now. There was no time to rummage through the Vault of Chronicles to hunt down the old accounts."

Now Ariana spoke up, reciting as from memory: "'In the month of Yularius, the second year from the founding of Colony Xandria; Tirshatha Kanadon, Governor, did commission Ard, of the house of Nimrim, to espy the unknown Northlands. Leading five hundred knights, Ard the Brave rode north from the Vale of Bacuth. On the second day, he discovered ancient buildings, which he deemed ruined towns and temples, encircling many hilltops. Of men, there were none; of Grishnaki there were but traces. But of strange sights there were many, including the plants that war. In the north for a fortnight rode Ard, passing along the edge of the Deserted Realm. So he came at last unto the far lands of the great Northland Grishnaki, where several battles were fought. South and east returned Ard, having endured hardship and perils previously unknown south of the mountains. Thus he came again to Colony Xandria with three hundred and three score and three knights. Recorded by my hand, Dothran of Demeritor, Scribe to the Tirshatha.'"

Ariana smiled. "At least, that's what one of the chronicles says. My first governess fancied history and had me copy old scrolls to practice my script. She preferred the ancient style of writing better than the new. Not very helpful, though, is it?"

"Maybe it is," Kiriath countered. "The Vale of Bacuth is well west of Watercliffe. We may not be quite north of it even now. So perhaps we haven't reached the eastward parts of the Deserted Kingdom."

"Or we're skirting south of it," Brand suggested. "After three centuries, the signs of it may have vanished. I suspect that it's been years since any of our people ventured this far over the mountains."

"Well, Sister, you're proving to be a helpful traveling companion. Do you know any other chronicles that might help us?"

Ariana closed her eyes, searching her memory. "I don't think so. I remember bits of a few old records. Genealogies . . . some miscellaneous accounts from the Mother Kingdom across the sea . . . things like that. But so little was ever written about the Northlands. Then the Grishnaki uprising came the year after Ard's expedition. There was just no reason to explore the north with so many problems plaguing Xandria itself. There are legends, some fables—nothing truly useful, though."

"I'm not sure I care for all of that first one," Brand said. "What's it mean by 'plants that war' and 'perils unknown south of the mountains'?"

This time it was Ariana's turn to shrug. "I don't believe anyone knows for certain. It wasn't explained in the scroll. Not that I know of, anyway. I suppose most of the knights who had been there and knew died early on in the battles against the Grishnaki."

All this while Kiriath had been sucking a blade of grass and listening. At last he rose and re-shouldered his pack. "No time to spare on speculation now. We'd better move out."

With Kiriath again leading the way, the trio resumed their hike. However, hardly had they topped a low mound overlooking their resting place when noises in the distance halted them again. At first no source for the sound was apparent.

The strange sound that grew in Kiriath's ears reminded him of something. What was it? Something he had heard once years ago. The plague of locusts he had seen when he was twelve? That was the year strong winds from the west had blown in great clouds of locusts, crawling, flying, devouring and devastating crops. This sound was similar, yet louder and somehow more supple in nature. Through it all came a cacophony of screeching birds.

"There!" Brand said. "Something's happening on that ridge."

The prince and Ariana stared in the direction their friend was pointing. Vast numbers of birds were rising and wheeling, passing over them now southward. Among the trees cresting the ridge, something else was taking place. It appeared as if hundreds of invisible hands in the branches of the trees were somehow shooting or throwing long scrolls of parchment at one another. But no one was there. In midair the scroll-like strands seemed almost to twist and writhe as they passed from the top of one tree to a lower bough of another.

Before long almost all the birds had disappeared. Only a few hawks circled and glided high overhead. Now other creatures—foxes, weasels, and badgers—were fleeing past the trio. One alarmed gazelle bolted quite near, nearly running into Brand, more alarmed by a danger behind than by the unexpected presence of humans.

"Could it be . . .?" Brand began. But that was as far as he got. He just stared at the descending shapes before them.

"Soaring Serpents!" Kiriath exclaimed, scarcely believing his own eyes. He had not heard those words uttered since he had been a child, when older defenders tried to frighten the king's son with myths and old fireside tales. The prince unconsciously shifted his hand to his sword's hilt.

"We can't stay here," Brand said. "They'll be swarming over us in minutes."

"Right," Kiriath agreed. "We'll have to run like the wind and better."

"The pond!" Ariana cried. "We'll be safe there."

Brand and Kiriath both turned to her, not understanding her meaning. She explained quickly.

"In the old stories. The Soaring Serpents swam through air but were helpless in water. If we swim to the middle—"

"Let's risk it," Kiriath abruptly decided.

The three of them pounded back down the slope, throwing down their packs at the water's edge. Next they kicked off their boots and dropped their cloaks. Ariana plunged into the pond first—tunic, leggings, and all—striking out with swift, smooth strokes. Each of the men, however, wore steel mail armor beneath their outer tunics. They removed these and cast them down before following Ariana's lead.

Treading water in the middle of the pond, the little group waited less than a minute before the slithering hoards began alighting in the surrounding oaks.

Wave after wave of green and brown mottled serpents soared into the branches and bowed them down with their weight. To the prince, the scene was both fascinating and repulsive. First, the snakes twisted and wound their way up a tree's trunk. Then, reaching the upper limbs, they slid along them and at last they coiled tightly and then flung themselves into the air. Once airborne, the creatures flattened their bodies and floated on the breeze. They twisted and writhed through the air just as a water snake ripples its way through a swamp.

Some of the creatures were a mere three feet in length, while others reached up to twenty. In the air, whenever a serpent began to lose altitude, it would maneuver into the lower branches of a nearby tree and from there back up the trunk for a new flight. Sometimes, just before alighting, a serpent would clamp its jaws shut on a petrified squirrel or some other prey while its body simultaneously coiled about a branch. From a distance, tree trunks seemed to pulsate with life as countless numbers of the reptiles slithered over each other and fought to climb upward. The very air around the swimmers reverberated with the crescendo of incessant hissing.

"It's incredible," Kiriath breathed.

"It's loathsome," Ariana countered. "They freeze my marrow to see them all around, watching us."

"Let's just hope they really can't take to water," Brand said.

As the companions watched, however, the serpents maintained their distance. Only occasionally did one dare to glide over an edge of the water. But from limbs that overhung the pond, cold, unblinking eyes like polished coal regarded the humans, while forked tongues slipped in and out of scaly lips and tasted the air.

Once, two younger serpents tried to glide over the pond from conflicting angles. At the last moment, the two saw each other and tried to swerve before colliding, but too late. Seeking support, the two serpentine bodies entwined together before splashing down. Instantly, they began twisting and squirming, struggling to keep their heads from submerging. It took some time before the human onlookers could be sure the two snakes were truly dead, for even after the immediate thrashing ceased, the slender bodies continued to twitch and wriggle on the surface.

Exuberant with relief, Kiriath laughed. "Ha! They really can't swim! There's more truth in old tales than even the storytellers believe."

"Look," Ariana called. "They're thinning out and moving past us."

It was true. The leading ranks had already passed even though many branches still bent and swayed under the weight of Soaring

Serpents. But these last were clearly stragglers, either older and slower reptiles, or else those that had eaten their fill and cared little for further hunting.

Kiriath guessed that they had tread water for nearly an hour before they finally saw the last snake creep away through the underbrush, too heavy to fly. Several bulges showed along its length: evidence of successful hunting. Even then, Kiriath waited a few minutes more before striking out for the shore.

"I never would have believed it if I hadn't witnessed it myself," the prince declared as he stepped, dripping, from the muck and onto the shore. "Soaring Serpents, of all things."

"Nor would anyone, I suppose," Brand agreed. "No one who hadn't seen them would believe such things could exist."

Ariana said nothing. She was moving slowly, laboriously. Brand put an arm around her and pulled her up onto solid ground.

"They made a mess of our packs," Kiriath declared, picking up his own. "The dried meat is gone, but the fruit and everything else seems to be here."

On his knees, Brand gathered the strewn remnants of his pack, helping Ariana find her belongings as well. "Kir, I recommend we wear our mail on the outside from here on. We'll look more like defenders than hunters, but that shouldn't matter anymore. Grishnaki would stick a spear in one as fast as the other. We won't want to lose any time, though, if more of those slimy monsters cross our path."

"Good idea." Kiriath buckled on his sword belt. He paused to take stock of the situation. "We've just lost a lot of valuable time. Let's be off and walk in our wet clothes. They should dry quickly enough in this sun."

The prince had just lifted his pack from the ground when he heard a slight noise, as if a leather belt were suddenly whipped out of its loops. Ariana cried out. Kiriath's head jerked up in time to see a last Soaring Serpent weaving out of the sky, jaws gaping wide, coming right at him. Its fangs curved downward like twin white scimitars, ready to clamp on the prince's head.

The thought of his sword flashed through Kiriath's mind, but there was no time to act on it. The gigantic maw would lock onto him before he could draw his blade. More out of instinct than deliberate strategy, Kiriath shielded his face with his pack, blindly shoving it into the serpent's mouth before flinging himself sideways.

The next instant the prince felt water splashing around him. He was already half-submerged before he realized that he had pitched himself into the pond. Flashing his sword from his sheath, he whirled around.

But the beast was no longer pursing Kiriath. The prince turned in time to see his attacker shaking his pack from its mouth. This was the largest of the serpents he had yet seen: as wide as a man and—but there was no time to guess how long. It now reared its head toward his friend and sister.

Naked from the waist up, Brand wielded his sword, gripping it in both hands. Sprawled on the ground behind him was Ariana, eyes wide with horror, apparently having tripped over a root. In the creature's side Kiriath saw a red gash and guessed that Brand had already struck a blow.

The prince pulled a stone the size of his fist from the murky bottom.

"Ho there, you!" he yelled. "Ugly one! Don't forget about me!" As the serpent turned, Kiriath heaved the rock. It struck near one lidless eye and bounced away. An angry hiss erupted from its gullet.

From the far side of the serpent, Brand struck another blow, then leapt back again. Instantly, the serpent's jaws snapped shut on the air he had just vacated. It drew back, poised to strike, but Brand stood his ground, steel raised and ready.

Seizing his chance, Kiriath rushed forward, shouting. This time the serpent ignored him, still preparing to spring on Brand, who had now wounded it twice.

Kiriath's blade arced through the air. The prince put all his might into the blow: Xandrian steel slashed through scales and sank deep. Another hideous hiss issued from the serpent, while a shudder shook through its length. Kiriath tried to wrench his sword from the snake's body, but it held fast. He couldn't draw it back out, and there was no time to try twice.

More slowly this time, the monstrous head began twisting toward its new attacker.

Kiriath's first thought was to rush back into the safety of the water. Immediately, however, he rejected it. He would not be able to help Brand and Ariana if he backed away now. On impulse, Kiriath lunged at the green scales of the serpent's back. Throwing both arms around his foe, he clasped both hands together just below the thing's mouth, for fear of its being flexible enough to drive a fang into him. Next he locked his ankles around it as well.

The sudden addition of Kiriath's weight shoved the creature's head down, driving its face into the dirt. Wildly, the serpent twisted and writhed, alternately flattening and rounding itself, trying to shake off its rider. Kiriath clung all the harder. Terror and determination combined with desperation to outlast the fiendish strength convulsing beneath him.

Massive sinews bunched beneath gleaming green and brown scales. One moment Kiriath was riding high as the serpent reared its head into the air; the next he was smashed into the grassy bank with the writhing creature atop him. With a strange detachment, the prince found himself noting that the serpent was not as heavy as it appeared. If a horse rolled over on him thus, he thought, it would crush him. He assumed that the monster's nature made it light but muscular to glide from the treetops.

A cry from Ariana brought Kiriath back to the present danger. He couldn't tell what she said, but he realized Brand was nearby, hacking and slashing with his sword. The serpent reeled and thrashed with renewed efforts. First it tried again to scrape Kiriath off on the ground; the next instant it was coiling and snapping for its other adversary.

One time Kiriath got a clear glimpse of Brand, who held a dripping, red sword and was just leaping clear as the tail snapped around. Behind Brand, Ariana was just loosing an arrow aimed at the creature's lower half. The vision jerked away as the serpent hissed loudly and gave a massive heave.

Water splashed, then closed over Kiriath's head. He had been caught off guard but held what little breath he had. Unwittingly, the monster had rolled into the pond and was now thrashing crazily. Suddenly the prince found himself thrown above the water's surface. Just as quickly he was dashed beneath again. Water lilies tangled about him, trailing from his neck and arms.

"Jump off," Brand shouted the next time Kiriath was tossed above water. "Jump!"

Simply letting go would have been simple for Kiriath, but jumping anywhere proved more difficult. He hesitated to loosen his grip. In its drowning agony, the serpent still twisted wildly, sometimes even biting the air or the foaming waves around it. If Kiriath should let go at the wrong instant, he might yet feel the monster's fangs digging into him. Or the serpent might coil about him, just as a drowning swimmer will sometimes clutch at a rescuer.

At last the creature flung itself upward again, giving Kiriath the opportunity he needed. He released his hold and pushed off. Half swimming and half running, he forced his way through the water lilies and toward the shore. Slapping into him once, the wildly craning tail nearly knocked him down, but the prince struggled on and at last reached shallower water. The next thing he knew, Brand and Ariana were on each side of him and helping him up the steep bank.

Kiriath, dropping down on the grass, panted hard. His arms and legs especially ached from the strain of gripping so tightly, but there were few parts of his body that didn't feel pummeled. He wanted nothing more than to lay unmoving.

Ariana knelt beside him. "Kiriath, are you all right?"

The prince nodded but didn't speak right away. "I feel like I've ridden a log over a waterfall," he said at last.

"Well, it looks like your mount is done for," Brand said. "If you want to ride, we'll have to find you another one."

Kiriath followed Brand's gaze into the pond. The hulk wallowed in the pink-stained foam it churned up. At last, it was slowing and dying.

Kiriath closed his eyes. "No, thank you," he said, responding to Brand's jest. "I've had enough riding for now. I'll walk the rest of the day."

"Just lie still and rest a moment," Ariana commanded.

Personally, the prince felt like complying with her command for the rest of the day. But even now his love for his father pressed upon him, and in his mind's eye he could see the sands of an hourglass slipping away with each delay. "I'm all right. Just had the breath knocked out of me—several times in a row. Give me a moment, and we can be on our way."

"Rest," Brand repeated more firmly. "We can't leave until we fetch your blade from that creature's hide. You might need it. Ariana has a few arrows to retrieve too. But I'm not going in there until that thing stops wiggling. By the way," he added, the mirthful note coming back to his voice, "what took you so long to come out of the water, anyway? Enjoying the ride too much?"

Still lying on his stomach with eyes closed, the prince smiled weakly to himself. He was glad for a friend who could stand and jest on the brink of peril. Playing along, Kiriath simply replied, "I was hot."

He heard Brand chuckle.

"He was an old one," Ariana said. "It might have been a harder struggle if he had been younger and faster."

Kiriath still lay with his eyes closed, but breathing more normally now. "He fought hard enough. If I ever see another one before I die, it will be too soon."

For a long moment, the only sound that came to Kiriath's ears was the soft swishing of water as the serpent's death throes slowed. Suddenly, he heard a loud hiss erupt nearby, almost at his feet.

The prince's eyes shot open, and he rolled onto his back, looking all about. But all he saw was Brand, crouching near his feet and grinning broadly. His friend slapped his knee and began to laugh.

"Brand!" Ariana scolded. "How could you!"

Brand, falling on his side, held his ribs and laughed even harder.

"Only one way to get rid of a sly snake," Kiriath said. Without warning, he shoved a foot against his friend's thigh. Brand vainly grappled at air as he tumbled sideways off the bank, splashing into the pond.

Ariana giggled and crossed her arms. "I don't see how you two ever accomplish anything when you're together."

Now Kiriath took his turn in laughing, half at his sputtering friend and half at his sister's mock indignation.

Still sitting in the water where he had fallen, Brand lifted a necklace of lily pads from his neck, looked at Kiriath, and burst into one last fit of laughter.

CHAPTER 8

A NIGHT IN THE DESERTED KINGDOM

"What do you suppose happened here?" Ariana asked.

Kiriath didn't answer right away. Like the others, he swept his gaze across the charred landscape that unfolded beneath the hillock on which they stood. Everywhere before them were black stumps. Charred tree trunks littered the ashen earth, some still jutting skyward as if in mockery of living, growing trees.

"Hard to say," Brand replied. "Lightning, maybe. But it's been this way for some time. Perhaps Grishnaki burned the approaches to their land to guard it more easily. What do you think, Kir?"

"I don't know. Maybe it's natural, but I don't know. Still, if Grishnaki did it to guard their valley, we'll have many barren miles to cross. We can't be near Vol-Rathdeen yet. On the other hand, they would also be driving away their food supply, which makes me think Grishnaki didn't torch it. At least not on purpose."

"Standing here guessing will get us no nearer to it," Brand said. "The scenery isn't pretty, but the traveling looks easy."

"Do we have to cross that burned mess?" Ariana wanted to know. "It looks so forlorn—and exposed."

"I think we'd better," her brother responded. "Look there to the south."

Pale purple mountain peaks paralleled their path, stretching to the west.

"There aren't many things we can be sure of," Kiriath continued. "But that's the same mountain range we left yesterday. I don't recognize them from this side, but I'm guessing that before long we'll be due north of Xandria's western boundary. If I'm right, it means that the northern garrisons that the Grishnaki have been harassing lie that way."

Ariana began to understand what her brother was getting at. "So we can't veer south lest we come too close to Grishnaki raiding parties."

"And going farther north around this waste would be throwing away time we may need," Brand added.

Ariana looked at the mountains again. "But don't you think the Grishnaki's recent boldness in the area was a feint, a trick to lure our attention northward when they really planned to sneak through the Gray Bogs? In that case, the brutes may not come anywhere near our borders again until they hear Mother's answer to Dar-kon."

"You may well be right," Kiriath said. "But we can't wager our lives—and Father's—on that chance. So, since we can't go around this wasteland, we'd better start crossing it."

"But Brother, how will you know when and where to turn south for the Valley of Grishnaki? You've never been to Vol-Rathdeen."

"You're right; none of us has been to their valley. But Brand and I have both been within sight of Saddle Mountain, which looms above their valley. If we can keep the mountains in sight, we'll see the saddle shape rising above the other peaks. But that's still many leagues ahead."

"And we have to go all the way by foot," Brand reminded. "Come, this standing around makes me uneasy. Let's be off and talk on the way if we must."

Without further comment, the trio marched down the hillock, crossed another dry watercourse, and stepped into the bleak landscape.

Contrary to Brand's suggestion to talk on the way, no one spoke a word now. An oppressive silence hung like a thick shroud. To even consider speaking seemed like an affront to this land's funereal peace.

Here and there scraggly weeds or bushes grew. Once, as Kiriath passed the blackened remains of a tree that still stood upright, a harsh cawing suddenly erupted overhead. Looking up, he saw an enormous crow gazing down at them from the tree's broken top.

That crow almost seems to be watching us with malice in his eyes, the prince thought. He concluded that he was just tense after the morning's fight with the serpent.

For the fourth time since he had left Shiralla, Kiriath noted the sun's slow descent toward the western horizon, and once more he reaffirmed the commitment he had made to himself the previous night. If it were at all possible, he must enter Vol-Rathdeen alone. *Especially now, with Ariana along*, he added to himself. *She must not fall into the stubby-fingered hands of any Grishnak.* Brand would have to safeguard her while he, Kiriath, sought a way to free Father. As yet the prince made no mention of his resolution. There was no point in provoking an argument earlier than necessary.

After about an hour of plodding through ashen waste, Kiriath paused and strained his eyes toward a hilltop to their left.

"Something wrong?" Brand asked.

"Not wrong," the prince replied. "Just different. Curious."

At first glance the gray hill hardly seemed different from any of the others they had seen in this dead land. But on second inspection there was a difference. Its sides were somewhat uneven, but in a patterned fashion, giving it a slightly terraced appearance. On its summit stood a jumble of rocks—no, not just rocks, but a former building of some sort and crumbling now with age. Farther ahead another hill was crowned in like fashion.

"The Deserted Kingdom," Ariana said.

"We're coming to it at last," Brand agreed. "My curiosity would have me to turn aside and rummage in the ruins to see what relics we might find. But we have less than an hour of sunlight left. No time for curiosity on this trip."

"Right," Kiriath said. "Let's press on while we may."

As they continued, Kiriath, Brand, and Ariana began to see more signs of a former civilization. They didn't speak anymore, save for an occasional whisper, but from time to time one of them would point out some edifice that hadn't yet wholly collapsed or the fallen remains of a statue, hopelessly weathered beyond recognition.

Before long, the friends struck upon a raised road, with granite posts periodically sunk in the earth along its right side. Bright green moss grew between the paving stones, but otherwise the road appeared to be swept bare by the wind. Since the highway was fairly level and went in a generally westward direction, they decided to use it rather than marching up and down over the burned hillsides. As they plodded along, however, more signs of greenery appeared in the landscape, and living clumps of trees gradually replaced the remains of the dead ones. The Deserted Kingdom became a land of rolling hills—still terraced as they had been in older generations—and silent, crumbling edifices that had housed . . . whom? Indeed, the remains of former manors, court-yards, walls, and temple-like structures became so numerous that no one pointed them out any longer. The three strangers simply hiked along, marveling at the grandeur that was still evident centuries after this civilization's decline.

"I wonder what kind of traffic once used this road under our feet," Ariana said at last. "It's incredible that such a kingdom existed centuries before Kanadon landed on this shore."

"*Incredible* is a word that scarcely begins to describe what I feel," Brand commented. "I wish I could see this land as it used to be. Maybe it would be like Illandria was before the cataclysm."

"Soon we won't even be able to see it as it is today," Kiriath reminded. "The sun is sinking fast. Let's find a spot to halt for the night. I'm still sore from my scaly ride, and I think we could all use a full night's sleep."

Ariana nodded. "Yes, let's. I know we mustn't waste time, but marching in boots all day makes my feet burn, as if I've been walking on hot coals instead of old ashes."

Brand pointed ahead. "Looks like there's a sort of dell up there, off to the right, where those trees stand. Let's make for it."

As the three drew near the spot, they left the road and scrambled down the embankment. The distance to the dell wasn't far, but the ground was uneven and strewn with rubble. When they arrived, they discovered that their campsite was a crumbling well surrounded by a venerable grove of apple trees of unknown age.

Vines as thick as a man's arm stretched from the ground into the branches, some vines reaching even to the topmost limbs.

"Apples," Brand said. "Those will help replace the meat the serpents stole from our packs." He jumped up and grabbed a branch over his head. Bouncing his weight up and down, he succeeded in shaking loose several of the fruit. Brand gathered up his harvest and gave two apples each to his companions.

"Delicious," Ariana said, biting into one. "They're still a little green, but they're the best wild apples I've ever eaten."

"I don't know if you could really call them wild," Kiriath responded. "Don't forget that someone once lived here. They must have cultivated them."

The prince stepped to the stone wall around the well and peered into its depths. "All we could hope for now would be a rope and bucket to fetch up some water, if there still is any down there. I haven't seen a drop since the glade with the pond."

"Rope?" Brand repeated. "My flask is the closest thing I have to a bucket, but I daresay we can make a good enough rope out of one of these thinner vines."

Immediately Brand pulled his sword from its sheath and slashed through the base of a vine as thick as his thumb. The entire plant quivered for a moment, then hung still. Next Brand pulled once, then twice, and finally a third time until the top of the vine came tumbling out of the tree.

"Rope!" he said, triumphant. "But look here. I've never seen anything like this before. The top of the vine is all curled about an apple with tendrils boring into it."

Ariana shook her head. "I've never seen such a thing either. I prefer a vine that bears fruit rather than eats it."

"Odd," was Kiriath's only comment.

Brand held up the slashed end for his companions to see. Pale, yellow fluid dripped from it. "It looks a little like the flodok vine, whose juice is sweet and good enough to quench any thirst."

He touched a drop of the liquid to his tongue, then quickly spat. "Bitter. Stagnant seawater would taste better."

Kiriath laughed and took the vine. Holding on to the gashed end, he dropped the tip, still gripping its apple, into the well. He let it down as far as his arm would let it, then pulled it back up.

"Dry," said Ariana, seeing the apple now covered with dust.

Kiriath let the whole vine drop back into the well. "Oh well. At least we won't have to go to sleep thirsty and thinking that water is just a few feet away."

Ariana sat down near the well and let her pack fall to the ground. "Small consolation. But thirsty or not, I'll be glad to get some sleep."

"I'm going to scout around the dell before we lie down," Brand said. "Be back in a moment."

When Brand had disappeared, Ariana looked up at Kiriath from where she sat on her cloak. "It won't work, you know."

The prince looked at his sister.

"What won't work?"

"Sneaking off to rescue Father without me. If that's what you're thinking, it won't work."

Kiriath stared at Ariana. Caught off guard, he realized too late that his expression must have betrayed him.

"You keep other people's secrets extremely well, Kiriath. But sometimes you reveal your own without realizing it—at least for those who know you well enough."

"Oh? And when did you become a reader of thoughts? Sorcery is too black an art for a king's daughter to practice."

"No sorcery. But ever since I joined you, you've held your peace for long spells, while Brand and I talked quietly. I knew that something more than Father's capture must be on your heart. Not until a little while ago, though, did I guess what it might be. Now your face has told me that I'm right, or at least nearly right."

Kiriath looked in the direction his friend had gone. "What about him? Does Brand know what I've been thinking?"

"Probably. We haven't talked about it, but I suspect he's guessed too. More than once I've noticed him regarding you closely. In fact, that was what started me wondering. We three grew up together, Kiriath. It's not surprising that we should understand one another more easily than others."

"If you see through me so perfectly, you should understand why I must go into the Valley of Grishnaki alone. I'm the one who conjured up this whole plan of rescuing Father. If it fails, only I should have to pay the price. After we left Xandria, I was even sorry that I'd let Brand come out here with me. How could I lead my own sister into that sinister place?"

"But we are here, and we're going in with or without you. And since that's so, isn't it better that your friend and sister should have your experience guiding them as they go into that valley? Listen, do you believe I would have turned back if both of you had been killed by that Soaring Serpent this morning? Well, I wouldn't. I couldn't. I'm sure Brand is of the same mind. You aren't dragging us to our doom, Kiriath. If death awaits us, well . . . it waits. But each of us has to go to meet whatever lies ahead."

"But if doom is there, it would be better for only one to battle with it and lose his life than for three to die in vain—four if you count Father."

"Where one can do battle and lose his life, two or three together might succeed. Isn't that why Brand joined you in the first place? Remember the serpent again! Could you have killed it alone? Could Brand? Or me with my arrows? Only by joining forces did we defeat it. How can you prophesy that it would be otherwise for wresting Father from Dar-kon's hole?"

Kiriath's mind and emotions struggled within him. Ariana's answers showed wisdom, yet he loathed the possibility of seeing her suffer at the hands of Dar-kon. "You shoot words as truly as you do arrows. But don't forget; if you're captured, your death will be as painful and horrible as the Grishnaki can make it."

Ariana dropped her eyes to the ground. "I know that."

"What would you do if you were to awake one morning to find that I had gone on alone?"

"Then I would have to follow, even if Brand were not with me. I told you before; my destiny is bound to Father's and yours. No matter what happens. This is what I'm meant to do. I can feel it."

Before Kiriath could make any reply, Brand reappeared between two massive tree trunks. "Kir, come have a look at what I've found."

Immediately, the prince and his sister followed their friend. Just a little below the clearing where the well stood, Brand stopped and pointed at the ground. There, in the deepening darkness at the base of an apple tree, lay two large skeletons.

Kiriath looked into Brand's eyes. "Grishnaki or men?"

"Grishnaki," came the reply. "Not the largest Grishnaki, but Grishnaki all the same. A few of the ribs on each one are cracked, but that's all the damage I could find."

Kiriath noted that the bones were weather worn and that the lanky grass grew up thickly between the ribs. "These aren't new."

"No. They died a good while ago. I'd say at least a year. Perhaps longer."

Finally Ariana spoke. "Even if they had been killed recently, surely we wouldn't have to fear whoever did it? The Grishnaki seem to be our mutual enemies."

"It's not that simple, Arie," Brand answered. "The fact that someone kills Grishnaki doesn't guarantee that he'll stomach our company any better. Besides, they could've been killed by fellow Grishnaki or by some dumb beast with no other thought than a quick supper. In that case we three could serve the same purpose."

Ariana shuddered. "This is a depressing spot. Let's go back to the well. Whatever killed them is long since gone; we should be safe enough."

"Perhaps these two thought they were safe too," Kiriath mused.

In twilight the tired travelers ate a cold meal, supplemented with apples from the trees around them. The sun had already set, and soon the fading light vanished entirely.

Kiriath volunteered to take the first watch. Ariana objected that he was the one who should rest first after his ordeal at the pond, but her brother insisted that he was fine and won out. The truth was that Kiriath actually felt more tired than he let on. In his opinion, however, the most dangerous time of night was in the early hours after midnight, when even rested men grow sluggish. He didn't particularly expect an attack, but the discovery of Grishnaki skeletons made him more cautious than ever. In his present bruised and tired condition, he didn't fully trust himself to stand guard during those dangerous hours. *Better to let Brand rest first so he can take charge later,* he thought.

In the deeper darkness under the boughs of an apple tree, Kiriath sat down with his back against a gnarled trunk. Under the starlit sky straight before him stood the well, with Ariana's shadow lying to its left and the dim shape of Brand just settling down to its right.

To Kiriath's mind, along with nightfall came a new and deeper dimension of the silence they had noted upon crossing into the Deserted Kingdom. Brooding hostility pervaded the night. *Once this Deserted Kingdom must have been a bustling, noisy place*, he thought, *filled with the sounds of men and animals both day and night. But now even wild animals seem to shun it.*

Only the stars above seemed to look upon the little troop with friendliness. Or did the prince mistake the familiar glittering lights as friendly when they were actually apathetic to what was happening in the wide world beneath them? He could not say. He did, however, like to consider them as old, familiar friends from home.

As the hours of his watch dragged by, Kiriath pondered what Ariana had said to him earlier. If, indeed, she insisted on entering the Valley of Grishnaki with or without him, certainly it would be better for them to unite their strength and watch out for each other. In that case it would be pointless for the prince to slip away alone. If only he could be more certain of their path. So much of their plan depended on legend, speculation, and hope.

At this point Kiriath's thoughts veered back to Vol-Rathdeen. One moment he would imagine the three of them overpowering some careless Grishnaki, taking their garb, and creeping into the caves in disguise. Minutes later his mind would be turning over the possibility of scouting out the mountain, searching for a secret entrance. The first method appealed to him as the fastest way to enter, but the second seemed like a safer approach. But then again, if no other entrances existed, the trio could waste valuable time and risk capture while lurking on the enemy's rooftop.

Too early to decide, he concluded to himself. *We'll try one or the other, but we won't know which is better until we can see the valley for ourselves. By that time there may not even be time to hope for secondary passages.*

Kiriath stretched. His eyelids were growing heavy, and the ancient apple tree's trunk bored into his back.

Almost time to wake Brand, the prince thought. *I'll give him just a few more minutes.*

At that moment something lightly brushed Kiriath's shoulder. Instantly, the prince craned his neck to see what had touched him. By starlight he could dimly discern a thick vine hanging alongside him. He relaxed and nudged it with his elbow. Yes, it was nothing more than a vine. *Strange, though*, he mused, *that it has hung there throughout my watch without my noticing it 'til now.*

Once more Kiriath settled back and felt his eyelids growing heavy as sleep struggled to win him over. He considered standing and stretching, but there didn't seem to be much point in it. In another minute he would wake Brand; then the prince would let himself succumb to the sleepiness tugging at him. Indeed, in the moon's pale light, the shadow that marked where Brand lay already stirred slightly.

Kiriath smiled to himself. He had always said that Brand had an hourglass built inside him. His friend ever seemed able to rouse himself from sleep when it was time to be somewhere. Soon he would be rising to take the watch.

The vine to Kiriath's left bumped into him twice more, only farther down this time, along his ribs.

Ah, that's why I never noticed it before. I feel it only when the wind moves it.

This explanation satisfied the prince. Gradually, however, his sluggish thoughts became aware of a problem with this reasoning. *But the wind isn't stirring tonight. Not a breath.* As the vine nudged him again, the truth burst upon him like the blare of a trumpet: the vine beside him was creeping under its own power.

With this realization, a rare sensation of chill fear streaked down Kiriath's spine. Was this truly a plant, or some sort of beast that merely masqueraded as a plant? In his mind he envisioned tendrils like those he had seen boring into the apple probing his own body. The prince wrenched his sword from its sheath and sprang to his feet. His one thought was to hack through the base of this hideous thing crawling so close to him. But no sooner had he gained his feet than the whole length of the plant came crashing down on him from above, driving him to his knees. Apparently aware that its prey was on the alert, the vine no longer crept slowly. Rather, it was twisting itself about Kiriath with dizzying speed. The prince could scarcely believe the weight and length of the plant tightening around his legs and torso.

"Bra—!" he started to cry out. But his voice was choked out. The vine was already curling around his throat and chest, immobilizing Kiriath's arms and steadily constricting every time he exhaled.

Kiriath's initial horror of the vine gave way to a swelling tide of indignation. Less than a day ago, a giant serpent had tried to make a meal out of him. He wasn't going to let an overgrown weed succeed where the serpent had failed! Summoning all his strength, he kicked against the ground and thrust outward with his arms.

The vine was still fastened about Kiriath's neck, but its hold on his body slackened for a split second. Already Kiriath felt it tightening again. While he still had the chance, he slashed awkwardly with his blade, gritting his teeth in frustration as the blade embedded itself uselessly in the dirt.

Now the prince was gasping for air. A high-pitched ringing filled his ears. The rough texture of the hoary thing gave an impression of the very tree above him reaching down and strangling him with bark-clad fingers.

Again he slashed aimlessly, hoping against hope to strike his predator. This time the blow proved true; a tremor rippled through the plant's length. But the grip around his neck did not weaken. Now the prince couldn't draw more than the slightest breath of air.

More weakly, Kiriath struck it a second, then a third time—in vain. Shimmering circles and stars danced before his eyes. His steel slipped from his hand. He ached to wrench the living noose from his neck, but now neither hand could budge. This would be a slow, suffocating death.

As if from far away, a sound came to Kiriath's ears, dully sinking into his mind. Again it came. Then again. Over and over, like the strokes of a woodsman's axe, came a solid thudding as if steel were gouging into wood.

Teetering on the threshold of unconsciousness, Kiriath vaguely sensed that his captor was trembling after each successive blow. The sound was coming closer. No, not closer, just clearer as Kiriath began to hear normally again. Sucking in lungfuls of life-giving air, the prince became aware that someone was standing nearby and rhythmically chopping the vine near his head with great strokes. But nighttime still reigned in the dell. Kiriath hoped that his friend did not misjudge in the darkness and lay his skull open with one of those blows.

The sword strokes ceased. "Not yet, Ariana," the prince heard Brand say. "Stay by the well. There may be another one."

Kiriath tried to stand up, but he could not. Even in death the vine remained tightly bound around him.

"One second, Kir," Brand said.

Soon strong arms were unwinding the vine from Kiriath's upper body, easing him to a sitting position. "Are you all right?" Brand asked, concern in his voice.

Kiriath's throat was so abused it wouldn't immediately respond. Finally, in a hoarse voice, he managed, "Yes. But let's get away from here. Now we know what happened to those Grishnaki skeletons with the cracked ribs."

Brand talked as he continued unwrapping dead vine from the prince's legs. "Yours is the second that I've hacked apart. I would have reached you faster if I hadn't been tripped up by a skinny young one. Maybe they come alive at night. There. You're free."

The prince found his sword but did not sheathe it until he and Brand reached the well, where Ariana was waiting. The three gathered their belongings, and Brand led as the three left the well and made their way back toward the road.

As they passed trees to the left and right, the moon illuminated slender shadows swaying in the branches. In Xandria Kiriath would have concluded that his tired eyes were deceiving him. But after his close escape, he knew that more nocturnal plants were groping for a meal of fruit—or flesh.

"Happily, none of those accursed things grow out here, away from the trees," Kiriath said aloud. He chastised himself for having grown careless and resolved not to let it happen again.

"Let's not go all the way up to the road," Ariana said. "I couldn't sleep in the middle of a road, even in a deserted land. Let's stop at the bottom of the embankment."

"Those are my thoughts too," Brand answered. "But I'm glad it's my watch. On or off the road, I don't know that I could sleep for a good while after dueling with a hungry plant."

"It's my fault," Kiriath said. "I should have been more vigilant."

"Nonsense," his sister retorted, "nobody expects a vine to attack him. Grishnaki, yes. An animal, maybe. But not an old vine."

Gaining the bottom of the embankment, Brand tossed down his pack. "You know, Kir, that makes two near disasters for you in one day. Maybe there's truth in the old proverb about the powers of evil striking first at kings and princes."

"Perhaps, although coincidences happen. But if you believe the adage, you'd better be on your guard: while this prince sleeps, you're the ruler here."

"I've never been so awake as I plan to be tonight."

"Yes, but don't forget to wake me for the third watch," Ariana put in. "My arrows might not stop a plant; but if you'll lend me your sword, I'll take my turn."

"You can be sure I will. Otherwise, I'll hear about it all day tomorrow. You're the only woman I'd trust to do it, though, outside of Lady Vandrielle herself."

With the mention of his mother's name, Kiriath settled down on his cloak, using his pack for a pillow. Brand and Ariana exchanged a few soft-spoken words, but the prince was too exhausted to listen. *What must Mother be feeling these days?* He wondered. *What must it be like to be the only one in the family left inside the kingdom? What would it be like?* Thus thinking, Kiriath, who thought himself fully awake, quickly settled into a deep and dreamless slumber.

CHAPTER 9

WATCHING AND WAITING

Queen Vandrielle sighed deeply. From her window casement in the Citadel, she could observe life going on as usual in Shiralla's streets below. Over in the market place, vendors were haggling over the prices of chickens, pitchforks, wagon wheels, and a host of other merchandise. On the battlements, defenders paced the walls, sunlight glinting brightly from their helmets and gear. In the towers above, Vandrielle knew, keen-eyed sentries kept watch on all approaches to the city. "Yes, life proceeds as normal for almost everyone in Xandria—for everyone who is not related to Jekoniah," she mused.

Vandrielle drew another deep breath. These days such a weight lay on her heart that even the simple act of breathing seemed more difficult, almost as though the air had become thicker and heavier since Kiriath and Brand had left. As if the tension surrounding their quest hadn't been burden enough to bear, she reviewed in her mind how later she had discovered Ariana's message on her pillow. Vandrielle still wondered if she would have been wiser to send a troop to find her daughter and bring her back. But no, that might have jeopardized the secrecy around Kiriath's plan. "Oh, Jekoniah. How I need you," she whispered aloud.

The queen let the linen drapery drop back into its place before the window and turned away just as a knock sounded on the door. "Enter," she called.

The door swung open, and a young maiden bearing a tray stepped in. "Forgive me, Lady Vandrielle," the lass began. "You haven't been eating well. I was worried about you and thought . . ."

"Thank you, Latasha. That was thoughtful of you, but I have no appetite these days."

"But you must keep up your strength for the good of the land. Please at least take some juice. They've been squeezing the grapes this week, and the flavor is especially sweet this year."

Vandrielle forced a wan smile for her handmaiden. "All right, Latasha, you win. Leave the tray, and I will enjoy the juice. If I can manage it, I might even eat a little."

"Thank you, Milady. It will do you good. You'll see."

"I am sure it will. You may go now."

Latasha hesitated. "Milady, I know I have no right to ask, but I can't help wondering. The prince came back to the city, yet he is not in his chamber. No one seems to know exactly where he is when we have need of leadership. Is he well?"

Vandrielle knew people would begin wondering this same question and had prepared an answer. "Rest assured that he is well, Latasha. But Kiriath is a man of action. He could not bear to sit in the Citadel idly passing time, and he begged my leave to go to the border with Captain Brand. Exactly where they are at this moment, even I do not know, but be encouraged that the good of the kingdom is ever in his heart and mind. He is not shirking his responsibilities."

Although the explanation was vague, the truth it contained was sufficient to assuage both the queen's conscience and her hand-maiden's curiosity.

"Ah, this is good to hear. May I pass that news along to others who wonder the same question?"

"Of course. That will be fine."

At that moment a slight sound as of a leather sole slipping over a floor tile came to Vandrielle's ears. "Is someone there?" she called through the open door behind Latasha. No answer. Going to the doorway, the queen stepped into the corridor and looked both ways, but no one was in sight.

"I thought I heard a footstep too," Latasha mentioned, "just as you were talking about Prince Kiriath and where he is. But perhaps it was just a dove fluttering outside the window."

"Perhaps," Vandrielle agreed. "That may be. Anyway, thank you again for the meal, but I think I would like to be alone for a while. Later I will come down, and we two can enjoy the sunshine in the gardens together."

"Good, Milady. Fresh air and sunshine are medicines always worth taking. I'll be waiting for you when you're ready."

After Latasha left, Vandrielle peered up and down the corridor one more time, then slowly closed the door. "Whatever that sound was," she told herself, "it was no bird fluttering its wings."

Chapter 10

A Fistful of Lightning

"Come on, Brother. Up. Time to be rising."

Kiriath felt a prod against his shoulder.

"Wake up, Kiriath."

The prince opened his eyes. Ariana was kneeling beside him. Full daylight glinted from the waves in her wind-swept hair. Despite his muscles' protest, Kiriath pulled himself into a sitting position. "Where's Brand?"

"On that closest hill, just over the road. He's scouting for water. We both agreed you could use a little extra sleep this morning."

Kiriath paused, counting in his mind. "This is the fifth day. Tomorrow will be the sixth. There's no time for extra sleep. Father dies on the seventh if we don't reach him." Thus saying, the prince heaved himself to his feet and gathered his pack. He noted that Brand's and Ariana's packs were latched and ready to depart.

"Well, no water in sight, but I suspect we'll be seeing more than we want before long." The voice was Brand's, who was just descending the embankment of the road.

"What's that, a riddle?" Ariana asked.

"No, just discerning the face of the sky. Hadn't you noticed?"

Brand gestured westward. In that direction dark, angry clouds lay in furrows on the horizon.

"We're likely to see rain today."

Kiriath straightened and set his pack on his shoulders, fastening the straps. "We'll need to get started right away. Have you two eaten? Well, I'll just munch on some bread and pears as we march."

"First, I have some good news," Brand said. "From the top of that hill I could see Saddle Mountain away southwest."

"That is good news indeed," Kiriath replied. "Time has sprouted wings since we left Shiralla. If Saddle Mountain is that near, then so is Father."

Ariana hoisted her own pack onto her back. "I'd like to go up and see this Saddle Mountain that I've always heard of. But I suppose we'll all see it well enough before long."

"Right," Brand agreed. "Judging from the sky, we had better be underway. Are you fully rested, Kir?"

"Yes. Let's go. I've slept like a corpse, but I feel much better now than I did at sundown."

"Better to sleep like a corpse than to become one." Brand cast a final look at the silent grove where they had begun the night, then turned and trudged up to the road.

The road beneath their feet stretched straight westward. Here and there portions of hills had even been cut away to let the road pass through. More than any of the ruins along the wayside, this fact attracted Kiriath's attention. He recalled the tales that ancient scholars had told about the mother kingdom, Illandria, as it was before the sea had swallowed it up. One account mentioned roads that ran as level and straight as this one, spanning gorges and rivers and burrowing through mountains. But even in Xandria roads followed the contour of the terrain, whether it were around hills or over them. Ever since the colonial years, other needs—such as defense—usually outweighed the desire to improve Xandria's roads.

Eventually, the three companions reached a point where the road forked, one branch veering northwest, the other southwest. Between the forks a building had once stood. Now, though, it was little more than a mound of mossy bricks. Along the way, other byways had intersected the main road at regular intervals. All of these had run directly north or south, so Kiriath had passed by them. Now, however, a definite decision had to be made.

"What do you think?" Ariana asked. "Angle to the north, veer south, or leave the road and go across country?"

Kiriath stood with arms folded, staring down first one road and then the other. "The fifth day," he murmured. "Let's leave the northern track alone. We want to come upon Vol-Rathdeen from the north, but each step we take in that direction has to be made up coming back. Time is against that route."

"That leaves the left branch or one of our own making," Brand commented. "My opinion would be to travel the road a little further and then to leave it as we draw nearer to the Grishnaki's territory. We're making excellent time on this track, but they're sure to know more about this land than we do. They may even travel on it themselves."

Kiriath nodded. "I'm inclined to agree. I just don't want to make any decision too quickly. Not with our lives and Father's at stake. There's always the chance of forgetting or overlooking something important."

A low rumbling echoed through the hills.

"You're both forgetting that a storm is coming to meet us." Ariana pulled the hood of her cloak over her head. "We can't stand here in the open road. If it's to be the left track for us, let's take it without delay. There's no shelter here at all."

Without further discussion, the three friends hastened onward, down the southwest road. Thunder continued to reverberate through the heavens, at first only in front of the trio, but soon all around them. The sky transformed into a cauldron of massive gray-black billows. A strong wind sprang up, and jagged tongues of lightning dueled back and forth overhead, sometimes stabbing down into a distant hilltop. Even though it was still midmorning, the murky twilight looked more like dusk.

Smaller, overgrown roads occasionally intersected this way, although not as often as on the main road that they had left behind. Along this route, the timeworn relics of ancient edifices were in better condition than any they had yet encountered. The prince almost felt that eyes in the shadowy doorways followed their passage, but, whenever he looked, no signs of life were to be seen. More often than not, the upper stories and roofs had long since crumbled and fallen in.

Finally the rain arrived. It began with but a few pinpoint droplets that moistened the travelers' hands and faces. Before long, however, it developed into a torrential downpour. Cloaks and hoods proved futile as the wind lashed the drops to and fro. Bolts of lightning, groping closer, shook the very ground with their thunder.

Water streaming into his eyes, Kiriath began looking more urgently for shelter. "We've got to get out of this," he shouted to the others, "at least until the worst is past. Keep your eyes open for some kind of cover. Anyplace."

Finding shelter proved to be more difficult than Kiriath had imagined. Even the ruined remnants of the Deserted Kingdom had grown increasingly fewer in number. *Should we backtrack to one of the more solid-looking ruins?* Kiriath wondered. At that moment a brilliant streak split the sky and exploded in the tops of the pines off to their left.

Now the road cut through another hillside. Here the winds did not blow so harshly, but great raindrops continued to pound down with a fury.

Slipping on a slick paving stone, Ariana collapsed onto the road. Together Kiriath and Brand helped her up. She didn't complain, but Kiriath hated seeing his sister so bedraggled. At this point he would have settled for even an overhanging rock to escape the storm's fierceness.

As they exited the far side of the cloven hill, Kiriath saw that, contrary to what he had expected, the road didn't continue into the distance ahead. Instead it ended in the broken gate of what must have once been a mighty fortress. Surrounding the fortress was a massive stone wall many times the height of a man and topped by decaying battlements.

Watchtowers evidently had once stood on the wall, but no longer. Kiriath saw two of them lying in heaps of rubble on the ground. Age had worked its crumbling spell on the stronghold, but the areas of worst destruction on the walls and arches were too strategic to have been caused solely by disrepair and the elements. Kiriath concluded that a great battle must have raged here in forgotten ages past.

"Let's go in," the prince shouted above the din of the storm. "But keep your eyes open."

Three abreast, with Ariana in the center, they picked their way over the fallen archway of the gate. Inside, shattered stone lay everywhere. Hesitant to step inside the main fortress too quickly, the three surveyed the scene, eyes and ears alert to catch any sign of habitation. Now and again lightning flashed, allowing them to see a short way into gaping doorways, but the place appeared desolate. Nothing could be seen through the windows above, which were tall and narrow, as they were on Xandria's border fortresses. Kiriath knew the Grishnaki had never built such defenses, but that fact wouldn't prevent them from sheltering in one.

"Come on," the prince called above the wind. "Be careful."

Swords drawn, Kiriath and Brand approached the main doorway, one on each side of it. Presumably there had once been a strong door here, but it had long since rotted or been burned away. Brand signaled in readiness, and the two rushed in. A stab of lightning cast their shadows onto the far wall, but otherwise the chamber was empty, save for a number of support columns and a flight of stone steps mounting up to the next level. The lightning passed, and the room relapsed into dim shadows.

Kiriath beckoned for Ariana to enter also. "Wait here for a moment. Brand and I will make sure there's nothing up above."

His sister flung back her dripping hood and nodded.

Kiriath was about to put his foot on the lowest step, but Brand motioned for him to wait and went ahead. The prince understood. His friend was indicating that, because Kiriath was prince, Brand was the more expendable and should go first.

On the second story the building was divided into a number of smaller chambers, all connected by narrow corridors. One by one, the two Xandrian men advanced through each of them. The only light filtered through the narrow window slits, but, as their eyes adjusted, this was sufficient. A thick layer of dust covered the floor, which was also generously strewn with an abundance of broken pottery and what appeared to be shards of swords, too corroded to be recognizable. In one of the chambers they found a number of clay tablets lying about, mostly broken.

Progressing up the final flight of steps, the men saw that a portion of the roof and wall had fallen away, exposing part of that level to the elements. Various sorts of birds had built nests and were even now sheltering from the storm. They all remained on their nests, but each stared menacingly at the intruders.

"Looks like the place is truly deserted," Brand said. "Let's get back to Ariana. She'll be wondering what keeps us so long."

On the way back down the steps, Kiriath paused long enough to pick up two of the undamaged tablets they had discovered. Arriving on the ground floor, they found Ariana where they had left her, still wearing her dripping cloak, but with an arrow notched into her bowstring.

"No need for that," her brother said to her. "Seems we're alone here."

"Good. I hope it stays that way."

Brand slid his pack off his back. "Let's get out of these sodden cloaks. Maybe we'd better have an early lunch too. We might as well accomplish something useful while we're delayed."

Kiriath agreed and opened his own pack. "Good thinking. If the storm eases up at all, though, I think we should press on. More delays might lie ahead of us. We just don't know."

Ariana peered back out the doorway. "You know, even though it's ancient beyond guessing and I've never seen it before, this place doesn't seem very foreign somehow. This whole fortress, I mean. The design of the wall, the cut of the stones . . . Old as it must be, everything seems oddly familiar."

"I've noticed the same thing," Brand agreed. "This place has the air of one of those early fortresses near the coast. But I'm sure our colonists never came this far. Besides, these buildings are older than Xandria itself."

"Yes, it's similar," said the prince, munching on one of Elead's pears. "But even so, I would have shrugged it off as an unimportant coincidence if it weren't for these." He passed the two tablets he carried to each of the others. "Recognize the markings?"

Brand stepped closer to the doorway and examined his tablet. All across the surface were rows of tiny wedge-shaped characters. "Not Illyrish?"

Kiriath nodded. "It's Illyrish all right. The classical tongue from Illandria. Who brought it here, I don't know, but that's what it is. I recognize the characters even if I can't read it."

"You're right," Ariana agreed, looking hard at hers. "See, this is the old symbol for the number three. And here's an old-style seven." She sighed. "What a mystery. Urijah once asked me if I'd be interested in learning Illyrish, but I said no, thinking it would be useless knowledge. How I wish now that I had accepted his offer!"

"I did the same," said Kiriath. "But foresight never sees perfectly."

Brand still studied his tablet, as if he might suddenly discover some key whereby he could understand its message. "It's a riddle, all right. To think that some of our own ancestors dwelt on this continent years before Xandria was even a colony. I've never heard of such a thing, not even in the oldest tales." He handed the tablet back to Kiriath. "It would be interesting to bring all of these back to Shiralla for Nethanel and Urijah to translate—if we make it back to Shiralla, that is."

Brand turned and looked about the chamber again. "If this fortress were really designed in the traditional fashion, though, there would be at least a small armory built on the ground floor. Nothing here but walls, though."

"Not just walls!" Ariana piped up. "I almost forgot to tell you. There's a round metal knob jutting out of the far wall, there in the deeper shadows behind the stairwell. I noticed it when the lightning flashed and went to look at it. I don't know what kind of metal it is, but it's dark blue and smooth, not rusted at all."

The threesome stepped over to the spot Ariana had indicated. Looking more like a stain on the wall in the shadows, there was indeed a round knob at waist height. Kiriath felt its smoothness. Then he pushed on it. Nothing happened. Next Brand pushed the stone around it while Kiriath tried pressing and turning the knob. Still nothing happened.

Finally Kiriath wrapped both hands around the object and gave it a hard yank. The knob shot out from the wall several inches, revealing a stem of the same metal. At the same instant, a door-way-shaped slab of stonework around the knob swung outward without a sound.

Brand let out a low whistle. "You don't often see craftsmanship like that. Solid stone and centuries old, but it still works like it was hung there and oiled yesterday."

"What's inside?" Ariana asked. "It's so dark in there."

"Let's find out," her brother replied. He stepped through the aperture, feeling the wall as he went.

"Careful there," Brand called from behind him. "Last time I saw you open a stone door like that, you led me straight down a long flight of steps. You'll be no good to us with a lot of broken bones."

"Nice of you to be so concerned about my welfare."

In the poor light the prince could dimly make out only vague outlines of objects, so he walked with his hands before him, feeling his way. Along the wall his fingers encountered numerous pegs that must have once held shields and weapons. On a stone shelf built into the wall, he could feel a score or more tablets like the two they had just been examining. Also, there was what felt like an empty candlestick holder. He picked up a tablet and handed it out to Ariana. "More of these."

Going in farther, Kiriath's boot bumped against something, sending it clattering along the floor. Bending down, he felt a round, light object. Not until his fingertips slipped into two holes did he realize that he was caressing a skull. Other bones lay nearby.

"Anything else interesting?" Brand called. His and Ariana's silhouettes were framed in the rectangular opening.

"Not much. This place could use some better air, though. It reeks of mustiness."

As Kiriath's eyes began adjusting to the darkness, he saw that in the middle of the floor stood a stone basin of some sort, beside which was a large cauldron. Both were empty, save for a layer of powder in the bottoms. Kiriath noted, too, that like the doorknob, the cauldron was smooth and not at all rusted. He wondered what kind of metal it was that it could endure time so magnificently. Then his eyes fell on a dark spot on the wall.

Going to it, the prince felt what seemed to be a metal plaque mounted to the wall. Its surface had writing etched into it. At waist height below the plaque Kiriath discovered another metal knob like the one that had opened the first portal. "Another doorknob. I'm going to try it."

Pulling the knob as before, he felt it slide outward in his hand, a rectangular portion of the wall following it. Inside, the blackness was complete; Kiriath could see nothing of what was there. He took one step to enter but stopped short when he noticed that the door was swinging shut behind him. Going back to the shelf with the tablets, he retrieved three of these and wedged the door securely open.

Upon entering, Kiriath immediately bumped his head on the low ceiling. This was a tiny chamber, no larger than a small wardrobe.

On the right he felt nothing but brickwork. On the left, however, his touch found two more stone basins filled with—what? He picked up one of the objects but could not fathom what he was holding. Feeling like cold glass, it was a small orb about the size of his fist. That was all. The surface of the orb was smooth, with no cracks or bumps to reveal its nature. He hefted two others, but they all felt identical.

"Brother?" Ariana called. "You're not going to believe what's on this tablet. Anything else in there?"

"Yes. Something. I'm not sure what, though."

Bringing three of the strange orbs with him, Kiriath started making his way back through the first chamber. This time, however, his eyes had adjusted enough to detect a long, slender shape near the bones he had come across earlier. Stooping, he immediately recognized the outline of a sheathed sword and brought it along too.

"This sword and about a bushel of these other things are all there is."

The prince handed the sword to Ariana and held up the three miniature globes. As he had suspected, the outsides were indeed fashioned out of clear glass, but inside of each was a dull-gray core.

Brand took one and shook it, listening. "Nothing. And there's no way to open it. If these were heavier and closer to the ocean, I might guess that they were part of a ship's ballast."

"I should think they're more important than that with the way they're stored away so carefully. I don't know, though. Ariana?"

"Hm? Oh, I wasn't listening. Look at this sword! The handle has some sort of milky-purple gem embedded in it! And even though it's who-knows-how-old, it isn't rusty at all. The edge is razor sharp. There's more Illyrish inscribed on the blade itself. What a puzzle. I wish I knew what lost people ever lived here."

"And what happened to them," Kiriath added.

Brand held up the tablet that Kiriath had found inside the armory. "That's one answer we have. We might have guessed, anyway."

In the hardened clay surface Kiriath saw a piece of rough artwork: a leering, naked creature that stood upright, ramming a spear through the figure of a man. Beneath it was a single cryptic line in the ancient script.

"Grishnaki did it." Ariana spoke in a disgusted tone, as she often did when faced with wanton waste or destruction. "I can almost hear the echoes of dying men and women."

Tight-lipped, Kiriath nodded. "Even the ancestors of our enemies weren't happy if they couldn't spill man's blood. So much for mysteries. We can't avenge the people who lived here, but we might yet rescue Father from their enemies' grimy hands."

"Aye," Brand agreed, "let's press on. The lightning is past, and the rain is easing up. Besides, next to their lust for slaughter, Grishnaki care only for their own comfort and pleasure. They're not likely to be out in such miserable weather as this."

As if to emphasize his contempt for the weather, Brand hurled his glass sphere out the doorway. A moment later there came an ear-shattering eruption, accompanied by bits of stone flying back into the entrance. As if in reply, thunder rumbled in the distance. An expression of shock sprang onto Brand's countenance.

Recovering himself, the prince looked down at the two remaining orbs with amazement. "A weapon! By all that's good, they're weapons!"

He hurried to the entrance and cast one of the spheres at the fortress's wall. On impact there instantly followed a flash and a deafening roar. Stone chips exploded from the wall.

"Ha!" Kiriath felt jubilant. "Let the Grishnaki try to swallow that! This is like owning a fistful of lightning!"

"Please, Kir," Ariana pleaded. "Don't throw another one. I know it sounds like the thunder, but I don't like it. Let's get away from here."

"We'll go," her brother agreed. "But we'll take some of these orbs with us." He looked back outside, where a shred of smoke still hung in the air. "Yes, just let them swallow that."

Before long, Kiriath and Brand each had two of the glass spheres stowed in their packs, and the two portals that had hidden them were resealed. Because she had no sword of her own, Ariana girt the ancient blade onto her belt but refused to carry any of the glass objects. "None of us will live to regret it if either of you stumbles and cracks one of those." she declared.

After finishing their meal, the friends stepped back outside. The rain had slackened to only scattered drops, and the clouds were thinning. Away westward, Kiriath even glimpsed a scrap of blue sky. The three travelers made their way through a breach in the fortress wall. The road and the Deserted Kingdom went no further. Instead, fog spread out in the distance before them, obscuring any sight of the saddle-shaped mountain that marked their goal. But Kiriath didn't mind. He knew roughly which way to go, and now they had a new weapon that might aid in their quest for his father.

As they plodded, three abreast, through the soaked meadowlands, the prince of Xandria turned his mind once again to King Jekoniah, wondering how his father was faring and pondering how the newly found weapon from the Deserted Kingdom might help in their mission to win him back.

CHAPTER 11

SADDLE MOUNTAIN

"There can be no doubt," Brand said. He was staring at the double peaks that rose from a single base above several others on the horizon. Between those two high points was a low, curved spot. "That must be Saddle Mountain."

"I never expected to see it from so close," Ariana said. "Nor from this northerly side."

"We'll soon see it from even closer," Kiriath replied. Even to himself, his tone sounded more ominous than he had intended. "If we keep up a good pace, we should be able to reach it by sometime tomorrow. From here on, we'll keep under cover of the forest whenever we can. If we come to any trails, we'll have to be doubly careful. This is undisputed Grishnaki territory. As far as I know, no one from Xandria has ever walked where we now stand."

Neither Brand nor Ariana replied. Both merely continued to gaze at the faraway mount.

"All right then, let's be on our way. Stay alert for any sight or sound that might warn of trouble."

As Kiriath had advised, the three travelers remained on their guard as they walked. Contrary to their fears, no sights or sounds gave immediate evidence of Grishnaki in the district. The terrain became hillier as they climbed out of the Lowlands back toward the mountains, and trees became more abundant, much as they had been directly north of Watercliffe. Before long there was no question about following the prince's injunction to stay under the trees, for poplars, oaks, chestnuts, sycamore, spruce, and a wide variety of others clustered thickly around them. A kind of fern grew there too, about two feet high and branching into three broad clusters of leaves at the top. So thickly did they grow in some areas, Kiriath noted, that one could have lain on the ground and had a convenient fern roof a couple feet above him.

Wildlife abounded in these woods. Overhead, squirrels hopped from limb to limb, while birds warbled their tunes and fluttered their wings. Foxes, weasels, and other animals sometimes peeked a wary head from their dens to watch the strangers pass. Kiriath was tempted to say how he would like to hunt in this forest but held his peace. Silence seemed better counsel in the enemies' backyard.

During the course of the afternoon, Kiriath had called only one brief halt. It was now somewhere around the twelfth hour of the day, and he was considering calling another when he noticed that the trees were coming to an end. Sunlight was shining more brightly through the branches ahead.

Advancing cautiously, he bent down a pine bough and discovered that they were on the outer perimeter of a fairly large, circular clearing. Not a natural one, however, for hacked stumps jutted upward throughout the area, some with rotting trees lying nearby where they had fallen. In an uneven ring, wooden posts stuck up from the ground, each one topped with the skull of an animal. In the center of the ring stood the blackened remains of what must have been a huge bonfire.

"What's this?" Ariana whispered. "Their picnic grounds, or a place for worshiping their demonic gods?"

"I'm not even going to guess," Brand answered. "I just hope I'm not around for the next celebration."

Kiriath let the bough slide back into place. "Looks deserted for now, but let's go around it. I don't think Grishnaki would go to all the trouble of clearing land if they didn't use it fairly often."

Taking the lead once more, Kiriath took them single file around the left side of the clearing. He made sure to keep two or three trees' distance from the fringe. They had nearly reached the far side of the circle when they came upon a trail winding out of the forest and emptying into the grizzly site. The trail was wide and not overgrown at all. In fact, the prints of bare Grishnaki feet could be clearly seen where they had kicked up the damp earth going both to and from the clearing.

"Footprints," Kiriath remarked. "They've been here since the rain."

Ariana regarded the prints over Brand's shoulder. "Which means we're where we don't want to be. Come on. Let's get away from this trail."

Brand looked at his friend. "The trail probably takes the shortest route to the Valley of Grishnaki. Have you decided whether you want to try sneaking in by night or take time probing for a second entrance to Vol-Rathdeen?"

"We could never reach the valley by tonight and still be cautious. Let's try to scale the mountain's shoulder tomorrow. Then by nightfall we can still try subterfuge if all else fails. Even if there is a second, less-guarded way in, we may have to wait until nightfall to try it."

"This isn't the time for a conference," Ariana hissed. "Let's go!"

"You're right, love," Brand answered.

"Come," said the prince. "Follow me. If we're heading for the mountain itself, we'll need to cross the path. Remember; step only in the Grishnaki footprints. Don't make any of your own."

Kiriath scrutinized up and down the trail one last time before he stepped out from their leafy protection. As he had told the others to do, he placed his own boots only in the much larger prints that the Grishnaki had scuffed into the moist dirt. Imitating her brother's lead, Ariana followed, and Brand crossed over last.

No sooner had the little troupe taken a dozen steps than a loud, harsh guffaw sounded up the path from the direction of the clearing. Kiriath felt a tingle run through his body.

"They're here," Ariana breathed.

Kiriath, jerking a finger to his lips, ordered silence. Slipping his sword from its resting place, he took three light bounds farther away from the trail. Here a large boulder, protruding from the earth, was topped by a moldering tree that had fallen on it untold years before. He motioned for the others to hide themselves behind it, lastly flinging himself to the ground beside them.

Kiriath wished that more of the little ferns grew there to conceal them better. It wasn't an ideal hiding place, but there was no time to seek another. Husky, grating voices were approaching.

Following Kiriath's and Brand's examples, Ariana now drew the sword they had found in the Deserted Kingdom. There was no time to string her bow. For a passing instant her brother noticed how the gem embedded in its handle appeared a brighter, more vibrant purple than when he had first fetched it out of that dark chamber many miles back. As Ariana adjusted her grip on the weapon, Kiriath thought he heard a voice, faint but undeniably Ariana's, saying, "Lead us well now, Brother!"

Perturbed, the prince gave her a light tap on the shoulder and put a finger to his lips again. He couldn't understand the puzzled look she gave him, but there was no time for idle wonder. He lifted his head just enough to peer through a space between the boulder and the tree trunk. Through tangled branches he could glimpse the trail.

The voices were almost close enough to understand now. More coarse laughter burst out, quite close to them.

"Yes," a croaking voice was agreeing with someone. "Will be a good feast time. Much to eat. Maybe much fun if Dar-kon gives us the man-kon for sport."

Another voice spoke up. "Maybe the man-kon be both sport *and* something good to eat!" At this remark a general chorus of croaking laughter erupted. "But I like my meat with less years and more fat on it!"

Kiriath could see the leaders of the band coming into view. They loped slowly, casually, carrying their spears over their shoulders.

"Not much chance of that," rumbled another.

As he had done while listening to Kroll back in the Citadel, Kiriath swallowed and wondered what it would feel like to have a throat capable of creating such scraping sounds. He could barely understand what the creature was saying.

"I heard Kroll tell another Grishnak. Dar-kon said he would give their putrid kon back for the secrets. So there will be no fun with him."

Two or three voices groaned, but others hurled abuses: "Stupid!" "Bashed-brain!" "Fool!" There were also other words that Kiriath couldn't make out at all. He assumed that they were either insults from the Grishnaki's old tribal tongues or badly corrupted words from the language of men.

"Grishnaki like you are why the big 'uns don't tell us more. Garg! Just 'cause Dar-kon tells 'em something, it don't mean he's goin' to do it. He'll keep the leader-man alive long enough to get the secrets. But after that—" Here the speaker forced a strained gurgling sound from his throat. "We'll have their miserable kon on a spit for supper!"

"And after we make many swords of steel, we'll all have a man or two on our spits!"

A spattering of applause broke out accompanied by gleeful shouts of "Yes, steel!" and "Feast! To the feast!"

The voices became too excited for Kiriath to understand much more. He saw, however, about two dozen others toiling behind, shouldering long poles from which several dead stags and some smaller game hung upside down.

The clamor gradually diminished, but the prince waited until he was certain there were no stragglers before he re-sheathed his sword and stood up.

"Typical," was Brand's conclusion. "Sickening, but typical. The only surprising thing is that they caught so much game. I've not yet seen the Grishnak that I'd call a good marksman."

"Disgusting," Ariana declared. "Did you hear how they talked about Father? At least we know he's alive."

"Yes, that's reassuring," Brand agreed. "But if they're planning some sort of feast, there may be others hunting in these woods. We'll need to look twice at every tree."

The prince agreed. "Right. We have only a couple hours of good light left for traveling. Let's be off."

As cautiously as they could, the three young Xandrians penetrated deeper into the woods. Occasionally, they veered out of their way if the terrain promised an easier or quieter passage, but for the most part they approached the saddle-shaped mount directly. Now they began to catch frequent views of the double peaks through openings of the forest's roof. Once Kiriath thought he glimpsed a wisp of smoke rising from a ridge high on Saddle Mountain's shoulder, but he couldn't be sure.

Their pace was much slower now than on previous days. However, the first stage of their goal was in sight, and their mission depended on absolute secrecy. Exchanging that secrecy for speed meant risking discovery and capture—folly to Kiriath's mind.

About the time that day began fading into dusk, they came upon another path, but this one was smaller and showed no trace of having been traveled lately. Each one of the three easily leaped over it and continued on. After they had left this second path far behind, Kiriath called a halt in a shallow ravine.

"Let's stop here for the night. We're losing our light. We can shelter under this outcropping of rock and get an early start before dayspring."

"Not long ago I wondered if we would even get this far," Ariana commented.

"I know the feeling," her brother agreed. "But by this time tomorrow, one way or another, at least one of us has to be inside the Grishnaki's den, trying to find where they're holding Father."

"No more talk about *one* of us," Brand said flatly. "As long as I'm alive, it's going to be at least two of us."

"Three of us then, as long as Ariana is alive," she put in.

Kiriath looked at Brand. "Are you sure you want this high-spirited woman for your wife? She has some lofty attitudes."

His friend sighed and smiled. "I know. But I've decided that it'll take a nobleman's son of my high lineage to keep her in line. It's all self-sacrifice on my part for the good of Xandria."

"And I might say that it will take all of a princess's might to keep in line that same haughty offspring of noble lineage," Ariana returned, taking Brand's hand.

"Well, if you two will faithfully keep each other out of mischief for the good of the kingdom, I guess it will be a perfect match. Let's hope it turns out that way."

The three passed the night peacefully enough, each taking a watch in turn. An overcast sky, coupled with the shade of the woods, kept the moon's light from finding them on the floor of the forest. Of Grishnaki they didn't hear or see any sign at all. But during the first watch Kiriath did notice one peculiar thing: miniature balls of luminescence dotted the ground here and there under the trees. Approaching the closest of them, he was surprised to find that they were mushrooms that glowed faintly, almost as if a fairy from some grandmother's fireside tale had painted each one from a thimble full of phosphorus. As the night grew darker, the little spots of light stood out all the brighter, giving the illusion of a whole forest full of watchful, unblinking eyes. He dismissed them as curious but neither dangerous nor helpful.

Hours later, with dawn's first faint light, the three were all awake and munching on a scant breakfast. The thought passed through Kiriath's mind that he was growing weary of apples, pears, and dried bread, but he ate mechanically, giving his meal no further consideration. He knew he needed the strength. Being familiar with Grishnaki, he knew, too, that in Vol-Rathdeen King Jekoniah would probably have rejoiced to have this food that Kiriath was taking for granted.

Fog had settled on the forest during the early hours before dawn. Kiriath was glad to see it, for now they could travel with less need for stealth. Also, he decided to march straight up the ravine, partially to further conceal them from any hidden observers and partially to make the climbing easier. There were fewer trees here, he noted, and since it seemed to provide a natural runoff for rainwater, it should lead them directly up the mountainside.

After they had steadily climbed upward for several hours, the sun finally rose high enough to dispel the last of the fog.

The words that the Grishnaki hunters had spoken about King Jekoniah came back to Kiriath as he climbed, tempering his resolve and fanning the flames of his indignation. "Put the king of Shiralla on a spit? We'll see."

"You say something?" Brand whispered.

"I was telling off a Grishnak in my mind. Sorry, I didn't realize I was muttering aloud."

"They deserve more than to be muttered at," Ariana put in. "But look; we're climbing straight to the base of a cliff. We'll have to turn left or right."

The prince stopped and looked up, surprised that he hadn't noticed the rock wall that would eventually stop them in that direction. "Let's go a little higher and then left. That should let us look right into the Valley of Grishnaki itself. I'd like a good look at it in the daylight before we plan our next move."

Following this course, the three continued upward, steadily placing one foot higher than the other over and over again. More than once the prince glanced at his sister to make sure she was faring well. Her stamina surprised him. He knew that she always enjoyed riding horseback and hiking around Mount Shiralla. Still, he usually thought of his sister as she appeared in the Citadel: dressed in a floor-length gown, with golden locks settling about her shoulders. Here her breath was a little more labored than his own, but she showed no signs of tiring. Indeed, the more he thought about it, the more stark became the contrast between how well Ariana fit in with life as the daughter of King Jekoniah and with life in the wilderness. The admiration he held for her rose even higher. *No king's daughter could do better or show more courage,* he thought.

Brand interrupted Kiriath's musing. "I don't believe it."

Kiriath looked in the same direction and saw carved in the cliff wall above them a great weatherworn symbol—in the ancient Illyrish language. Beneath it were the remains of an arched entrance into the cliff's face. But the entrance had long since been blocked up with massive stones.

"They were here too?" Ariana whispered aloud.

Drawing nearer, Kiriath found that the area directly in front of the blocked entrance was fairly level, as if it had once been used for some purpose. As for the entrance itself, there was nothing else to note, save that a crude mortar had been used to seal the stones securely in the mouth of the entrance.

Kiriath turned, looking back down the mountain slope they had walked up and at the green carpet of treetops spreading out below them. Whereas the surrounding slopes were rugged, the trail up the ravine was comparatively smooth and free of solid obstacles. "We haven't been climbing a natural wash at all. It's some sort of grown-over road or walkway. But this gate into Saddle Mountain hasn't been used in years."

Brand put one hand on the stones blocking the entrance. "If these were smaller and the mortar more crumbly, we might try reopening it to make our own way in. But it's too much heavy work for the time we have."

"Our glass spheres might help us to unblock it. But every Grishnak within miles would hear us doing it. We wouldn't get far."

"Let's continue on and spy out the valley," Ariana suggested. "Even without a cliff in the way, we couldn't go any higher without losing the protection of the trees. Even this high they're becoming shorter and stubbier."

As they edged along, Kiriath noticed that here, too, was a smooth, narrow space that may have once been a path made by some ancient people living on the mountain. Time's hands had loosened rocks from the slopes above and deposited them here, but the way was still passable and less difficult than the ground above and below them. From where they now walked, only one of the mount's two peaks was visible, towering high above them on the right and blocking out all sight of the second one.

Presently they came within sight of yet another sealed entrance, identical to the first save that a different symbol marked it and that stunted bushes grew out of the crevices, partially obscuring it. As they walked past it, Ariana paused, sniffing the air. "I smell smoke."

Now Kiriath noticed it too. He stepped closer to the former entrance. "It's coming from here." Through a chink between the boulders the prince felt a slight breeze emerge. Mingled with the air from within the mountain was the definite odor of burning wood.

"Perhaps they've already started their feasting," Brand suggested. "Tomorrow is the seventh day, when Queen Vandrielle is supposed to answer Dar-kon's offer. They must think they've already got Xandria rolled up and ready to cast away."

"Let's go on. There's no way in here."

Smelling the smoke from inside the mountain raised Kiriath's hopes. Lately he had begun to consider the existence of any secondary entrances into the Grishnaki's caves a whim of wishful thinking more than a realistic possibility. In fact, his main reason for climbing this high on the mountain was the opportunity it would afford to spy out the valley. But if there were only one entrance, surely the enemy would not burn wood inside—to do so would turn their hole into a smoldering pit, choking and blinding them all.

Still determined to see the valley, he led them onward. But now the walkway disappeared altogether. Either it had never extended so far, or it had long since eroded away. At any rate the traveling became more difficult, and the mountainside steeper.

As they crawled along, the smaller mountain that formed the far side of the Valley of Grishnaki came fully into view. Through the tree branches Kiriath could see where the valley wall on that side dropped off sharply, almost as if cut straight down with a gigantic cleaver. He thought he could also see some dark holes in its face, but it was too distant to be sure. "Let's go down a way and take a closer look."

Descending carefully might have proved difficult had it not been for the many pines growing on the slope. As it was, by sliding from trunk to trunk, they could descend the mountain fairly quickly—almost too quickly. Kiriath stepped out from the shade of one tree's boughs and found himself standing not five feet from the edge of a sheer precipice similar to the one across the valley. Far below he espied a multitude of dark shapes moving along the valley floor.

"Down!" he whispered, dropping to his stomach.

Without hesitation the others followed his example. For a long moment Kiriath lay unmoving, straining to hear if any alarm were being raised below. Nothing happened. No one had seen him.

On their stomachs Brand and Ariana inched forward to join their comrade. Kiriath pointed through the scraggly undergrowth that separated them from the brink. "The valley. They're everywhere down there."

Raising his head just a little now, the prince took a long look at the Valley of Grishnaki. He discerned thousands of figures far below. Off to the left, a thick wall stretched across the valley, running almost uninterrupted from the perpendicular base of Saddle Mountain to the wall of the unnamed mount across the valley. Kiriath's gaze found that only a thin, meandering stream interrupted this barrier in its center. Lining the wall itself was a host of Grishnaki with spears, bows, and other weapons. Squinting and looking far off to the right, the prince made out the dark line of a similar wall at the other end of the valley.

Evidently there was at least one opening in the mountain face directly below the three, for Grishnaki seemed to be moving in and out of it. However, Kiriath dared not creep forward to improve his view.

"So many," Ariana whispered, amazed. "I never quite realized . . ."

Brand's observations were on an earthier note: "The wretched place stinks. They've turned the whole valley into a dunghill."

"More important is the question of how to sneak in." Kiriath swept his eyes up and down the valley floor, memorizing its features. "The wall is pretty heavily guarded, but none of the others seem to carry any weapons. I wonder . . . Do you think we might swim past the wall under darkness without being spotted?"

Brand picked a blade of grass and stuck it in his mouth. "Maybe. We'd have to use floating logs or something to help us get close before going under. But it's risky. Only one Grishnak needs to see one of us poke a head out of the water to raise the cry. And the stream looks shallow. There might be staves lining the bottom to prevent tricks like that."

"We'll be risking our throats no matter which way we try it," Kiriath countered. "But I don't suppose that even torch light would help us pass for Grishnaki if our clothes are dripping wet. Let's scout around some more."

At that moment a shout went up from below. The three instantly flattened themselves where they lay. But, the cry had nothing to do with them at all.

"Dar-kon! Dar-kon!" chanted hundreds of throaty voices. "Dar-kon!"

Raising his head slightly, Kiriath could see some sort of procession winding up the valley. At its head loped a dozen Grishnaki, shouldering a sort of platform of poles lashed together. Upon the platform sat a figure larger and more muscular than the rest. Mobs of frenzied Grishnaki thronged about the group, joining in the cry: "Dar-kon!"

"Dar-kon himself!" Ariana whispered. "If Father's life weren't at stake, I'd be tempted to try an arrow from here."

Slowly the procession made its way closer, finally stopping almost directly below where the three onlookers lay hidden. Kiriath could barely see Dar-kon stand to his feet on the platform and raise both arms high. The tumult died instantly. The Grishnak chieftain was addressing his followers, but the prince couldn't make out any words from this great height. Here and there he caught the echo of a syllable but little more.

As suddenly as the noise had ceased, the tumult erupted again with redoubled volume. "Dar-kon! Dar-kon!"

The Grishnaki leader leaped to the ground and led a procession toward the cliff, evidently entering the mountainside somewhere below. A band of Grishnaki followed, but most remained outside, continuing to shout "Dar-kon" and other unintelligible phrases before they finally turned away.

Kiriath motioned the others back to the safety of the nearest pine boughs. "Vol-Rathdeen. Dar-kon's cave is beneath our very noses," Kiriath said.

Brand plucked his blade of grass from his lips and threw it away. "But without a rope to climb down, we're still no closer to reaching your father."

"Here's my counsel," Kiriath offered. "Let's go back and scout out the side of the mountain past the ravine where we first came up. Maybe I'm clutching at false hopes, but all the signs point to another way into Vol-Rathdeen. Whatever Illandrians or other people who once dwelt here created other passages than through the valley. We've seen two of them already. I'm guessing there are more that aren't blocked up, or maybe not blocked very well."

Ariana protested. "But even if such ways exist, they'll be guarded."

"You're right. But by how many guards? Besides, how alert will they be? Remember that Xandria has never attacked the Valley of Grishnaki. Any watchers on the upper slopes may have grown lazy after years of no threats from our side. I trust my intuition that the enemy thinks of power only in numbers. They won't expect three people to approach their den from the direction we've come. With the advantage of surprise, two or three with sharp swords can go where an army could never penetrate. Besides, we certainly can't get in from here. We have to explore all the possibilities."

"All right. Lead on." Ariana shifted her weight to stand up. In doing so, however, she dislodged a loose stone, which rolled down the slope and clattered over the edge where they had just lain. All three crouched low, frozen motionless.

A minute passed, then two. Kiriath raised his head ever so slightly to see if there was any commotion below. "Slowly, one at a time, crawl back up the slope. Ariana, you go first. Stay in the shade."

In his mind the prince envisioned scores of Grishnaki rushing up the mountainside and hewing the little group to pieces. As hard as he knew how, he hoped none of the enemy had seen them or guessed their presence. Finally both his sister and Brand had reached a safe distance.

"I'm sorry," Ariana blurted when Kiriath joined them. "I feel so foolish. I almost destroyed us all."

Brand took her hand. "Accidents happen. Any of us could have loosened a stone. Besides, if a tile fell off the roof of the Citadel in Shiralla, would you suspect a Grishnak was up there? Me neither. They're probably used to stones breaking loose and falling now and then."

Kiriath agreed. "That's my opinion too. Let's go back, though, just in case they're smart enough to search the area as a precaution."

The return trip went more quickly than had the journey to the valley's brink. They passed the second blocked entrance, then arrived at the first one, where they had first scaled the mountainside. Continuing now to the far side of the mountain, Kiriath discovered that its far face was not nearly so steep as the area they had recently clambered over. The trees, too, became more abundant on that side, for which he was glad. He didn't relish prowling in the enemy's territory without a generous mantel of woodland to obscure them from hostile eyes.

As they trudged along, Brand looked skyward. "Past midday. If we don't find something in this direction soon, we'll have to go back down and search for whatever way we can to enter the mountain through the valley."

"Perhaps," his friend answered. "But there's no reason to stroll through a bear's den before you've hunted for a path around it. Let's go a little farther. If there's nothing there, we'll have a quiet meal then turn back."

"Glarpk! Hurry up, yer filth!"

The prince froze in midstep. It was unmistakably a Grishnak voice, and not too distant.

"Glarpk! I'll bust yer back if yer don't get up here! I'm sick of waiting on yer."

A second voice shouted in response, too far away to make out.

"They're just down the slope from us," Ariana breathed. "There's no place to hide!"

Muttering "Come on!" Kiriath bounded forward. Second to the prince's desire not to let these Grishnaki see him was his wish to observe them and see which way they passed. He hastily searched for a place to conceal themselves, but his sister's words proved to be prophetic. Not so much as a bush or fern was to be seen—only tall, slender trunks supporting branches high overhead.

"Glarpk!" The booming voice was nearer now, though still downhill. There was no time to waste.

Kiriath whipped out his sword. "Through this clearing, then crouch behind a tree trunk. It will have to do. Ariana, have your bow ready when they come, just in case. Let's go!"

Still leading the way, Kiriath ran into the sunlight of the clearing. He had almost gained the shade of the far side when, for half an instant, his mind registered that there was something wrong about the ground. Too late! Kiriath couldn't check his speed, and already his left foot was plunging downward, disappearing through the soil. Flinging away his sword, the prince grappled for a firm handhold at the side of the hole he was tumbling into, for the ground wasn't ground at all but a covering of twigs and leaves over a blanket of animal hides. Kiriath thudded to his knees in the bottom of a pit, while a clanging noise above shattered the stillness. An animal trap!

"Kiriath!" Ariana cried from above.

The prince looked up but immediately had to shield his eyes: leaves and loose dirt were still filtering down on him. In the hole's bottom, three deadly-sharp stakes pointed skyward. The prince's left leg had nearly come down on one of them.

"C'mon, yer swine! The high trap just sprung. If yer don't help carry . . ."

Even from the bottom of the pit Kiriath could tell that the angry Grishnak was almost upon them. "You two get out of here! Run!" he commanded.

"But—" Ariana began.

"Go! Now! Brand, get her out of here!"

Kiriath's last glimpse of his companions was of Brand putting a firm arm around Ariana's shoulder and forcing her away from the gaping hole above. Rising now to his feet, the prince tried jumping to grasp the edge of the pit, but he could not. It was out of reach. He tried again, then again, still with no success. He was just about to try kicking some steps into the dirt wall when he heard the noise of footsteps approaching. A shadow fell over the hole.

"Now let's see what kind of meat we've caught," a rasping voice said.

Kiriath looked up. Staring down from above was one of the huskiest Grishnaki the prince had ever seen, its yellow eyes wide and staring. As he gazed at the creature, the look of wonder on its face changed to one of malice. Its thick tongue slipped out of its mouth and slowly began moistening its lips.

CHAPTER 12

VOL-RATHDEEN

The creature above Kiriath cupped his hands to his mouth and bellowed louder than ever. "Glarpk! Come! Run! We got a man in the trap!"

Several times in border skirmishes Kiriath had looked into Grishnaki's eyes filled with the venom of hate. But even though this one was clearly the master of the situation, his malice was still mingled with astonishment. He seemed uncertain of what to do. The creature had probably never seen a man without a host of companions with him, let alone a man on Saddle Mountain itself.

"Garg! Yes, I said a man. No, I'm not lyin' to get yer to hurry, yer sniveler!"

Kiriath heard more footsteps hastening. Soon another, less brawny Grishnak was peering into the pit. This one carried a bow and wore a cap of animal hide over its head. Now accompanied by one of his fellows, the first brute put on a braver face.

"Where did he come from, Sgtar?" Glarpk rasped, all out of breath.

"How'm I to know?" the first rumbled back in his deeper, gravelly voice.

"Why don't you just ask the man?" Kiriath suggested.

Sgtar took the bow from Glarpk and notched an arrow, pointing it at his captive. "All right, wise little scum. Speak. Where d'yer come from? Why're yer here? This is Grishnaki land."

"I've come from the north," Kiriath admitted. "And this is not Grishnaki land, for my kind lived on it years before yours settled here."

Sgtar's eyes narrowed. "Yer lie. There's no men-kind in the northlands. Yer a Grishnaki killer from across the river."

"I've come from the north. Or had you forgotten that another land of men lies in that direction?"

"The Spirit Place!" Glarpk exclaimed. "That's where he's from. The old ones said they'd come back. That's what they said."

With a loud smack, Sgtar slapped his broad hand across Glarpk's face. "Quiet! Let me think, swine-dog."

Glarpk stepped back, anger blazing in his eyes. But something on the ground immediately arrested his attention. "Look. A sword!" Glarpk retrieved the blade and carved circles in the air over his head. "I found a steel sword. I am Glarpk of the Steel Blade!"

"Yer'll be Glarpk of the Busted Teeth if yer don't give me that!" Sgtar snatched the blade and shoved the bow into Glarpk's face. "No sniveler gets a steel sword. Yer've never even killed a man. Go up toward the door and yell for Grud. But don't go all the way up. Just yell. Run!"

Muttering under his breath, Glarpk stalked away, evidently unwilling to run at Sgtar's bidding.

Kiriath's neck was getting sore from craning it to look up out of the animal trap. "Say, Sag-tar," he said, unable to properly frame the Grishnak's name in his mouth, "how about helping me out of here?" He lifted an arm as if he expected the enemy's assistance.

"Stop. Don't move!" Sgtar jumped backward, brandishing Kiriath's sword. "When Grud comes down from the door, we'll tie yer up and take yer to Dar-kon. He'll decide what yer skin's worth." An evil light gleamed in Sgtar's eyes, and his tongue moistened the little fangs protruding from his lips. "I'm bringin' in a live man. No single Grishnak has ever done that kind of thing. Dar-kon will give me a big reward."

Kiriath feigned ignorance. "Dar- who?"

"Shut up yer tricks, puny man. Yer can't fool Sgtar. Yer're not from the Spirit Place. They were killed long, long ago. My tribe did it. Grishnaki songs tell the story. Now why're yer here? Where're the others?"

"What others?" Kiriath carefully avoided the first half of his captor's query. "If I had come with friends, would they have left me in a Grishnaki animal trap?"

Sgtar's eyes narrowed, as if trying to see through any deception. "If yer're a coward or a weakling, they would. Like Glarpk. Garg! Useless rot. That's what I think. Yer're a sniveler man spy that was left here to die. Now tell me: where're the men who came with yer?" Growing bolder, Sgtar bent down on one knee, threatening with the sword.

"There are no other men," Kiriath admitted, truthfully repeating the plural.

"Liar-mouth! Garg! Off with that thing on yer back. Give it to me quick! The pouch on yer belt too."

The idea of hurling a glass sphere at Sgtar occurred to the prince, but he instantly suppressed it. The Grishnak was too close: Kiriath himself would be swallowed up in the inferno of his new weapon. Dutifully he tossed up the pack and smaller pouch.

As the prince expected, Sgtar pulled the two glass spheres out of the pack. "What're these?"

"I can't explain it to you. You would probably call it terrible magic from the Spirit Place."

Despite a snort of bravado, Sgtar respectfully set the spheres on the ground and rummaged among the remnants of Kiriath's food. Next he opened the pouch, spilling the contents in his hand: a small knife, a smaller pouch of nuts, a few Xandrian coins, and a yellow glass bottle.

"What's in the bottle?"

"Poison—for me to drink." Actually, Kiriath had never expected to use Urijah's gift on himself, but he couldn't resist baiting his captor's anger.

"Double liar-mouth! I'm getting sick of yer. Don't try me. Menkind don't drink poison. It's man's wine. Say it!"

At that moment Glarpk came loping back, puffing hard. "Sgtar, I don't think Grud's at the door. I yelled and yelled, but he doesn't come."

"Double garg! That fool. Why does Dar-kon give me filth to work with? I know Grud. He's taken the others down to the feast. I warned him. He'll lose that flabby head this time."

Glarpk saw the yellow object in Sgtar's fingers. "What's in the man-bottle? I get some too. I helped."

"Get away! Yer deserve nothing. It's the puny man's wine, but it's my secret now. One word to Dar-kon about this, and I'll lop off yer head, right after Grud's. Now help out. We'll take the prisoner alone. Jump down there and tie him up."

"No! Not in a hole with a Grishnaki killer!"

"Get down there. I'll guard him so he can't hurt yer."

"You tie him up, and let *me* watch him," Glarpk argued.

"Don't tell me what to do. Maybe another hole in yer skull would let us stuff some brains in there." Without warning Sgtar smashed the flat of Kiriath's sword over the crown of Glarpk's head.

With a howl, Glarpk crashed to his knees.

"Yer're not hurt. Now obey! Into the hole."

Far from obeying, however, Glarpk appeared to have a new idea, accompanied by the kindling of hatred burning in his gaze. "No. You obey this time. Sgtar—die!" Glarpk's arrow plunged deep into Sgtar's chest, driving him stumbling backward.

But the wounded Grishnak wasn't finished yet. "Wretched little . . ." Sgtar lunged and swung the sword feebly at Glarpk, missed, and fell to the ground at the lip of the pit. The Grishnak lay there unmoving.

Glarpk snatched up the sword and the yellow bottle. Leaping onto the fallen one's body, he laughed with a frightful glee. "Ha! Mighty Sgtar is fallen! Glarpk the conqueror!" Bending down, he ran his stubby fingers along the arrow tip protruding from Sgtar's back and then licked them off, savoring the taste. "Glarpk the Winner!"

Kiriath looked on in horror and revulsion as one Grishnak tasted the blood of another. He had never realized that their savagery could also be directed against their own kind.

"Well, Glarpk? What now? Will Dar-kon approve of your killing Sag-tar?"

Glarpk ceased his prancing and looked into the pit. He seemed to have momentarily forgotten the man who stood so near. Then his lips parted in a cunning grin, revealing his large, crooked teeth. "I did not kill Sgtar, O man. You did it. When you tried to escape. That's what I'll tell Dar-kon. And I had to kill you before you got away. Yes. That's right. No one will know. Glarpk will get the reward—prob'ly the beautifulest Grishnaka in Vol-Rathdeen. Ha!"

Throwing back his head, the Grishnak let out a hideous gurgle of delight. Then, jerking the cork out of Kiriath's bottle with his teeth, he dashed the brown liquid into his mouth and swallowed. "Ha! A reward for Glarpk. A reward for Glarpk!" Almost chanting the words, the delighted Grishnak began keeping time by hopping up and down on Sgtar's lifeless corpse.

Suddenly the dance stopped, and an expression of pain mixed with terror came over Glarpk's countenance. His eyes rolled upward in their sockets, and a spasm shook his form. He put a hand to his throat. "You!" he screamed at Kiriath. "It wasn't wine!" Gripping the sword in both hands and sinking to his knees, the Grishnak hefted it, as if to deliver a crashing blow.

The prince tensed, prepared to dodge. The sword was too short to reach him if Kiriath were to crouch, but in his rage Glarpk might even fling it as a deadly missile. But the blow never fell. Instead a silver shaft with white feathers whistled into Glarpk's chest. His eyes closed, and he collapsed atop Sgtar.

Kiriath immediately understood where the silvery arrow had come from. Moments later he heard more footsteps approaching. Brand and Ariana appeared at the top of the pit.

At first Brand looked concerned, but then he broke into a grin. "Why, Arie, look who's in this hole. Digging for gold, Kir?"

"Brand! Help him out!"

Kiriath shook his head. "I'm not ready for jests. Lend me an arm for a minute and I'll forgive you both for not letting that arrow fly sooner."

"Glad to oblige." Brand stretched himself out on the ground. Reaching down, he was able to grab his friend's hand. "You were in no danger, though. Ariana had an arrow aimed all along. And I trailed Glarpk to make sure he never met whomever he was shouting for. We would've come sooner, but we thought you were enjoying the chat."

"How are you, Kiriath? Are you hurt?" his sister asked.

"I'm fine, Ariana. I'm in your debt for your arrow. You make a good companion to have around." He pushed Glarpk over and pulled the shaft from the body, wiping it on the grass. "Here, put this back in your quiver. We may need it again."

Brand began removing the animal-skin tunic from Sgtar. "Here are two outfits for the occasion, Kir. From what I gathered from this big brute, the doorkeepers have deserted their post for some kind of feast. We wanted Grishnak clothing for disguises, and here we are."

"My idea, exactly. Phew! The clothes stink as badly as the owners."

"I'll stand guard under that soursap tree while you get in your disguises," Ariana offered. "But hurry. Whoever Grud is, he may decide to come back to his post after his belly is filled."

Shortly, one woman and two thin, would-be Grishnaki advanced through the woods.

"This is the way Glarpk headed," Brand said. "That looks like a path. It must lead to the door they were talking about."

Cautiously, the peculiar-looking trio continued up the trail. They hadn't gone far, however, before the woods ended abruptly. The trail continued through the sparse mountain grass and entered a gaping fissure in the mountainside. As before, carved above it was a weathered Illyrish numeral.

"Just like the other entrances," Ariana said. "Even the Illyrish character."

"But not blocked up," Brand noted. "That's the important thing."

"You two wait here. I'll go ahead and scout out the entrance."

"Wait a moment, Kir. That's a job for a patrol captain, not a prince."

"It's a job for a man who has no wife and isn't betrothed to receive one, as you are. Besides, captains aren't supposed to tell princes what to do."

"Sorry," Brand returned with his customary grin. "A fellow forgets when the prince is a close friend. Be careful, Kir."

Imitating the Grishnaki gait as well as he could, Kiriath began crossing the space between the woods and the rock face before him. He was glad Glarpk's fox-skin hat was too large for him. Even so, he wished he could pull it down farther to mask his features better. He was painfully aware of his very un-Grishnakish face and hands. His heart was thumping hard in his chest.

I suppose I could have just stayed in the woods and shouted "Grud" to find out if he's here, he thought to himself. *But no. I could never duplicate the grind of a Grishnak's voice. I might as well cry, "Here's a man; come and slit his throat."*

Directly before the gaping fissure was a huge mound of ashes, remnants of untold numbers of fires for cooking or for nighttime guard duty. Even now thin wisps spiraled upward from a few warm embers in the center of the mound. Upon approaching the entrance, Kiriath discovered that what he at first had assumed to be nothing more than a cave was much more: inside, about ten feet back from the entrance, was a barrier of stonework. Set in the barrier was a door propped open by a short log. Because the sun was now in the western sky, its rays slanted in nearly to the door. Kiriath spotted a dark, circular doorknob and recognized it as the same style as those he had seen in the Deserted Kingdom. Evidently men had indeed lived in the mountain in past centuries, probably long since destroyed by Grishnaki.

Standing just outside the open portal now, Kiriath paused, listening. He could hear his own pulse pounding in his ears but nothing else. Narrowing his eyes to slits to adapt them for darkness, he waited a few more moments, then quietly slipped through the doorway.

Inside, the prince discovered a fairly smooth-cut tunnel that sloped downward. At wide intervals along the left-hand side of the passage, torches flickered dimly in their brackets. Not having been tended in some while, they were burning low, some on the verge of sputtering out. The smell of smoke lingered in the air. On neither side could Kiriath discern other passages or portals save one: a rectangular patch of black, opening not twelve feet before him on the right. Stealthily, Kiriath edged toward it.

Gliding within inches of the hole, the prince paused. His ears caught a slight sound. Then another. And another, as of someone breathing slowly, rhythmically.

If that's Grud, it sounds like he's sleeping, Kiriath decided. *After so many years of never seeing a man on the mountain, he must assume there's no danger. Bad assumption!*

Backing out the way he had come, Kiriath beckoned for Brand and Ariana to join him.

"Inside the passageway there's an unlit chamber of some sort on the right. I think Grud is in there sleeping. If he isn't expecting visitors, we should be able to flit past quickly without disturbing him."

"Shall we draw our swords?" Ariana whispered.

"Not yet. Torches line the tunnel. Swords might reflect the light. Carry your bow fitted with an arrow, though. You two go first, and I'll keep my hand on my hilt until you're past it."

Brand led Ariana into the tunnel. Kiriath saw him stop just outside the dark opening; then with two quick strides he was on the other side. Next Ariana slipped by, and Kiriath came last. There was no cry of alarm. Instead, rising and falling in pitch, gurgling snores echoed from inside the darkened chamber.

Wordlessly, the trio continued down the tunnel. At one time, Kiriath noted, the tunnel's floor must have been a marvelous set of stone steps. Now, however, the centers of the steps were worn down to rounded ridges of rock; only at the sides did the sharp angles of the old stonework remain.

As they proceeded downward, Kiriath noted that the dark gaps between the torches along the left became wider. Strangely, however, this fact didn't seem to affect his ability to see. In fact, rather than becoming darker, the tunnel ceiling and walls grew lighter the farther they went. For some while he was not able to account for this phenomenon, but gradually he became aware of an increasing amount of lichen growing on the damp tunnel walls. Like the luminescent mushrooms he had noticed the previous night, this species of lichen emitted a sickly pale-green light all its own. In these lower levels the lichen grew so thickly that the torches ceased altogether, yet he had no trouble seeing at all. Only the floor remained dark. Kiriath assumed that the frequent tramping of feet kept the peculiar lichen from growing there.

At one point the tunnel intersected with another at right angles. Directly past that spot, the steps plunged downward more steeply. Hoping that the downward path led to the main cave, Kiriath led the others in that direction.

With each step downward, the prince became more apprehensive, a knot forming in his stomach. Would there be Grishnaki guarding the inner end of the tunnel? Or what if there was no main cave but simply a network of chambers and passages? In such a case it would prove impossible to locate Father without being detected or losing their way.

Kiriath's impression was that he was descending down into the very bowels of the world; yet he realized that they must still be fairly high above the valley. At one point a dribble of water issued from a crack in the wall to the right. Flowing into a little channel beside the steps, it raced down the tunnel ahead of them.

From somewhere below an increasingly loud din echoed up to the trio's ears. Whether it sounded more like revelry or the preparation for war, Kiriath couldn't decide. He remembered, however, the Grishnaki's mention of a feast and concluded that this was what he heard. The jumble of sounds seemed to reach a crescendo as the friends approached a corner in the passageway.

"Wait here for a moment," Kiriath told Ariana. "Brand and I will go ahead. If anything goes wrong, you run like the wind back the way we came. Save yourself. Understand?"

Ariana nodded and backed against the wall, an arrow at the ready. Satisfied, the prince peered around the corner and led Brand down the last score of steps. As Kiriath descended, his mind was racing. Should he have begged Ariana to remain outside in the woods? *No. She wouldn't have stayed,* he reminded himself. *She is the daughter of King Jekoniah. She determined what she would do back in Shiralla. Only death could have stopped her from following us.*

As the two gained the bottom step, Kiriath caught his breath: Vol-Rathdeen. This was the heart of the dreaded place he had heard about since childhood, but none of the tales or rumors had prepared him for the actual sight.

No mere cave was this. Vol-Rathdeen was an enormous underground vault, a dome of rock lined with the little lichens that illuminated the whole place with their sickly, greenish glow. Off to the right lay a vast, underground lake, into which the channel of water beside them now flowed. Even though many miniature waterfalls in the cavern's roof and walls continuously dribbled more water into that black lake, it still wasn't full to capacity. Indeed, the high-water mark stood at least a half dozen feet above the surface.

Off to the far left a road of sorts burrowed through a high-arched tunnel. Kiriath guessed that the exit to the valley lay in that direction. But straight before the two comrades stood the heart of the Grishnaki's realm. A magnificent fortress of stone reached almost to the very roof of the vault. To each side of this main edifice were a number of smaller block-shaped structures of similar workmanship, but simpler in design. Finally, clustered in a vast semicircle before these main buildings was a sea of crude wooden hovels, apparently little more than branches crisscrossed into rough dome shapes with gaps left on one side for doorways. The total effect was of a cramped underground town, one part beautiful in its antiquity, and the other repulsive in its shabby, unkempt state.

The Grishnaki's merrymaking was still in progress. Peering between the wooden huts, Kiriath could distinguish a sort of clearing in front of the fortress. In the midst of this area blazed huge fires, where whole animal carcasses were roasting on spits. The smoke billowed upward and curled about the roof before escaping into cracks and fissures in the rocky dome. In a wild frenzy, untold numbers of Grishnaki danced and shouted in rings around the fires. Other than these, no other enemies were in sight.

"They didn't build this," Brand whispered. "Not that fortress, I mean."

"No. This is the work of men."

"So many little hovels. Where do you think Dar-kon would keep your father?"

Kiriath shook his head. "I don't know. I wasn't expecting this. Maybe in that fortress? Doubtless that's Dar-kon's own home. He might keep Father nearby where he could taunt him all the easier."

"As good a guess as any. We might sneak along the edge of the lake and get in the back." Brand paused, gazing at the enemies that heedlessly danced so nearby. "What about Ariana? We can't leave her on the steps. She'd be caught if Grud's boys decided to go back to the door."

The prince considered this idea. "I don't like it, but we'd better take her with us. She wouldn't stand a chance alone."

Minutes later, Kiriath and Brand in their Grishnaki garb led the way toward the narrow strip between the nearest hovels and the underground lake. Ariana, still outfitted in hunter garb, walked on the far side of them for concealment. Despite his tense muscles and sweaty palms, Kiriath strove to look natural in imitating the Grishnaki's lope to deceive the eyes of any casual observer.

Approaching the nearest hut, the three became more careful in their actions. Flitting from dwelling to dwelling, they skirted between the rim of the Grishnaki shanties and the edge of the lake, gradually working their way around to the fortress. At one corner Kiriath paused to watch the frenzied dancing. He had never seen a female Grishnak—or more properly, a Grishnaka—before, but both males and females were gyrating wildly in the frenzied celebration. Grotesque caricatures of femininity these latter seemed to him, with long, matted hair and cruel eyes. The slimmest one he could see had a girth much greater than his own. In the prince's eyes, the only positive quality about them was that they were more nimble on their feet than their male counterparts.

By this time the trio had nearly reached their destination.

"Quick, around the next hut," Ariana whispered.

From the urgency in her voice, Kiriath knew to act without question. When they had safely gained the far side of the next dwelling, she explained. "A band of Grishnaki left the feast. They headed the way we just came."

Risking a peek back around the corner, the prince saw that about a dozen Grishnaki were indeed loping across the stone floor toward the distant tunnel that had led the three uninvited guests here. The group moved casually, however, and seemed in no hurry to reach their destination. Two of them carried large joints of meat.

"No danger for the moment, except maybe for the one they call Grud. But we might have a hard time fighting our way back out, if it comes to that."

Bracing himself to slip behind the next hut, Kiriath threw a quick glance toward the feasters. What he saw, however, froze him in place. Immediately before the fortress steps, less than one hundred feet away, stood a man with graying hair, stripped naked from the waist up—his father.

The king's wrists and ankles were tightly bound. On either side of him a burly Grishnak gripped him by his arms. Many of the dancers in the ring carried spears and wildly thrust them within inches of King Jekoniah's chest as they cavorted past him. Unflinching, Jekoniah stood his ground, resembling a tired parent patiently waiting for a group of children to finish their mischief more than a captive in danger.

Behind the king, Dar-kon himself sat in a huge crudely fashioned chair, probably the Grishnak notion of a throne.

He's so huge! Kiriath marveled to himself. *I've never seen such a powerfully built Grishnak!*

Although Dar-kon's skin still bore the bark-like appearance of his race, the prince noted the muscular cut of the Grishnak's arms and chest. His primitive animal-hide garb did little to conceal the creature's obvious strength. In one hand he held a joint of meat, in the other a wooden bowl from which he periodically guzzled some sort of drink. Over and again his booming voice erupted into a wicked, gurgling laughter that rose above the clamor of the revelers.

"Well, Kir?" Brand whispered, looking over his friend's shoulder.

The prince hesitated. He had hoped to find his father in a guarded chamber or cell of some sort, where they could surprise the guards and overpower them. Obviously, though, they couldn't approach him at all while hundreds of Grishnaki were looking on. Furthermore, the three would-be rescuers certainly couldn't linger long in their present predicament: crouching behind a hut of sticks made for a poor hiding place. The prince was about to suggest slipping into the hut beside them when he heard a shout from Dar-kon.

In response to their leader's command, the two Grishnaki flanking King Jekoniah swung him around and brought him face to face with the Grishnak ruler. Dar-kon spoke something, but Jekoniah didn't move or respond at all. Suddenly one of the creatures holding him kicked the rear of the king's knees, forcing Jekoniah into a kneeling posture. Dar-kon roared with glee. Then he emptied the rest of his bowl over Jekoniah's head.

"Vulgar vermin," Brand muttered.

Next the two guards scooped up Jekoniah by the shoulders and dragged him away. Instead of taking him to the fortress, however, they approached a low squat building beside it. The three disappeared within. Moments later one of the Grishnaki returned to

Dar-kon's side, but his comrade remained inside with Jekoniah. Meanwhile, the feasting and dancing carried on unabated.

Kiriath tipped his head in the direction of the building where King Jekoniah was being held. "This may be our only chance. The longer we stay, the greater our chance of being discovered."

Every sense on the alert, the three Xandrians slipped past the final huts that stood between them and the king's prison. Although he wouldn't have wagered on finding a rear entrance into that stone cell, Kiriath would have rejoiced to see one. Reaching the back of the structure, though, he found only a plain stone wall without even a window.

The only way in lay in full view of the whole company of Grishnaki. The prince weighed the odds of entering without raising an alarm. In her hunter's garb, Ariana must remain out of sight at all costs and Brand with her. But in his Grishnak clothing, he reasoned, he just might be able to flit in before any enemy eyes could get a good look at him. Indeed, the Grishnaki horde seemed too engaged in their feasting and dancing. But if he failed? The prince swallowed hard.

We've come this far, he thought to himself. *Either we attempt it and succeed, or we attempt it and fail. But we can't cower here waiting until someone spots us.*

Kiriath put his mouth to Brand's ear. "Wait here with Ariana. I'm going in. I'll try to overcome the guard and put his clothes on Father. If anything happens, don't wait. Make your way back to the tunnel and bolt up it like lightning!"

As the prince turned away, Brand caught his shoulder. For a second Kiriath thought his friend was going to speak. Instead Brand looked his friend in the eye and gave his shoulder a hard squeeze. In that brief moment, he communicated volumes of meaning that time would not permit.

Kiriath steadied himself for the next step. For a full minute he stood transfixed behind the corner of the building, watching the Grishnaki. Finally, he could see no one looking in his general direction. Swiftly he loped around the corner and slipped through the doorway.

The prince had no time to worry whether anyone had noticed him. In the dim interior he saw the Grishnak guard—who had been bending over and facing the other way—straighten and turn around. Instantly the brute's eyes shot wide open in bewilderment.

Kiriath dared not give his foe a chance to shout. Whipping his sword from its sheath, he lunged. But this Grishnak was fast, possibly faster than any Kiriath had encountered before. He dodged the lethal blade and fastened his huge hands on Kiriath's forearm, crushing him to his knees. With a vice-like grip, the Grishnak squeezed hard and began twisting his hands in opposite directions. The look on the monster's face was one of perverted enjoyment, the expression of one who delights in inflicting pain on the helpless.

And Kiriath did feel pain: torture, excruciating agony. Any moment, he thought, the bones in his arm must snap, and still his opponent squeezed. The sword dropped from the prince's hand. He jerked and pulled, then rained blows from his left hand on the Grishnak's arms. But his foe held him fast, his long, hairy arms keeping Kiriath at bay.

Feeling victory within reach, the Grishnak paused long enough to summon up a mouthful of phlegm, leaning forward to spit into the prince's face.

Kiriath seized his last opportunity. Clenching his left hand into a fist, he rammed it under his foe's chin and connected with the thing's throat.

Instantly, the Grishnak released Kiriath's arm and threw back his head, his muffled gasp of pain sending rivulets of scum streaming down his chin.

Pressing the attack with Tara-Ni, Kiriath leapt into the air and snapped his right boot into the Grishnak's belly.

The adversary sprawled prostrate on the stone floor, but didn't concede the battle. Lashing out both hands, he grabbed Kiriath by the ankle and bared his teeth for a bite. But the prince was ready. He had witnessed a wounded Grishnak attack a man with its teeth once before on the battlefield. With both hands locked together to form a mace of muscle and bone, Kiriath slammed down on the base of his foe's head.

The Grishnak's face dashed against the stone floor. He lay unmoving.

Breathing hard, Kiriath snatched up his sword and whirled to face the door in case other enemies had appeared. Nothing happened. Outside, the dance surged on uninterrupted.

Next the prince's eyes returned to where the Grishnak had been bending over when Kiriath first entered the chamber. There lay King Jekoniah, still bound at the wrists and ankles, silently regarding him.

Solemnly, the old king nodded. "So you have come after all. In my heart I was afraid that, if you were alive, you would try."

Chapter 13

Out of Darkness

Kiriath rushed to his father's side and slit the leather bonds with his sword. "Father! Are you all right?"

"Yes, I'm all right." The aged sovereign's voice was steady but much weaker than usual. "Dar-kon wanted me alive. Of course, that did not keep them from knocking me about and defiling half my food before they threw it at me. But you should not have come."

"I had to. I could not live without trying."

The elder man nodded again. His weary eyes were full of understanding. "I know. Twice I tried to escape to spare you the trouble. Each time they hauled me back and lashed my back for the attempt." He stood stiffly and began massaging his wrists. "You are alone, I take it?"

"No. Brand volunteered to come with me. He's waiting for us."

"For a friend, Brand sticks closer than a brother. You won't find another man like him."

The prince hesitated to make his next statement, but he couldn't avoid it. "Ariana, too, has come. She followed us out of Xandria and caught up with us in the Lowlands. I couldn't send her back alone, so we let her join us."

King Jekoniah's eyebrows lowered, and the weariness vanished from his eyes. "Ariana, you say? She should not be here! Where are they now?"

"Waiting on the other side of the wall behind you. We sneaked in through a tunnel on the west side of the mountain."

"Yes, I have seen several such tunnels. Some of them are blocked up, but at least three are still used, not counting the main entrance out to the valley. Was the tunnel not guarded?"

"Not well. Two of the guardians are dead in the forest. We slipped past a third while he was asleep. The rest were down here feasting until a few minutes ago. We spied a group of them heading back up the way we came."

The king absorbed all this news quickly. The fatigue melted from him, his attitude quickly resuming that of King and First Commander of Xandria. "Then we dare not go back the way you came. Is there any chance they will find the two dead ones?"

"Possibly, though not right away. The bodies can't be seen from the outer entrance, but they aren't too distant from it. It's a long climb from here to the outer exit. They can't have reached it yet."

"Mixed tidings, both bad and good. We have a few minutes to plan but little more. Dar-kon is unpredictable. He sent me away at a whim. Often he unexpectedly orders for me to be dragged back to him just to spit on me or to make me witness some grotesque deed. Quickly, tell me all you know about the mountain and the region about it."

"All right, but while I talk, let's take this fellow's clothes; you'll need a disguise too."

It didn't take Prince Kiriath long to relate all that he had learned about Saddle Mountain and the Valley of Grishnaki. At intervals King Jekoniah raised a quick question on some point or other. What he seemed most interested in was his son's passing mention of the Deserted Kingdom.

"So you crossed the Deserted Kingdom? Did you happen to notice . . ." But the king cut himself off and returned to the danger at hand. "No time for idle talk now. We must escape while we can."

"Listen, Son, I counsel that we not go back the way you came in. Even without the guards up there, my body has been sorely abused, and my sleep has been little. It will not be able to climb back up that tunnel very quickly."

"But what other way? Brand and I—"

King Jekoniah put up a hand. "In the Grishnaki's home they outnumber us and have the advantage of knowing the place. Even if none of them notices us leaving this spot, we will not be gone long ere the chase is on. There is some risk in my idea, but I believe it will give us a chance to escape from Vol-Rathdeen alive."

"I'll take any fighting chance you think worthy."

For the first time King Jekoniah spared a weak smile. "That's my son. Now, did you observe the low level of that lake just past the Grishnaki's huts? It is growing shallower. Probably not enough rain on the mountain to keep it up. I would guess that it has dropped half a foot in just the week I have been here."

"Is that good?"

"For us, yes. On my second attempt to escape, I reached the far end of the lake and saw enough to confirm my suspicion— there is a hole, an outlet through which the lake drains out of the mountain. Natural, perhaps, although with these ancient buildings down here it is hard to be certain."

"And you think we can escape through this opening?"

"That is my hope. It seems the only way. It will mean swimming some though. Breathing may not be easy once we go through the culvert."

"We don't need it to be easy; just so it's possible. And since Grishnaki can't swim, they won't be able to follow us. But what stopped you from getting out that way before?"

"Another tunnel opening such as the one you came through lies at that end of the lake. I had barely reached the spot when a dozen Grishnaki sauntered out of it. Just coincidence, but it could happen again. Wait. Someone's coming."

Father and son took positions at either side of the doorway. Seconds later a massive shape stepped inside.

"Mudj? Dar-kon wants the—"

The Grishnak never finished his sentence. Crumpling under Kiriath's blow, he dropped beside the still form of his comrade.

"We are out of time, Son. Dar-kon must expect that one to haul me back to him. It is the same nearly every time. We must all flee—now."

"I'm with you. Lead the way to your escape hole."

As the prince followed King Jekoniah out the doorway, he glanced up in time to see the Grishnak king looking straight at them. Dar-kon jerked himself to his full height and bellowed hideously.

"Follow us!" Kiriath blurted to Ariana and Brand. "This way out!"

Another shout went up from Dar-kon.

The little group bolted in the direction of the lake. But in his weakened condition, the king wasn't able to run as fast as he once could have. Kiriath looked back just long enough to see a vast host on a fast lope in their direction. In that brief instant he even saw Dar-kon himself, wildly gesticulating and shouting as he pursued with a spear in his hands.

The cavern's stony floor was not perfectly flat and easy to run on. Rather, it resembled rolling ocean waves suddenly petrified under some spell. As they ran, the escapers came upon dark cracks that gaped open at their feet, and once they had to leap a narrow chasm that snaked across their route. Casting another backward glance as he ran, Kiriath saw that the enemy was gaining on them. But weakened as he was, King Jekoniah could run no faster. If something weren't done quickly, they would all be captured.

"Brand, we have to slow them down. Let's throw some spheres!"

Brand held up his hands, letting his friend see the two shiny globes he already held. He carefully passed one to Kiriath as they ran. "Thought we might need some help. I pulled them out while you freed the king."

"Let's do it. Ready—now!"

In unison, the two men stopped abruptly and turned toward the approaching hordes. As they hurled their glass orbs, Kiriath could see Dar-kon's muscular form bearing down on them, leading the charge, a maniacal anger contorting his features. Suddenly the foremost ranks of Grishnaki exploded with a flash and a roar. Then a second explosion erupted. Guttural screams echoed through the cavern.

"That did it. Let's go!" Brand shouted above the noise.

Near the far end of the cavern, the prince thought he could discern the opening through which the lake emptied. Also, ahead and a little to the left, he made out the arch to the tunnel that had been the downfall of his father's previous escape attempt. With all his heart he hoped that none of the enemy would appear there just now.

"They're catching up again," Brand said. "No time to dig out your spheres. Where are we going?"

"Through the water. No time to explain. Follow Father."

"The way out! There!" Jekoniah shouted, pointing. Barely showing above the water line of the lake, the opening in the cavern wall was less then impressive. Still, water was definitely flowing steadily through it. The king slid down the slick stone into the dark waters and struck out for the hole.

Brand had his sword in his hand now. "Quick, Ariana, behind your father."

"Wait!" Deftly fitting an arrow to her bowstring, Ariana drew the string back to her ear, closed one eye, and aimed into the approaching horde.

"Ariana! It's not worth it! Let's go!" Kiriath couldn't understand his sister's sudden gamble to stop one Grishnak when countless numbers of them were approaching.

The arrow sprang away, a glistening needle of silver arcing through the perpetual greenish twilight. Suddenly Kiriath grasped his sister's plan, for in the distance he saw Dar-kon's form falter and collapse, disappearing amongst those that had followed him. A cry of shock and dismay went up from the Grishnaki.

"Good eye, Arie! Now into the water. We're right behind you."

Ariana dived into the lake and struck out after the king, who was halfway to their goal.

Momentarily stopped by Dar-kon's fall, the lead Grishnaki now screamed wildly and surged on with redoubled fury.

Brand cast off his Grishnak cloak and slapped Kiriath's side. "Into the water, friend. Can't do any good here."

The prince had already lost his hide cap while running, but now he flung away Glarpk's tunic and followed Brand down the slippery stone. Diving into the deepest-looking spot he could see, Kiriath was startled to find himself sinking deeper rather than rising to the surface. Was this some enchanted pool, dragging him down with cool, liquid fingers? Equally eerie was the feeling that he had been through this experience before.

But then the truth struck him: he was still wearing his chain-mail shirt! There was no time to remove it; even if he could, his nigh-empty pack still hung on his back, and Kiriath wasn't ready to lose the other two glass spheres inside it. Kicking the water with renewed vigor, he finally broke through the lake's surface and gulped the air. Just ahead of him, Brand too lay deep in the water as he stroked his way along.

"Miserable time to have armor on," Kiriath shouted to his companion.

"If they catch you, it'll come off!"

Kiriath didn't try to answer. The weight dragging at him made it too difficult even to breathe without inhaling water. Besides, spears were pelting the water all around them now. Instead, he concentrated on the dark mouth opening ahead. Kiriath considered the fact that the water's escaping the mountain this way didn't guarantee that people could. For good or ill, though, the escapers had no other choice but to risk it. In the next instant, his father disappeared through the hole. A moment later Kiriath saw Ariana approach the opening and pick up speed just as she was swept through it.

A distinct *chink* and a pain in his back told Kiriath that a spear had found its mark. For the first time since he had entered the lake he felt glad for the steel protection he wore. Remembering the spheres in his pack, however, he kicked his legs even faster, lest another shaft blast him to the bottom of a watery tomb.

Brand now gained the opening and disappeared from sight. Not wanting to become separated from the others, Kiriath put on one last burst of speed. Nearing the hole in the cavern wall, he now saw that it was even smaller than he had supposed. It was about three feet wide but scarcely a foot and a half deep under the water. Just a slim gap of air space showed above the water's rippling surface.

Kiriath had intended to slow down and enter the stony maw cautiously. Caught in the out-flowing current, however, he felt his body being flung through it with irresistible force.

In the next instant darkness engulfed him, and Kiriath was sliding down an incline of slick stone. Without warning, he felt as if he had lost his stomach as he plunged downward through darkness.

Quickly he shielded his head with both arms. The tactic soon proved unnecessary, however, for he had not fallen far before he splashed into another pool. Struggling once more to the surface, he tread water, catching his breath. Absolute darkness surrounded him. "Father?"

"Here. Follow the sound of my voice." By the loud echo the prince knew that the cavern they were now in could not be large. Striking out in the direction where King Jekoniah's voice seemed to come from, he soon found footing on the bottom of the pool.

"This way, Kir," Brand's voice encouraged. "I just found them myself."

When the water was only knee-deep, Kiriath bumped into someone and realized he had found his family and friend. "We've lost them, Father. You certainly know how to make an exciting departure."

"Always enjoyed drama," the king's voice replied.

From the strength and cheerfulness he detected there, Kiriath was assured that his father was unhurt. "Is everyone all right? Ariana? Brand?"

"I'm fine. Just a little bruised," Ariana's voice answered.

"Me too. I feel like a water rat though. The water seems to follow a definite channel. Let's see if it leads us out of here."

"One more moment," Jekoniah said. "I'm older than you three and not used to exercise. Tell me the secret of your fire and lightning while I catch my breath. I thought the mountain was collapsing back there."

While Brand and Kiriath removed their mail shirts, Ariana found two pears in their gear and gave these to King Jekoniah, who accepted them gratefully. Then she briefly recounted how they had found the glass spheres.

"Ah," the king sighed upon hearing of the exploding orbs. "I have heard of such weapons. Then 'tis true. The Ancients of Illandria really were related to the ones who built the Deserted Kingdom. Your grandfather suspected that it might be so. But the dangers from the Grishnaki always outweighed the risks of exploring the ruins."

"I've never heard such a tale," Ariana said. "Who were these Ancients? How did they get so far from Illandria?"

"You have heard of them, Ariana. You just do not realize it. The Ancients are mainly remembered as a community of scholars in the common folklore. They were men of learning in early Illandria, studying the sun by day and the stars by night. Plants, animals, soil—they studied all of these and learned to do amazing things with them. But the uneducated people feared them and persecuted them as sorcerers.

"Now there truly were unclean sorcerers, of course, mumbling to shadows over bubbling cauldrons, but these that I call the Ancients were not of that number. The ancient men of science, however, were merely misunderstood. Preferring not to be stoned or burned alive, they elected to band their families together and leave Illandria. They set sail and were never heard from again. At least, that is how I have pieced the story together."

"So they came to our shore years before the colonists?" Brand asked.

"Apparently. Until I saw Vol-Rathdeen and heard your tale, I merely speculated. Now it seems certain."

Ariana spoke up next. "Now the descendents of the Grishnaki who destroyed them seek our doom as well. Some things never change."

"Righteousness and evil never change," King Jekoniah agreed, "only those who work them. Evil will remain with us until the end of the age."

Kiriath stood up in the darkness. "Come. We should be going. Are you rested, Father?"

"Yes. Let's continue."

Wading in the cool water of the stream, they followed it down, down twisting corridors of night. Most of the time they could stand erect with no trouble. But as Brand led the way, he occasionally warned of an obstacle or low-hanging rock. Their feet met no obstacles at all, for the flowing waters of untold years had polished it smooth and clean. As they progressed, King Jekoniah asked many questions concerning the Grishnaki's extortion proposal, Vandrielle's response to it, and the reaction of Xandria in general. Kiriath shared his suspicion that someone had betrayed them, to which Jekoniah made no comment. After what seemed like hours, Kiriath noted a dim light ahead of them.

"We must be nearing the outside," Ariana said.

When they reached the source of the light, however, there was no exit such as they had hoped for. Instead the stream ended in another pool of water, through which filtered a hazy light that danced and shimmered on the ceiling of a little chamber. No exit hole or tunnel was to be seen.

Brand stepped into the pool. "Looks like another swim. Stay here. I'll be right back—I hope." Thus saying, he took a breath and disappeared into the pool. Kiriath watched his friend's silhouette knife beneath the surface, disappearing at the point where the light seemed brightest.

"There may be Grishnaki waiting to meet him," the king commented.

Ariana nodded. "That's why he didn't give us a chance to stop him." Her tone was of pride mingled with concern.

Minutes passed in silence. Ariana began to fidget. Even Kiriath began to feel uneasy. At last a shadow reappeared against the light in the pool, and Brand broke through the surface.

"This is it. There's no sign of Grishnaki about. I checked."

King Jekoniah was skeptical. "Are you sure? Surely they know where the stream from their own abode flows."

"Perhaps not, Sire. For this pool connects to a lake outside of the mountain, and a brook flowing down the mountain empties into that. From the outside no one would even guess that the place where we are standing exists."

"Grishnaki don't swim, so they would never find it." Ariana was almost jubilant. "For all they know, their lake may drain into the very core of the earth. They'll have no idea where to begin looking for us."

"Let us hope so," the old king said. "But let us not cast caution to the breeze either. Since your arrow pierced their leader, it will take more than our four lives to satisfy their blood lust. It is Xandria that I worry about now. The Grishnaki can be demons in battle when the madness for revenge is on them."

Kiriath agreed. "The sooner our kingdom has her ruler back, the better off she'll be."

Once again following Brand's lead, the little company swam through the pool and emerged from the lake outside the mountain. Still seeing no trace of the enemy, they struck a fast pace, hoping to veer well south of the direct approach to Xandria in case pursuers were prowling for them. The day was far spent, and night soon descended upon them, but still they marched on through the open lands.

As Kiriath feared, King Jekoniah was showing signs of fatigue, but the sovereign refused to stop. He accepted Brand's last battered apple and a long draught from Ariana's flask but wouldn't even debate slowing down or stopping for the night.

"No," the monarch replied, "I have observed the ways of Grishnaki for longer than any two of your lifetimes added together. I underestimated their ability to sneak into the kingdom, but I won't underestimate a Grishnak's lust for vengeance. To Xandria, with all speed!"

Around midnight Ariana urged her father to take a short rest, and the king at last relented, provided it was not for more than ten or fifteen minutes. Even at that, his decision sounded more like it was out of consideration for the others than himself.

Kiriath took advantage of this respite to ask a question he had been turning over in his mind. "Father, when I spoke about a possible traitor earlier, you said nothing. What do you think of that idea?"

"I believe your guess is true. I loathe to accept the thought, but there were too many coincidences the day I was taken. There is a scoundrel in our realm."

"Do you have any ideas of who it might be?"

"No."

"Then how can you be sure?"

"Sometimes enlightenment comes even from the blackest of enemies. Dar-kon tried to break my spirit. Thrice he told me outright that 'one of your own,' as he put it, had told him when and where to find us while we two were out riding."

"Couldn't he have been lying to goad you?"

"That was my first thought. But he stuck to this story as he tried to torture me with his words. To prove his knowledge, he described the very roads that you and I traveled the morning they captured me, including the various ones we might have used had we finished our ride. He was not guessing. Someone has observed your favorite haunts and passed him the information. Whether willingly or under torture is another question."

"Then it was me they wanted after all."

"No, though I do not doubt they would have seized you if they could have. Somehow it was known that I would be with you that day."

"I don't see how. We planned our ride only a few days in advance and never spoke of it more than a couple times. I remember one time in the Citadel courtyard—"

"And once on the stairway near your room. You never spoke of it to anyone else?"

"Never. You said that you would let Mother know, but I never spoke to anyone else of it. Not even Brand knew."

"I thought not. I had planned to ask you just to make sure. Well then, Son, in my mind it is definite: one of our own citizens gave or sold the information to Dar-kon. Whoever it was must have access to the Citadel, for knowing your morning routines would have been worthless had not someone overheard our specific intentions for that morning."

All this time Ariana and Brand had been listening without comment. At this conclusion, Ariana broke her silence. "Is there no other explanation? Many people live or serve in the Citadel, but I can't think of a single one that I wouldn't trust. The only person I don't always feel at ease with is Shiralla's chamberlain, Bered."

"Do not doubt Bered," Brand urged. "He's a good man. Grim, yes, but that's only because he witnessed with his own eyes how the Grishnaki brutalized his parents when he was a boy. I should be just as sober-faced myself had I been there when they slaughtered my family."

"I can think of no other explanations," Jekoniah concluded. "Apparently Dar-kon's boasting was truthful; someone that we consider a friend has betrayed us. My heart burns knowing that this person is comfortably going about his life in Shiralla while we four shiver in the wilderness in damp clothing. Enough talking. Let us cut straight east to cross Border River."

Obeying the king's wishes, the four of them continued their march. A waning moon did its best to illuminate the open land, and only occasional clusters of trees dotted the terrain. The group made good time despite the night. Although he had sometimes crossed the river marking Xandria's western outskirts, Kiriath couldn't recall ever traversing this particular region. During the night, King Jekoniah permitted only two more brief halts before the Eastern horizon began paling.

Ariana was especially happy to see the dawn. "At last. Dayspring comes."

"The seventh day," Brand noted. "For a week we have dreaded what might happen to you on this day, Sire."

"Do not stop dreading. Only change the emphasis from me to the kingdom. An enraged Grishnak is a fearsome thing, and we have stirred up a whole nest of them."

The day dawned clear and sunny, still with no sign of their goal, the Border River. Kiriath wondered at this, but then he remembered that Border River didn't flow straight. Rather, it meandered in a broad curve as it wound its way to Lake Prochorus in the South. He judged that they must be approaching it at a point where it looped eastward toward Xandria.

Before much longer, however, Brand exclaimed, "The river! We're almost home."

True enough, in the plain before them twinkled the watery ribbon that designated the edge of the realm in the west. The river was now narrower and shallower than it was in less dry years, but it was a welcome sight nonetheless.

When they had drawn closer, Kiriath finally recognized exactly where they were. On the far bank and a little north of their location a gray fortification topped a low rise.

"Fortress Diligence," Kiriath announced. "We've come out of the wilderness at a good location."

"Yes," Jekoniah agreed. "Commander Draik makes the Diligence garrison worthy of its name. Kiriath, see if you can signal the watchmen from here."

The prince pulled out his sword and held it straight up in front of his right eye and extended his left arm, his upright thumb aligned with the fortress. Twisting the sword from side to side, he reflected the rising sun's rays back and forth over his thumb, which guaranteed that the glinting should be visible by the garrison watchmen. "There. They ought to have seen that."

Hardly had the prince finished speaking when a troop of horsemen issued from the fortress, galloping in their direction. The riders forded the low level of the river and charged up to the little group. The company's leader reined in directly before them, while the defenders behind divided and closed ranks from each side to circle around the four on foot.

The commander held up his hand. "Halt and be recogni—" Suddenly the man's mouth froze as his eyes fixed on the four in front of him. Clearly he had indeed recognized those whom he addressed. "My liege, you're free! And the prince! Lady Ariana and Captain Brand!" Quickly he swung from his saddle and dropped to one knee. "We expected messengers from the wilds, but not the royal family itself."

Without wasting time King Jekoniah took over the situation. "What tidings in the kingdom, Draik? What do you mean by messengers from the wilds?"

Experienced in military brevity, Draik spoke quickly, supplying Jekoniah with all the information he needed. "Yesterday morning, about this hour, a rider from the Westrock garrison arrived with tidings from Lady Vandrielle. She warned us to be especially alert in case three or four men on an errand in her service approached from the land of Grishnaki, whether by day or night. We were cautioned to withhold our arrows until we knew for sure that it was not her couriers who approached."

"That would be us," Kiriath explained. "She wanted to keep anyone from targeting the king by accident after all the labor we've had to free him."

"More ominous were the latest tidings from Westrock. Shortly after sunup this morning, another rider arrived, saying that thousands of Grishnaki had overrun the Shallowford fortress and that they were proceeding toward Westrock. The queen herself was there and bade us send any able riders that we could spare but not all, in case other Grishnaki cross over to attack us here."

"It is as I feared," Jekoniah said. "Vandrielle is in Westrock, then?"

"Yes, Sire. At least she was when she dispatched the rider to us. The queen, Nethanel, Urijah, and Commander Carpathan, among others. We heard that they arrived yesterday to await Dar-kon's emissary. But instead of one Grishnak coming in truce, thousands of the black-hearts swarmed to the attack without warning!"

"All evil news. The only good I hear is that Carpathan is there to organize the defense. If the enemy overcomes Westrock, there is no limit to how many of our citizens they may butcher."

King Jekoniah's mind jumped to a decision. "Draik, carry us to the fortress, and immediately prepare all your men to ride into a battle like they've never seen before. No one remains behind. There will be no carefully planned second attack this far south. Dar-kon has fallen, and the enemy thirsts for vengeance. Dispatch your fastest riders to the garrisons at Oakdale, Southmarche, and Highmount. Have them all do the same and meet us at Westrock. Let the word go forth: The King of Xandria has returned and rides ahead to the battle!"

CHAPTER 14

BATTLEFIELD WESTROCK

Draik had wasted no time in fulfilling the king's orders. Couriers had galloped off to summon the other garrisons, and the Diligence Fortress had mustered her three hundred remaining horsemen. Thanks to the queen's earlier messenger, the muster required little more than scant minutes, for the garrison's horses had already been saddled, and its men were eager to aid their fellow men-at-arms.

Since King Jekoniah could not be dissuaded from going to the battle, Kiriath had convinced him at the least to eat a quick meal, lest he fail from hunger if not from a Grishnak's blow. More surprising to the prince, however, was that his father had granted Ariana's plea to ride along.

"If we do not stem the Grishnaki tide today," Jekoniah had said, "there is nowhere where any woman or child will be safe. But stay in the middle of the company, Ariana. If Westrock still stands, you can serve as my aide during the battle."

But all of that had been many miles ago. Since then, the company had reached Rapid Shoals and Windemount, the last fortresses before Westrock. King Jekoniah had stopped at each only long enough to summon their riders to follow him northward but would not so much as wait while they mounted their steeds.

Pressing onward, the company surrounding the king was now but minutes away from Westrock.

All eyes locked on a black column of smoke billowing in the distance before them. Only the torching of a small village—or a border fortress—could create such smoke. Each man knew that no villages were situated so near the frontier. Would they be too late to rescue the men of Westrock and the queen?

Cresting a hilltop, King Jekoniah threw up his hand with fingers spread in command to halt. From that higher ground they could now see that the smoky billows rose not from Westrock but from Shallowford, several miles beyond. Atop another hill slightly larger than the one where they now stood was Fortress Westrock, intact, but besieged by countless Grishnaki carrying torches, ladders, and primitive weapons.

At the gate of the fortress a multitude of the enemy huddled in a compact mass. Although Kiriath couldn't see it, he guessed there must be a battering ram at work there. On the small plain between the two hills, horsemen wheeled and spun their mounts, slashing and hacking at the Grishnaki hordes that surrounded and vastly outnumbered them. Already the scattered corpses of hundreds of men, Grishnaki, and horses littered the field.

King Jekoniah shouted to Commander Draik. "Wedge formation! Drive the enemy from the gate first. Leave Ariana and me there; then turn back to join the battle below. And send your swiftest rider toward the northern fortresses for more defenders. Here is where Xandria stands or falls!"

Draik nodded and spoke to the young standard-bearer beside him, who blew three quick blasts on a trump. Within moments the three hundred horsemen formed themselves into a spearhead formation with King Jekoniah, Ariana, and Kiriath in the center. The prince was about to spur his steed into the point with Draik and Brand when Jekoniah beckoned him to stay back. "Nay, Son. Not this time. Kings and princes cannot always do as they please in battle. If you or I fall now, many others may lose heart and despair. Stay with me as far as the gate; then be my eyes and ears outside the fortress. I will send word if I have any special instructions."

Reluctantly, the prince fell in beside his father and sister. The advice was sound, he knew, but for Kiriath to watch comrades in battle without taking an active role was more difficult than being in the thick of the fighting.

Everyone was in place. The young man with the trump sounded the charge, and as one body the mass of three hundred men and one woman thundered down the hill, pounding straight toward the fortress. The very air vibrated with the staccato hammering of twelve hundred hooves. Incredibly, the forward tip of the wedge had already started up the next hill toward Westrock before anyone noticed their approach. A tremendous shout of joy and jubilant trumpet greetings sounded from the beleaguered battlements. It was followed by guttural cursing and shouting from the attackers on the ground.

Now Kiriath could see that a group of Grishnaki was swinging a tree trunk against the fortress gates, while other Grishnaki sheltered its bearers with Xandrian shields gleaned from fallen defenders. The prince knew that all of Xandria's border outposts were fortified with stout gates of oak and iron, but he also realized that none of them was impregnable against constant battering. He hoped this one still held strong.

As the king's host surged up the hill, a few Grishnaki of slighter build deserted their comrades and fled. Most, however, turned to face the foe, determination and hate blazing in their eyes. Draik's trumpeter blew the call to arms, and three hundred polished swords sprang from their sheaths, glittering like a wave of stars in the morning sunlight. King Jekoniah had no blade, but in midcharge Ariana passed him the ancient sword with the purple gem she had borne since the Deserted Kingdom.

An ear-shattering din erupted as the onslaught of men and horses slammed into the wall of Grishnaki. Steel swords flashed, parrying wooden swords and cleaving Grishnaki flesh and bones. In response, Grishnaki spears hurtled into the human throng, and bludgeons thudded into horses, armor, and human flesh.

Here and there a hastily fired arrow chanced to lodge in some unarmored part of a defender's body. Above and throughout the entire scene of carnage, an unintelligible din of men crying out in agony mingled with the neighing of horses and the gurgling howls of wounded Grishnaki. Indeed, the Grishnaki struck at the riders' mounts as often as at the riders themselves, so great was their fear and hatred for these beasts that gave men such speed and strength in battle.

Having lowered their shields and turned to face the horsemen's assault, the Grishnaki suddenly became vulnerable to the archers atop Westrock's battlements. These were now rapidly raining arrows into the ranks of the enemy.

To Kiriath's mind, the chief goal for this moment was to get his father and sister inside the fortress. But the enemies before them were as ferocious and untiring as they were enormous. His mind raced, searching for a way to break their stand quickly, before more of the creatures came upon them from the battle below.

Unexpectedly, a voice similar to the king's sprang into Kiriath's thoughts: *Those spheres, Son! Throw the last spheres from the Deserted Kingdom!* For an instant he thought his father had truly spoken to him, but although his father was watching him intently, Kiriath knew he had heard no such words. With the clamor of battle all around them, no one could have spoken so clearly to another.

But there was no time to dwell on such thoughts. Yes, the spheres! Sheathing his sword, the prince ripped open the pouch on his belt, pulled out one of the glistening orbs, and hurled it into the center of the Grishnak pack. The ensuing blast and roar flattened the foes around it and terrified many other Grishnaki. However, the flash and explosion also struck fear into many riders and horses.

Standing in his stirrups, the prince shouted above the tumult, "Xandrian lightning! Feel the wrath of Xandria!" Pulling out his last sphere, he held it aloft so the men could see it, then cast it at the Grishnaki nearest the gate. Just as suddenly as before, the explosion ripped into the Grishnaki's ranks, felling a half dozen. With a howl, the enemy dropped their weapons and scattered from these fire-wielding men.

The defenders above cheered wildly. But Kiriath knew better than to waste an instant before the battle was won. Cupping his hands around his mouth, he shouted to the men on the wall. "Open! Open your gate for the king and the Princess Ariana!" Several faces disappeared from the battlement, and shortly one half of the double gate began creaking outward. Draik, forming the horsemen into a protective half-circle before the entrance, waited for the monarch to reach the safety within.

Before entering, however, King Jekoniah leaned close to Kiriath. "Listen! When my thoughts come to you in the battle, do not be afraid. It is not witchcraft."

"What?" Kiriath shouted back, not comprehending. His father made no sense. Had his head been struck in the battle?

"The sword. The sword Ariana gave me. The handle contains one of the thought-casting stones of the Ancients. As long as my hand is on that purple stone, I can cast my thoughts into the mind of anyone I can see."

Kiriath hesitated. Could such a thing be true?

To illustrate his point, King Jekoniah held the blade up by its gem-embedded handle. Despite the king's closed lips, Kiriath undeniably heard his father's voice, as if echoing down a long hallway, saying, *I will guide you in battle. Do not be afraid. Do you understand?*

The truth was that Kiriath didn't understand at all. He had never heard of such a trick and was genuinely astonished. Nonetheless he nodded a hasty *yes* and swatted his father's horse to speed it into the fortress. Ariana followed, and the gate swung shut again.

"To the battle below!" Kiriath shouted to Draik. The commander nodded and rallied his men. Once more the group thundered downhill, their blades held aloft as they charged. Simultaneously, a much larger host charged into the fray from the opposite side—the garrisons from Rapid Shoals and Windemount, which they had passed along the way.

The sea of Grishnaki that had encompassed the horsemen below still outnumbered all the men of war, but it was also true that they were afoot while each of the Xandrians rode a war-horse. Rather than shrinking back, however, the enemies braced themselves and ran screaming to meet the oncoming soldiers.

Once more the air around Kiriath filled with the noise of pure battle: slashing, clashing metal, and voices from both sides raised in anguish. Now there were three centers of battle: one where the Westrock fortress was besieged, another where Kiriath and Brand fought with the men from the Diligence garrison, and a third where the other garrisons hacked and hewed at the far fringes of the sea of Grishnaki.

Remembering his father's words, however, the prince held himself back from the main fighting so that he could foresee what orders to give. Only now and then did he suddenly spur his horse forward to aid a defender who had been surrounded or knocked from his mount. Draik, too, stayed near Kiriath with the standard-bearer who also served as trumpeter.

Do not let them keep our forces divided, Jekoniah's voice said from nowhere. *Being on horseback is to our advantage; keeping us separated is to theirs. Concentrate your men and cut through to where Carpathan fights with the men from Westrock! They are faltering.*

As before, Kiriath marveled that he could hear his father's voice inside his mind. Had there not been a battle raging, the prince might have been troubled by this feat. The counsel was wise, however, and no sooner had the voice ceased than he acted on its commands.

"Draw in the flanks! Let's push in to join the men from Westrock."

Obeying, the standard-bearer sounded the trump, and the men on the flanks gradually backed as they fought, drawing together around Kiriath, Draik, and the standard-bearer. Briefly, Kiriath reflected that he didn't even know the name of this man who was calmly trumpeting out his orders, but he admired the young defender's cool-headedness in the midst of chaos.

"Now the charge!"

Again the trump sounded, and the mass of men surged forward. It was hardly a charge, for that was impossible in such close-packed conditions. Still, they were making progress, steadily grinding into the enemy ranks. Horses in the front line often reared up, crushing the Grishnaki before them under their iron-shod hooves.

At last the men from Diligence reached the beleaguered men from Westrock, merging with their ring and lending much needed support to their flagging strength. Seeing their example, the six or seven hundred riders from Rapid Shoals and Windemount also began penetrating deeply into the Grishnaki ranks. As the battle raged, every minute added more corpses to those already heaped on the ground.

"Ho, Kiriath! Welcome home!" It was Carpathan who spoke as he reined in his mount alongside the prince's. In contrast to Carpathan's cheerful tone was the man's appearance, for his armor was dented and stained with scores of red streaks. Sweat dripped from his hair and face.

"Good to be back," the prince returned. "Father is in the fortress."

"Yes, I saw," was the soldier's reply. "You've done a mighty deed!" Charging forward again, he hewed through the arm of a Grishnak preparing to behead a fallen defender.

Now the horsemen from the two other fortresses began flowing into the ring of men. Their position was now solidified, but the minions of Dar-kon still outnumbered them beyond counting. Yet now, at least, the men were unified rather than warring in fragmented islands.

"Were you able to get off a rider to the north?" the prince asked Draik.

"Two. Both north and east."

"Well done."

It would take time for a man to reach the garrisons past Shallowford, he knew, and even more to return with aid. But at least more defenders of the realm would be coming, regardless of whether Westrock stood or fell.

From nowhere Kiriath once more heard Jekoniah's voice: *More help is on the horizon. Do not let the men lose heart!*

At first Kiriath couldn't see what these last words meant. His gaze swept the rim of the plain, but the low hills round about limited his field of vision. Then, on the very rise where they had begun the charge toward Westrock, there appeared a long line of horsemen. Even from a distance Kiriath recognized the standard of a green tree in a yellow field.

"Oakdale!" he shouted to no one in particular. "They must've ridden like the wind! The men of Oakdale are here!"

Others took up the cry even as the Oakdale horsemen came careening down the slope, crashing into the sea of the Grishnaki. The newcomers had to fight with all their might for every foot of ground, for the enemy was now more dogged than ever to keep the soldiers apart. Eventually the men from Oakdale also reached their compatriots at the heart of the battlefield. But even with these fresh forces, the number of Xandrians seemed discouragingly small by comparison. Even as the prince watched, more Grishnaki, evidently having lingered at Shallowford to partake in looting or other devilry, were still approaching from the direction of the burning fortress.

Never in his life had Kiriath witnessed such a battle. But if the Xandrians were outnumbered, they took heart in the fact that only those Grishnaki in the forefront of the battle could participate in the fight. Those in the rear could press forward only after their comrades fell under the riders' blades. Of course, the enemies' greater numbers also meant that most of them could rest while only the Grishnaki closest to the soldiers labored in the battle. The men, on the other hand, had no rest as they constantly labored under their swinging blades.

The hot sun burned friend and foe alike. Thick clouds of dust swirled upward to choke throats and sting eyes. The air stank of sweat and unwashed Grishnaki hide.

Kiriath noticed that the enemy was again battering Westrock's gates, the fortress's weakest point, but then he watched with satisfaction as the defenders above poured flaming oil on the adversaries, which sent them shrieking away in pain.

However, the prince was not so certain that the defenders on the plain could hold out for long. Most of the original defenders of Westrock had fallen in combat. Of the few score who remained, most were sorely wounded and physically exhausted; they had to take frequent rests in the center of the ring before rejoining their brothers. And each time they did so, the circle of men grew smaller, tighter.

As before, Jekoniah's voice occasionally spoke into the prince's mind, advising him to fill a gap or to reinforce one side of the ring, but even sound advice would be useless when no men were fit to carry it out. Gradually but surely, the sea of Grishnaki was wearing away the mound of men who withstood them. Even Draik was now dead, having at last begged Kiriath's permission to engage the enemy with his men. And where was Brand? Kiriath had lost track of him in the mêlée.

"Did you hear me, Prince Kiriath?"

Suddenly Kiriath realized that someone had been speaking to him. Forgotten beside him was the faithful standard-bearer, one hand still holding his banner—a brown hawk on a blue field—that represented Fortress Diligence, the other hand clutching his brass trump. "My prince, if you have no further orders, I ask permission to join the battle."

Now looking at this young one more closely, Kiriath considered him little more than a boy—very tall and muscular, but quite young nonetheless. "Have you fought Grishnaki before, young sir?"

The man seemed pleased that the prince of the realm had honored him with a *sir*.

"Yes, during a skirmish about six months ago."

Kiriath didn't answer immediately.

"Please, Prince Kiriath. My family lives in Jessex. It's the first village east of here. If we fail— Well, I want to keep as many of the enemy as I can from reaching them."

Making a quick decision, Kiriath sheathed his sword and extended his hand. "Give me the standard. You can't hold this and a sword at the same time."

"Thank you, my prince."

"Do not thank me. It's no service to give a man a chance to die. Fight well!"

Unleashing his sword for the first time, the young man shouted, "Xandria!" and plunged his stallion into the fray.

Just then an especially gigantic Grishnak succeeded in ramming his spear through a soldier who had fallen to the earth. A wail of anguish escaped from the dying one's lips, while the Grishnaki thumped his own chest with his fists and croaked with glee.

The prince's wrath kindled. Lowering the standard of Diligence horizontally like a lance, he dug his stirrups into his charger's flanks. An instant later the Grishnak's laugh ended abruptly as he crumpled under the fury of Kiriath's assault.

Letting the standard drop, Kiriath could restrain himself no longer. He redrew his own sword and finally joined the men in the heat of battle—slashing, stabbing, and chopping any Grishnak who dared approach him. One of the foes managed to cripple the prince's horse with a swing of his stone battle-axe, but the prince leaped to the ground, thrust his steel into the same Grishnak, and clambered aboard a riderless horse that was prancing and circling in the confusion.

No longer did the human warriors number over a thousand. At the most only several hundred remained, and their circle was dwindling as the enemy relentlessly whittled away their ranks. So certain of victory had the enemy become that many of them who were unable to share in the killing now loped off to help besiege Westrock.

Never before had Kiriath sensed doom in combat, but this time it seemed inevitable. All he could do was imitate the example of the standard-bearer whose name he didn't know: stop as many of the enemy as he could from overrunning the realm. No doubt other defenders would eventually arrest the Grishnaki onslaught, but the more enemies who stayed here this morning, the fewer there would be to massacre the innocent. The resolve within him hardened, and he determined to fight his best to the end. No wound would stop him. Not before death closed his eyes would he drop his sword.

So, like a man obsessed, the prince of Xandria now threw himself into the conflict with every ounce of his skill and strength. He used each lunge, parry, and counterattack his father and Carpathan had ever taught him.

Seeing the prince's example, the nearby defenders also took heart and fought with renewed vigor. "For Xandria!" and "With Kiriath!" went up the cries, each man striving to fight as long and as well as he was able. And while it was obvious that men were falling in battle both left and right, for each one who perished, several Grishnaki also dropped.

Once, when a mountain of a Grishnak swung his battle-axe toward the prince, Kiriath had no time to dodge. Using his sword as a shield, he swung it hard to intercept the blow. The maneuver was successful, but Kiriath's sword snapped in half under the force of the axe. Lunging with the remainder of his blade, he pierced his adversary and left him in the dust.

Continuing the struggle with his stump of sword, Kiriath lost sense of how long he had mechanically cut and thrust before he became aware that Jekoniah's voice was once more speaking into his thoughts.

They're coming! They're coming at last, Son! From the north and the south—Southmarche, Highmount, Raven's Peak, Lake Crest. They are flying on the wings of the wind! Hold on!

From the low ground where he stood, Kiriath couldn't see the vision his father had observed from Westrock's tower. He knew he should try to encourage the men, but he no longer had energy for shouting, only to fight for his life.

In Kiriath's mind he kept hearing his father's last words: *Hold on!* He didn't know whether he was repeating them to himself or if his father was continuously willing this message to him. But it made no difference: Kiriath continued to strike and block, doing his utmost to *hold on* as long as possible.

All at once, through the dust and the din of battle, throaty battle calls of "Xandria!" could be heard from afar. Trumps blared, and the earth rumbled afresh with the pounding of hooves. Down a grassy mound to the north came the most welcome sight Kiriath had ever seen—horsemen, thousands of them surging toward the battle. One company broke away to sweep the enemy from around Westrock's walls; the rest drove straight toward the enemy in the plain. From the approaching newcomers sounded a trumpet call to arms, and the onrushing garrisons whipped out their swords and broke into the enemies before them.

With the appearance of these fresh defenders, the Grishnaki's lust for vengeance seemed to drain out of them. Fear now replaced their earlier fanaticism. Thus, with victory suddenly wrenched from their grasp, untold hundreds of Grishnaki bolted and fled south or west toward the river. But out of the south roared another multitude of Xandrian riders, several garrisons strong. More trumpets blared from that direction, and the new hosts poured into the plain.

As animals caught in a trap, Grishnaki bellowed in mingled fear, anger, and frustration, each forsaking the others and fleeing for survival. Within minutes, the near defeat for Westrock became a rout of Grishnaki. All over the plain and on the surrounding hills, Xandrian riders were pursuing or clashing with the enemy. Here and there some of the huskiest and boldest Grishnaki huddled in compact islands, but the well-trained horsemen were already hacking apart these stands of resistance.

Like those around him, Kiriath was too exhausted to shout or laugh—too exhausted to do anything but sheath his broken sword and watch his comrades drive away the foe. He started to wipe the sweat from his eyes and then froze at an unexpected sight.

Suddenly finding the strength to dismount, Kiriath stepped over the dead, simultaneously hurrying yet dreading to approach the sight that had caught his eye. Stopping, he knelt where a brown, bloodstained cloak like that of a Xandrian hunter showed from beneath a lifeless Grishnak.

With all the might he could muster, the prince heaved away the Grishnak's massive frame. The sight beneath was more than the exhausted prince could bear.

"No!" he cried. "Not like this!"

Hot tears welling in his eyes, Kiriath broke down and wept over the still body of Brand.

CHAPTER 15

FINAL DUTIES

The persistent sound of a cock's crowing in the distance dragged Kiriath out of his slumber. Daylight was not yet fully come, but a few of those who had lain down near him outside Westrock's wall the night before were already stirring. Every muscle in the prince's body ached from the previous day's ordeal, especially his sword arm. Studying his hand, he found it sore and blistered from wielding his weapon.

Rising stiffly from the trampled and stained grass, he looked down into the plain. There the watch fires that surrounded the horde of Grishnaki taken captive were burning out. In contrast to the Grishnaki, who primarily squatted or lay on the ground, all around the ring rode vigilant sentries from among the garrisons that had arrived during or after the battle's end. Other men still searched among the fallen for wounded survivors, while others yet were reverently laying the bodies of lifeless Xandrians in long lines, to be buried.

Stepping carefully over the still-sleeping defenders at hand, the prince made his way to the splintered gate of Westrock. Entering the fortress, he paused to look over the courtyard, where hundreds of soldiers lay side by side, all of them wearing red-stained bandages on various parts of their bodies. Physicians and fellow soldiers went from man to man, changing bandages and doing all they could to ease the pain. Many there called out for water or moaned in their pain, and it grieved the prince to think that so many of these before him this day would not survive to see the next.

Noticing an aged soldier who lay nearby eyeing the prince's water flask, Kiriath untied its leather string and handed it to the man.

"Thank you, my prince." He put it to his parched lips and swallowed several times.

"No. You are the one to be thanked. I don't know your age, but I'm sure you could have signed out of the king's service with honor long ago. Instead you stayed on and helped to hold the line. It's to men like you that Xandria owes the most."

"The struggle against evil is for both the young and the old. The battle never ends."

"You're right. But, when many consider their own comfort more important than the battle, defenders like you shine ever brighter. Keep the water, and rest."

Going on to the central stronghold, Kiriath stepped inside and saw even more wounded men that were being tended. These within were injured more seriously than those outside. Ariana and his mother were there helping, as was Counselor Urijah and even the aged Nethanel. Vandrielle saw her son enter and made her way over to where he stood.

"How is Brand?" he asked.

"Better, I think. The healers said it was good that you brought him when you did. The gashes in his arm and thigh were not deep, but he lost much blood. He must have fought until his body simply collapsed. But his wounds have been cleansed and bound up. They believe he will mend well."

"I was afraid it was too late when I found him. I'm glad he was spared. Can I see him?"

"He's asleep just now, but he's on a straw pallet behind this building if you want to stop by."

Kiriath nodded. "I'll wait. I'm sure he's in good hands as long as Ariana knows where to find him. What about Father?"

"Up in the tower. He has been there alone all night, deep in thought."

"I'll speak to him."

"Do you think you should interrupt him?"

"Better me than someone else."

So saying, the prince left Queen Vandrielle to her work and mounted the circular stairway up the center of the stronghold until at last he reached the little watch chamber high above. Rapping the door twice with his knuckles, he pushed it open and entered.

"Good morning, Father."

King Jekoniah continued to stare out the window before him. "You would have done better to say only *morning* without the *good*. Indeed, your father is full of mourning this day. Mourning and sorrow. For what has been and what is soon to be. We lost Carpathan too, you know."

"I heard last night. I can still hardly believe it. But at least we were successful in stopping them. Think how much more sorrow there would be today if the enemy had conquered us here and pushed on to the interior of the kingdom. Who can tell how many women and children might have been hacked to pieces? This is what all those who died gave their lives to protect."

King Jekoniah sighed and finally turned away from the window. "I know it. Do not mistake me for a near-sighted fool. The enemy had to be stopped; there was no other way to do it. Still, life is precious. As king, I grieve for every one that has been lost. I even feel sorrow for the shed blood of the enemies. Knowing that it was wholly unnecessary, knowing that some Xandrian citizen who has been counted faithful enough to serve in the Citadel has betrayed us with his treachery makes my grief even deeper."

"And we may never know who it was."

"Perhaps not, but then again we might. I have thought long and hard about it, both before and after you rescued me."

Kiriath was immediately interested. "Do you have an idea?"

"Nothing more solid than that—an idea. As my thoughts have drifted from man to man and from woman to woman, even you have not escaped my consideration. I do not like to think in such a way about those closest to me, but each time my suspicions have come to rest on one individual."

Kiriath grew impatient speaking in such vague terms. "But who, Father?"

King Jekoniah shook his head. "I will say nothing as yet, for I have no proof. If we are to determine the guilty one, he must not suspect that we are on his trail. Better it would be for him to believe we suspect nothing for the present, so that I may watch him all the more closely. Say nothing to anyone of this matter."

"As you wish."

"There is something else on your mind." The king phrased his words more as a statement than a query.

"Yesterday. You spoke to me in my thoughts. You said it was not witchcraft, but how—"

The king nodded. "True, it was not sorcery; it was science. Or a lost skill, or a lost art, or a natural characteristic little understood, or whatever you may care to name it. I did not have time to explain." King Jekoniah pulled out the sword he had received from Ariana. "You came across this in the Deserted Kingdom, I take it?"

"Yes. We wondered that it had not corroded long ago, and we marveled at the gem in the handle, but even so a sword is just a sword. The glass spheres seemed much more important."

"The spheres are also of unknown design, but I deem this sword more valuable than dozens of such spheres. Did you never learn to read Illyrish?"

"No. Not much more than a smattering of words, anyway. Military stratagems always seemed more practical."

"We shall have to remedy that. If you had, you would have understood what you held when you discovered this. Interpreted, the words inscribed on the blade just above the hilt say, 'A gift for the eminent Stephanius. Grasp the handle and think to whomsoever you will.' Of course, I had read of such things before in the Vault of Chronicles."

"I have seen no such records."

"You have, but you could not have read them. They are in the collection of Illyrish scrolls, which you say you cannot read."

"But how did you know it would still work after so many centuries? And how does it work for that matter?"

"To answer your first question, I did not know. Not until I tried it. When I told you in my mind to throw your glass spheres and you heard me, then I knew that the gem's virtue was intact. To answer your second question, I do not know how the thing works. It simply does. Whether it draws energy from sunlight, the air, the warmth of the carrier's hand, or from one's own mind, who can tell? I am not even sure if the gem is natural or an invented thing. This is knowledge that has passed from the world."

Kiriath made no reply. His question had been answered well enough.

All that remained now was for the king to render judgment on the enemy, and as if coming to a decision, Jekoniah took a deep breath and stood up. "Let us go down. Everyone will be expecting us soon."

When father and son entered the open air of the courtyard, Kiriath paused. "Excuse me, Father, but I'd like to turn aside for a moment to see if Brand is conscious yet."

"Of course."

Kiriath found the pallet where Brand lay, right where his mother had said he would be. Ariana was there too, aiding the physicians who tended the many wounded, but she often cast glances in Brand's direction. Although he was still asleep, Brand already looked much better to the prince than he had the previous evening—less pale and more like a man in slumber than one who is lifeless.

"He's resting well," Ariana said, coming up behind Kiriath.

"Has he awakened since last night?"

"Twice. Each time he wanted only a long drink of water. The second time he managed a smile, though, before he closed his eyes again."

"Good. I won't disturb him. Just wanted to see how he was doing. Father is almost ready to pronounce judgment. You'll be expected to be there."

"Yes, let's go. The healers are doing everything possible; now only time will tell who will live."

Just then a physician picking his way through the crooked aisles of bodies stopped and addressed the prince. "Excuse me, Prince Kiriath, but there is a gravely wounded man. They found him on the battlefield this morning. He says he knows you and wants to speak to you."

"Oh? What's his name?"

"I believe he said it was Cheneniah, but he is so weak. It is difficult to hear him."

"I don't recall any Cheneniah, but take me to him. I'll meet you on the field, Ariana."

The healer led the prince back outside the fortress to where a pavilion had been erected during the night. There the last of the wounded lay side by side in rows. "That is the one," the man said, pointing to a defender in the center of the pavilion. In a lower voice he added, "We don't expect him to last long. Took a spear in the stomach. We've made him as comfortable as we could."

Now Kiriath understood. Before him lay the standard-bearer from Fortress Diligence. The young man opened his eyes and nodded weakly to the prince. Cheneniah moved his lips, but Kiriath couldn't make out the words. The prince moved closer and bent down. "I'm sorry; I couldn't hear you."

"Thank you . . . for letting me fight. Wanted . . . to do . . . my share."

"You have done your share and even more. I don't lie when I say that your example inspired me to battle more fiercely than I ever have before."

"I'm not going to make it, am I?"

Kiriath hesitated to tell the truth, but neither did he want to deceive one so courageous. "They don't think so."

"It's all right." A series of coughs gripped the man for several moments before passing. "Just wish . . . I could say farewell to my family. Could someone send word?"

"Yes, of course. You said that they lived in one of the nearest villages, didn't you?"

"In Jessex."

"Very good. From what house do you come, Cheneniah?"

"The house of—" Another series of coughs gripped him. Kiriath felt helpless and was about to call for the healer when the fit eased again. "The house of Tymon."

"Ever a small house in Xandria, but ever a solid one without blemish. I don't say you will not live, Cheneniah; but, if anything should happen, I promise to visit your family personally. I'll tell them of your valor and how they were in your thoughts both on the battlefield and after."

"My thanks, Prince Ki—" Cheneniah broke into a final coughing spell, and a spasm of pain swept over his face. The next second his body went limp, and his eyes closed a final time. Finding no breath in the young man, Kiriath removed his own tattered cloak, draped it over Cheneniah's still form, and walked back out into the sunshine.

Down on the battlefield, more horsemen were already lining up around the prisoners and preparing for the coming of King Jekoniah. All those in Westrock who weren't needed to tend the injured were also walking in that direction to hear the king's judgment upon the prisoners. In silence, the prince fell in step with these and tried to forget the young man who would never return to the family he so loved.

On the plain, Kiriath found his mother and Ariana beside Nethanel and Urijah. He joined them in waiting for his father. When everyone had gathered, King Jekoniah, coming last of all, rode down from the gates on the black stallion that had borne him from Diligence. All the Xandrians parted, allowing the king a clear approach to the Grishnaki. Drawing up before them, he stopped to survey first his subjects, then the battlefield—still littered with shattered weapons and the dead—and finally the Grishnaki before him.

"Servants of Dar-kon, listen to me." Resonant and strong, the king's voice carried easily to all in attendance. "For three hundred years your race has sought to wipe out my people. Our fathers greeted your fathers in friendship and received death in return. We did nothing to deserve your hate, unless being different is a crime. Now, in these latter days, your purpose has not changed, for you have held me hostage and abused me, hoping to force my people into giving you the secret of making steel, with which you could destroy us more easily." He gestured to the plain around them. "You see what your hate has brought you—death for many men and death for even more Grishnaki. Is the fruit of your hatred sweet?"

"You killed Dar-kon!" a gravelly voice shouted.

"We never wanted enemies, but you desired our destruction anyway. Since you sneaked into our land and stole me away, is it any wonder that some of my own should risk their lives to enter Vol-Rathdeen and free me? If Dar-kon has fallen, he forged his own death. Had he left our kind in peace, he would be alive today. Had Dar-kon not molested us, these thousands of your fellow Grishnaki who are now dead would also be alive.

"Have we ever stormed into your land to see how many of your females and young we could destroy? You know that we have not. Yet your kind have done so to us many times down through the years. It is madness. Folly! Those who live to sow death shall reap their own destruction. Look again at your dead brothers. Were their lives worth the cost? Our kind produce offspring often; in a few years we shall have back the number of men we have lost. And even though Grishnaki live longer than men, you know Grishnaki conceive and bear young slowly. How many years will it take to raise up again as many of your kind as those who have fallen? Reconsider your ways.

"Three hundred years ago we were a small people. Today we are a much stronger nation. Do you truly wish for us to hate you as much as you have hated us? I think not, or our sons, who will be more numerous than we, will be forced to exterminate you for their own safety."

No Grishnak spoke or moved, so the king continued.

"Now we come to the end of the matter. To your own undoing, you have wrought much killing among us. In our land the penalty for causing intentional death of any person is death in return, for so we remove from among us those unwilling to live in harmony. Because your slaughter was committed on Xandrian soil, by our law each one of you deserves death."

The crowd of prisoners began murmuring and stirring uneasily.

"Indeed," King Jekoniah continued quickly, "we did not need to spare you even this long. But we are also a merciful people. If you will consent to lay down your weapons forever and live beside us in peace, there is no reason for enmity between your kind and mine. The land is wide enough for both our kingdoms."

"You keep the best places. Let us live with you in your lands!" one cried out.

"Nay, not yet. A time may come when we shall dwell together in one kingdom, but not yet. In truth, I do not expect you to quickly let go of your hatred as an old bone when all the meat is eaten. Even before yesterday, you had done us enough harm to keep us from fully trusting you for years to come. We have learned not to believe what the Grishnaki leaders say, but to watch what they do. Dwell peaceably in your own lands for now, and set aside war, and later we shall see about dwelling together. Can we not live as neighbors without being continually at one another's throats?"

The king paused, but still no answer was offered, so he resumed. "You have little choice. I repeat: if we truly wanted to do away with your race, we could start by annihilating this assembly now. But we do not love to shed blood. If you learn to refrain from war, we will amend our law and help you. My people will teach you to tame the land as we do, growing crops for seasons when the hunting is poor. But I warn you in advance: we will have no more stomach for murder without cause. If any of us hurts one of you without just cause, then you shall watch as the offender is punished. But if you shun the ways of peace and seek war again, our mercy shall evaporate quickly. What say you then? Shall it be peace? Or shall it be war?"

The prisoners broke into stony-throated murmuring with each other. Either none of them were leaders among their kind, or none of them would admit to the fact. At last one of the huskier ones called out, "You are right, O man-kon: we have little choice. Let us return to our valley in peace. We will not hunt men-kind again."

"Good. If you speak sincerely, you show wisdom beyond any Dar-kon ever possessed. You know the way. Go in peace. We shall bury your dead after we have attended to our own."

At first the Grishnaki seemed unable to believe they were free to depart. The riders surrounding them likewise maintained their positions, as if in doubt that the king truly granted liberty to these that had wrought so much havoc.

"Stand away!" Jekoniah called to the guardians on horseback. "I am sending them home. Escort the prisoners as far as Border River; then return. Grishnaki, you may depart. Only remember well what has been said today."

Slowly at first, then with increasing speed, the Grishnaki began loping past the horsemen toward Shallowford, where they could return to their valley across the river. All the bystanders on foot drew back, keeping their distance, tacitly agreeing that even now an irate Grishnak might strike a final blow if given the opportunity.

After the contingent of defenders broke away to follow the Grishnaki, King Jekoniah addressed the listeners who remained. "People of Xandria, if I seem overly lenient, it is only because I am hoping against hope for an age of peace. Doubtless some of you think it folly to let the Grishnaki escape with their lives. But I say that if we slay all these for vengeance or on the possibility that they may harm us in some future year, we make ourselves little better than savages such as they are. For the moment, we have another matter to consider."

The king's eyes searched among the crowd and lighted on the little group where Kiriath stood. "Nethanel, of the house of Nethrod, stand apart please where I may see you better."

Nethanel stepped forward, and bowed his gray head toward Jekoniah. The prince was confused, not comprehending what purpose his father could have.

"Nethanel, listen to me. In your youth, you grew up near the region of the Gray Bogs and know the area well. It was through the Bogs that the Grishnaki traveled when they captured me and nearly killed my son. Later, when the emissary from Dar-kon came to Shiralla, only you spoke up to request more information on what else besides my release Xandria might receive, which brought the additional offer of the Grishnaki's legendary elixir of long life. When my son, Prince Kiriath, suggested that he and a friend attempt to sneak into Vol-Rathdeen to rescue me, you encouraged the idea when some others warned them that the plan might result in their deaths."

King Jekoniah paused for breath. Everyone's eyes shifted between the king and the wizened counselor, whose eyes had slowly been growing wider. Kiriath could hardly believe what his father was implying. Still, though the evidence was scanty, the combined circumstances did point at least a finger of suspicion toward Nethanel.

"My king—" Nethanel began, but Jekoniah cut him off.

"Please hold your silence a moment. Urijah," the king called. "You have heard all that I just said to Nethanel. Before these witnesses, I call upon you now as my counselor to give your appraisal concerning all these facts."

Urijah stepped forward and cleared his voice. "It hurts me to say it, Lord Jekoniah. It pains me, indeed. But I am afraid you have correctly discerned the guilt of the traitor who betrayed you into the enemy's hands."

"Jekoniah, it is not so!" Nethanel cried. "If anyone has done such a deed, it was not I. I vow it. You have my word."

King Jekoniah hunched forward a little in his saddle, for all appearances as a man with a great burden on his back. Kiriath detected, too, a deep sadness in his eyes such as he had never before seen in his father.

"Sire, I am innocent," Nethanel called again.

"The king is merciful," Urijah said to Jekoniah, "but the voices of the dead cry out that you not delay in meting justice to him who is the author of so much misery." He turned towards Nethanel and spat at his feet. "Traitor!"

Jekoniah straightened himself in the saddle. "In this you are right, Urijah. Justice must be done, and for betrayal that has led to the shedding of fellow citizens' blood, a Xandrian king may not pardon even those whom he has regarded as family. But let not the wheels of justice roll too quickly lest they crush one who is innocent. Tell me, friend Urijah, who ever said aught to you of a traitor?"

"Why . . . of course, I assumed . . ."

"Nay, Urijah, for you are too intelligent to quickly assume a conclusion on so weighty a matter—a matter on which the life of a respected counselor depends. Never in your service to me have I seen you base any conclusion on assumption. I want to know how you knew beyond doubt that I was betrayed into Grishnaki hands."

The expression of a cornered animal flashed across Urijah's face. Suddenly he laughed. "But this is preposterous, Sire. Surely you are not accusing me . . ."

"Yes, I do accuse you, Urijah. Of the same crime for which you were so quick to condemn Nethanel. Only the evidence against you is greater, for no one in Xandria save the traitor himself could have been positive of how my capture came about. Even I would not have been sure had not Dar-kon himself boasted that one of my own had sold him the necessary information."

"I do not know why you are bluffing so, Sire. Dar-kon could not even—" Urijah stopped in mid-thought.

"Dar-kon could not even *what?* Know your true name? Go back on a bargain and implicate you in the crime? Here is the truth: I never suspected Nethanel at all. I merely wanted you to condemn yourself so that I would not have to."

With astonishing speed, Urijah snatched the reins of a horse from a confused defender standing nearby and swung into the saddle.

"Seize him!" Jekoniah thundered.

At once Kiriath and several others, leaping after Urijah, pulled him down and pinned him to the ground. The king rode up and stared at the counselor with an expression of mingled outrage and hurt. "Let him stand."

His eyes still fixed on Urijah, King Jekoniah uttered a single word: "Why?"

His mouth clamped shut, Urijah gazed only at the ground.

"I asked you a question, Chief Counselor. I command that you answer. Why would a man that has served me faithfully for years—a man whom I have trusted above so many others—suddenly betray me to those that hate us most? Why?"

Finally Urijah raised his eyes in defiance. "He would not. You think yourself so wise, O Jekoniah. But you are not. I have not suddenly deserted you. When I was young, I naively served you faithfully, as you say. But as the years passed, I feigned allegiance so that all Xandria might have opportunity to see that it was my wisdom that governed your decisions, to recall that it is I who should have the throne. You are not descended from the kings of Illandria, but I am. It is my family that should have ruled Xandria all these years. But you deceive the people. You make them think that my counsel is your own wisdom. You blind them to the truth that I am the one who should rightly hold the reins of power."

As long-pent waters suddenly bursting through a dam, Urijah's words flowed with increasing speed, his face filled with scorn.

"I played your puppet for years, but no more. I knew Vandrielle would not rule without you . . . If you and your son were to disappear tragically, then the people would restore me to my family's rightful office. I never believed Kiriath's foolish plan would succeed, so I let him go wandering in the wilderness. And even if I couldn't gain the kingship, I would have still won if I could trick Dar-kon into giving us the elixir of long life! Still, I have not betrayed the realm. In truth, I have made it easier for Xandria to see who should be its rightful head: I, Urijah, of the house of Unnalon!"

For a long while King Jekoniah only looked at Urijah, sadness etched into the lines of his face. At last, he shook his head slowly, solemnly. "More than anything I have suffered during my sojourn in this life is the pain you cause me now, Urijah. Not the pain from the Grishnaki's abuse, but the pain of knowing that he whom I had considered my own familiar friend, a companion of my latter years, is the one who has cared the least for my well-being and orchestrated a plan for my death. So how did you arrange all this with your Grishnaki companions?"

Urijah seemed almost to boast as he explained how he had carried out his scheme: "You saw fit to make me go and observe border patrols with the garrisons. After a small skirmish, I found a wounded Grishnak. I gave him water—and a proposal to deliver to Dar-kon. The rest was simple."

The king shook his head. "You speak of blindness, but how far the wise do fall when pride blinds their eyes. Your precious elixir is a myth. It was a Grishnaki deception from the beginning, for Dar-kon personally boasted of how his kin deceived our ancestors. They have no elixir. They live long lives simply because that is their nature.

"Concerning my lineage, it is no secret that my ancestor Kanadon was only the Tirshatha, a governor of the Xandrian colony and not blood kin to the kings across the waters. But when the cataclysm struck and Illandria sank forever, only a cousin of the Illandrian king dwelt on this hither shore. This cousin—your ancestor—was not fit to rule our infant kingdom, for he was a half-wit."

"So say you!" Urijah shot back.

"Nay, so said all those who knew him. They decided to appoint Kanadon as king, and that was the end of the matter. I have often reflected how odd it was that a man as brilliant as you should descend from one whom the people considered so dull of mind. But I see now that your thoughts are not so deep as I had imagined. You are no true counselor. Actor extraordinaire, I dub you."

Urijah glared back, unable to find the words to vent his rage.

"Urijah, how can it be that you have lived with a king and provided counsel for a king—even for your own interests—for so many years and still not have realized what it actually means to rule? I do not grip the power of Xandria like the reins of a horse. The citizens of the realm entrust me with my duties. If I prove unfit to carry them out, then they must invoke the right of petition and choose another. Your concept of a king is like that of the Grishnaki: a selfish individual who rules through cunning for self-glory and pleasure. But with us it is not so. Though they name me *lord*, I am the chief servant in the kingdom. No soldier, cook, or handmaiden has more lords than do I, for the king lives to benefit every citizen, not the other way around. How would a man become great among our people? By putting away selfish ambitions, humbling himself, and serving others. Those are the signs of a great leader."

Now Kiriath spoke up. "What are you going to do with him, Father?"

"As he himself said, the voices of the dead cry out that justice be done. Witnesses of Xandria, from henceforth, Urijah, of the house of Unnalon, is barred forever from our borders. We will give him water and a pack of provisions, then deliver him straightway across Border River. If he perishes in the outlands, then so be it."

"But I am no hunter. You seek my death in the wilderness without soiling your own hands!"

"To the contrary. I temper the judgment with mercy. But even if you were to die this morning, this very instant, would not justice be done? Have you so soon forgotten that you are the chief author for that blood staining the grass under your shoes? Did you count my life dear when you told the enemy where and how to capture me? You cast your lot with the Grishnaki. Let them love you, if they will. Only never again set foot inside the borders of Xandria, or a tight noose will be your punishment. Lead him away."

Binding Urijah's wrists, a handful of soldiers trudged away with him, taking him first to Westrock to carry out the king's command to provision him. Most of those who stood by followed. Others returned to the task of gathering the dead until only the king, his family, and Nethanel were left. King Jekoniah dismounted.

"My apologies, Nethanel," King Jekoniah said, "for using you as the bait to catch a traitor. But I saw no other way."

"No harm done, Milord. You did best. I was startled though. I must confess that I never would have considered Urijah capable of such wickedness."

"Nor did I want to. Indeed, had he told me to my face that the circumstances I cited were mere coincidences and that you, too, could have nothing to do with the enemy, I would have regretted ever doubting him. In his haste to assign blame elsewhere, he gave himself away."

Now Vandrielle spoke. "But whatever made you suspect him in the first place? You called him an actor, and he played his role perfectly."

"Yes, but even though a few circumstances pointed suspicion toward Nethanel, Nethanel had nothing to gain through unfaithfulness. Even gold does not sway him, for I have often seen him contributing to the orphans' home. On the other hand, I had noted more than once that Urijah places undue importance on family history. Also, though, two times he encouraged me to change my routine and to catch a breath of fresh air with my son. It occurred to me in Vol-Rathdeen that he might possibly be appointed king if Kiriath were not alive. But even then I did not seriously doubt the man."

"It's so hard to believe," Ariana put in. "One of the most trusted in the kingdom, a traitor."

"Daughter, there are lusts that move both men and women to commit shocking deeds. Urijah's bane is the pride of life—and his yearning for an extended one. He fooled us for a long while; yet no one can perpetually harbor lustful ambitions without revealing them. Remember that, Kiriath. A sovereign cannot afford to forget it."

"Yes, Father. But what of the Grishnaki? Do you think they will truly put away their lust for slaughter? And is it true that there never was a secret elixir to explain their long lives?"

King Jekoniah sighed. "As for their blood lust, who can say? I would not have wanted this battle to happen—even had I known that we would win it. But for now they have lost a huge number of warriors. They have no choice but to accept our terms for the moment. Only time will tell if a Grishnak can learn peace. Perhaps your reign will decide, Son. But remember, too, that victors are usually more willing to forget grudges than are the vanquished.

"Now, to answer your other question, it is true. No secret elixir of long life ever existed. Dar-kon laughed when he told me, calling us simpletons for having believed the tale for so many years. Grishnaki live long lives simply because that is normal for their race."

"Come," Vandrielle suggested. "Let's go back to the fortress. Many men need a compassionate hand today."

King Jekoniah shook his head. "You all go ahead. I will wait here and mourn the dead until Urijah has departed. He has wounded me sorely; I have no wish to see his face again."

Vandrielle, Ariana, and Nethanel started up the hill. Seeing Kiriath hesitating, Ariana called back. "Coming, Kir? Brand may be awake now."

"Not yet. If he does awake, give him my best wishes, and tell him I'll be back soon. But I made a special promise to a dying defender named Cheneniah. With your leave, Father, I'd like to borrow your horse and visit his family in Jessex."

His eyes still sad but with a trace of a smile on his lips, King Jekoniah handed the reins to his son. "You are a son any father would be proud of. I hope your heart remains as tender toward the people when I am gone."

Not knowing exactly what to say, Kiriath simply embraced his father and swung himself into the saddle.

"One moment, Son."

"Yes?"

"Xandrian tradition dictates that the king should have at least one counselor. Today we have Nethanel, but his days are numbered. Because my time as the sovereign is more than half spent, I would like you to name Urijah's successor. Whomever you choose will have access to the king's ear and will play a vital role in decision making, so pick carefully. Find someone who understands the nature of man—someone who can win the respect of both the commoners and nobles while seeing into the hearts of each. He should be a man who is able to lead as well as he follows."

"I'll have to give it some thought. But already one name comes to me. They call him Elead; he serves in the Watercliffe garrison."

"Elead? The name is only vaguely familiar. But do not be hasty. Weigh the matter well. Then speak to the one you choose and let him do the same."

"Yes, sir, I will."

"Stay a moment more, Kiriath. Where is your sword?"

"Broken in the battle yesterday. I dropped it in the field."

Jekoniah unbuckled the sword belt someone had given him and slid off the sheath that held the ancient blade with the purple gem in the handle. "Take this one back. It doesn't appear fitting for a prince to ride without his weapon. Besides, there might yet be some insane Grishnaki skulking in the grass, waiting for a chance to swing an axe at a man."

Kiriath accepted the weapon and attached the sheath to his belt. "Thank you, Father. I'll be back soon. Farewell!"

So saying, the prince nudged his stirrups to the horse's flanks and guided the stallion eastward. Gaining the summit of the first knoll, he halted and turned to survey once again the silent plain where ear-ringing battle had so recently raged. Solitary and motionless, the king still stood where they had parted, in lonely lamentation for the fallen. Gazing at his father, a thought appeared in the prince's mind.

Wrapping his fingers around the purple gemstone, Kiriath pulled the Illandrian sword from its resting place. Concentrating on the distant figure of Jekoniah, he thought, *You are a father any son would be proud of. I love you, and I hope to rule as wisely and ably as you when my time comes.*

Down below, King Jekoniah lifted his head to see Kiriath and raised an acknowledging hand.

Then, with a flip of the reins and another nudge of his stirrups, Kiriath called to the steed. "Let's go, my friend. To Jessex!"